SOLOMON'S SON AND JOHN SOLOMON:

THE ADVENTURES OF

JOHN SOLOMON, VOLUME 9

H . BEDFORD-JONES

SOLOMON'S SON
AND
JOHN SOLOMON
THE ADVENTURES OF
JOHN SOLOMON, VOLUME 9

H. BEDFORD-JONES

COVER BY
P.J. MONAHAN

STEEGER BOOKS • 2022

SOLOMON'S SON

.

CHAPTER I

HIRAM KING, OF NOWHERE

THE CITY clerk of San Francisco was a busy man, but his assistants routed him from his private office without ceremony.

"There's a boob out here you'll have to handle, chief. Wants to register; been out of the country for the last year. Don't know his name, age, birthplace, or anything else. He's got us up a stump."

"Eh? Is he a lunatic, then?" demanded the city clerk in surprise.

"You'd think so all right. But he ain't. Will you take him over?"

"Send him in," was the resigned answer.

Five minutes later the city clerk was listening to his strange caller. A young man was this, with wide-set eyes of china blue, fairly bronzed features, and medium height; one to attract no second glance; a very average fellow in every respect.

"Suppose you let me tell my story as I know it, sir, then set me down as you think best," said the visitor. "In June of 1892 Captain Hiram King, of the P. & O. line, picked up a ship's boat off Malta; in the boat were two dead men, a dead woman, presumably my mother, and a baby of about six months—myself. The names of these people or of the ship whence the boat came were never discovered.

"That is my genesis as I know it. I'm about twenty-five now, was adopted by Captain King, and am a sailor. My adopted father died in 1900. I came to this country as a boy after his death, worked my way up, and now hold an American board-of-trade license as captain. Also I'm part owner in the West Coast Commercial Company, of this city; rather, I *was*."

"Oh!" The city clerk raised his brows in surprise. "You're Hiram King. I've heard of you, of course. Cleaned up some big money when this present boom in ships came on."

"You might put it that way. You probably know that last year the West Coast Company went out of business—sold out lock, stock, and barrel to an English concern and is now being operated by the Britishers under the same name? Well, I undertook to make delivery of our freighter *Ajax* at Vladivostok—took her over myself; smashed our crank shaft in a typhoon, got blown up into the arctic, was held in the ice, and stayed there six months until—"

"By George, I remember now!" cried the city clerk, holding out his hand excitedly. "Shake! Glad to meet you! Why, the papers were full of that story last month! So that's why you're getting in to register months after the big day, eh?"

"That's it. Never heard about registration until I got to Vladivostok with the ship, and I just got back to San Francisco last night on the *Hinyo Maru*. So here I am, and I want a ticket."

"Well, you'll sure get it," laughed the city clerk. "Here, smoke up while I'm writing down that stuff, captain. By George, I'm proud to make out this card of yours!"

In this wise did Hiram King, of nowhere, secure the little, bluish-gray card which made him a man among men. His present residence he gave as the Palace Hotel. He was out of the West Coast Commercial, but before the day was over expected to meet some Englishmen who had secured a line on him through the concern which had taken over his late company with a view to a new business.

Half an hour after leaving the city clerk's office, Hiram King fought his way against a buffeting San Francisco wind, striding down Post Street and aiming for the Union Square entrance of the St. Francis. He was smoking, with evident enjoyment, a large, wonderfully browned old meerschaum pipe.

As he turned the corner of the building at Powell he ran slap into another pedestrian who was turning the corner in the opposite direction. Both men, their heads down under the buffets of he gale, came together blindly, and then staggered up against the building under the shock.

"You confounded fool!" cried out King sharply. "You've smashed my meerschaum!"

With dismay and keen grief striking through him, he looked down at the fragments of his shattered old friend. Then he saw, as it were mingling blood with blood, that with them lay strewn the shreds of what had once been a villainous old clay pipe, and the voice of the other man came back at him, with acerbity equal to his own:

"Dang it! If you ain't been an' busted me old clay! This comes o' beatin' up against a gale without no lookout for'ard— Dang it! You danged careless young blighter. I—I—"

The speaker paused, wheezing for breath. The two men stared at each other angrily.

King checked his too ready fist. He saw that the man facing him was old, gray-haired, and seemed a little unsteady on his feet, holding one leg stiffly. Also the other was a bit shorter than himself, had a singularly expressionless face, and wide blue eyes which just now were blazing with anger.

"You! You and your clay pipe be hanged!" snapped King. "If you weren't an old man with one foot in the grave, I'd knock the tar out of you!"

The other snorted indignantly, then spoke with premeditated insult:

"If you wasn't a werry tough-looking bloke I'd soil me 'ands on your bleedin' mug. But you'd dirty me up, just like that. It don't never pay, I says, to touch wermin, 'cause why, they ain't no respecter o' persons. You bloody swab, that there old clay pipe was—"

"Beat it, you panhandler, before I kick you down the street!" With difficulty King repressed his desire to seize the old man and execute his threat. "My meerschaum was worth more than your whole dirty hide! Why don't you look where you're walking? Shut up and beat it away from here! Cockney, that's what you are, playing the gentleman in America."

The little cockney fairly shook with inarticulate rage. At this instant, however, a burly policeman swung around the corner and interposed his bulk just as the old man was shaking a pudgy fist under King's nose.

"Come on—what d'ye think this is, ye two? Break! On your way, both of ye!"

With more regard to authority than to ways and means, the "cop" took King's arm and propelled him away with a violent shove. Five seconds later the right hand of Captain Hiram King landed flush on the big jaw of the astonished copper, who quietly threw up his hands and went to sleep.

"Dang it! Now you 'ave done it!" shrilled the little cockney. "Duck! Run for it!"

King felt the little man seize his arm, and with amazing agility urge him around the corner. Instantly dismayed over his action, and realizing full well the consequences, King flung aside two or three hesitant citizens who attempted to stop him, and a moment later the cockney whipped him into a doorway.

"Quick! In 'ere, sir. Dang it, if we ain't goin' to do it all shipshape yet! Do what I says, an' do it quick!"

The antagonists of a moment previous had, by the magical effect of human nature, been converted into allies. King laughed to himself as the cockney urged him through a corridor of the hotel, and so into the bar.

"Right 'ere at this table; lay off that 'ere coat!" commanded the little man, with so evident an authority in his voice that King was astonished.

In a few seconds the two were seated at a table, hats and coats removed. When presently several men entered the doorway and a swearing policeman ran his eye over the men before the bar, he quite overlooked the two at the corner table; to all appearances they had been there for some time, and the removal of hats and overcoats makes a wonderful change in the looks of mankind.

"There! Gone, 'e is," and the cockney drew a wheezy sigh of relief. "Let's 'ave a drink, sir. Liquor is all werry well in its place, says I, and this 'ere is the place for a drink, just like that. I'd like werry much to know, sir, just 'ow you 'it that 'ere bobby. Dang it, I 'adn't thought it was in you!"

"I've time for one drink." Smiling whimsically, King glanced at his watch. "Sailors learn to hit hard, my friend."

"I'm by way o' bein' a seafaring man meself," announced the little cockney complacently. "Now, if you 'ad the time to spare, I'd like werry much to 'ave a bit o' talk—"

"I haven't got it," returned King. "I'm late now for an appointment here with Sir James Mowbray, an Englishman who—"

He paused, the words dying on his lips from stark amazement.

At his words, it seemed as though a little shudder had run over the pudgy cockney. The little man stared at him, his round face suddenly devoid of all expression, blank, wiped clean. Then, rising, the cockney spoke in a queer voice:

"Sir James Mowbray—'im! I'm werry sorry to say, sir, as—as I can't 'ave that 'ere drink with you—"

Abruptly the little gray-haired man took down his hat and overcoat, turned, and strode away, walking a little stiff-legged. He passed out the door and was gone.

King stared after him in blank astonishment then as the waiter brought the ordered drinks, tossed a coin on the table, and reached for his own hat and coat.

"Crazy—stark, staring mad!" he thought. "I might have known it; he acted queer from the first. A queer un right enough! Yet he pulled me out of what might have proven a bad mess. H'm! I guess I'd better move along upstairs and interview those Britishers."

Had he been privileged to follow the queer little cockney and to closely observe his subsequent actions, Hiram King night have been confirmed in his opinion—and again he might have been shaken in his opinion.

For, upon gaining the street, the little cockney moved out to the curb, and stood there gazing at Union Square for a moment. A taxi, as though awaiting him, swiftly approached; the pudgy little man entered, and the taxi sped to the British consulate.

There, inquiring for the consul, the cockney learned that the official in question was at the St. Francis Hotel and would be back in an hour. The cockney glanced at a surprisingly handsome watch, returned to his taxi with a subdued exclamation of "Dang it!" and ordered his chauffeur to drive to the beach and back. One hour later the cockney reascended the stairs to the consulate, and this time found the consul at home.

The official received the card which was brought in to him. It was an odd card to be received by the English consul in San Francisco, for it bore the following inscription:

JOHN SOLOMON
Ship's Stores
Surabaya,   Java.

It would appear, however, that there was something electrical about that card, for it extracted a low whistle from the consul, an amazing alacrity in bidding Solomon be shown in, and a marvelous cordiality in placing a chair for the little cockney.

Solomon dropped into the chair and fastened his mild blue eyes on the consul, who was expressing great pleasure at meeting him.

"We had no idea that you were in the city, Mr. Solomon," went on the consul. "If we had only known—"

"A werry good job as you didn't know, then," said Solomon testily. "Look 'ere, sir! Mebbe as 'ow you know I 'ave a stand-in, so to speak, wi' the foreign office?"

The consul smiled.

"I know, Mr. Solomon," he returned, "that until you retired from the service you had the reputation of being the most wonderful secret agent ever possessed by Downing Street. I know that among the standing instructions given all representatives of his majesty's government is one that any request or order from you shall meet with instant compliance."

"Werry good," interrupted Solomon. From his pocket he drew a brand-new clay pipe, regarded it a bit sorrowfully, and filled it with vile black sailor's tobacco, evidently cut beforehand from a plug.

"Then there's no need of explanations."

For a moment he sucked at his pipe, and his face was very blank.

"Twenty-odd year ago, sir," he said very slowly, "I knowed a man by the name o' James Mowbray; younger son, 'e was, of old Sir Stewart Mowbray, o' Bristol, and a werry bad egg 'e was likewise. As I recollect, sir, 'e was said to 'ave died in Egypt in the early nineties. Well, sir, a little while ago I 'ad a bit of a shock when I 'eard a friend o' mine speak o' Sir James Mowbray bein' in San Francisco. If I might make so bold as to be askin' of you whether—"

"Certainly, Mr. Solomon." The consul leaned forward smilingly. "Old Sir Stewart died just before the war broke out, and his eldest son was killed in Belgium a few weeks later, dying without issue. As you say, the younger son had dropped out of sight; he was advertised for very extensively, of course, and, contrary to all expectations, he was found to be living under an assumed name in South America."

Solomon nodded. He suddenly appeared very old; wrinkles lined his pudgy face; the fingers that gripped his pipestem were trembling visibly.

"I may say, however," went on the consul, "that Sir James has completely redeemed any—er—irregular features in his past life. He is one of our solid men, Mr. Solomon; heavily interested in shipping and so forth."

"Rich?" inquired Solomon, his voice husky.

"Immensely so."

There was a moment of silence. Then, wheezily, Solomon sighed.

"I've been out o' touch with England these late years," he said almost with an effort. "Me life 'as been spent in foreign parts, and—and—" He paused, and changed the trend of his speech abruptly. "And 'ere I be, fifty-eight year old, one wooden pin under me—"

"Fifty-eight? Why, you're young!" The consul laughed a bit nervously. He obviously did not understand his visitor, and obviously wanted very much to say the right thing. It was therefore quite natural that he should say the wrong thing. "I'd have taken you to be quite a bit more than that, Mr. Solomon—"

"I dare say," cut in Solomon bitterly. "I'm gettin' on in years, and I ain't what I used to be."

The consul smiled, as in duty bound, but Solomon did not smile at all.

"I'd be werry glad, sir," he went on, "if you'd up an' tell me what this 'ere Sir James Mowbray is a-doin' in San Francisco; who's with 'im; why 'e's interested in seafarin' men, and where 'e's a-goin' from 'ere. All about 'im just like that!"

He leaned back in his chair and set his pipe between his white, even teeth.

"Sir James is here on business connected with his son's interests in China and—"

The consul halted abruptly. Solomon had heaved himself from his chair, clutching at the desk edge for support. He stared at the consul from a face suddenly stricken an ashen hue; great beads of sweat stood out upon his forehead.

"You said—'is son?" he repeated in a terrible whisper. "Son? Where did 'e get 'im?"

The consul looked ill at ease.

"Er—quite honestly, I believe, Mr. Solomon, Sir James had married in South America; his wife is dead; his son, Horace, is twenty-two years of age and is manager of the Mowbray interests in China?"

"Since when?" demanded Solomon hoarsely. "And where in China."

"During the past year, I believe. His headquarters are at Hangchow, where the Mowbray and allied interests have large holdings in the silk industry. Confidentially, of course, he has not met with success. Sir James is going there himself to consolidate certain shipping lines and also to take personal charge of certain concessions in Chikiang province, west of Hangchow, given the Mowbray corporation by the republican government."

Solomon resumed his seat, and motioned the consul to go on.

"There is one other gentleman associated with Sir James, but his name has not been mentioned; I believe he is now at Vancouver, also on his way to China. Sir James had me in a few moments ago to assist him in engaging a captain for his steam yacht, which is now in harbor here. We were fortunate in securing Mr. Hiram King who is to—"

"What!" Solomon looked up again. "Not a blue-eyed chap, werry 'ard with 'is fists, as 'as quite a way with 'imself?"

"That possibly describes him. Mr. King is a young man, but prominent here in the city, and a keen business man. Sir James found he had capital to invest, but wished an active share in the work; therefore, he was engaged on the rather irregular basis of skipper, friend, and partner. The yacht, *Halcyon* by name, sails to-morrow. That, sir, is all that I know."

"And werry much obliged I am," said Solomon. "You'll not mention to a soul about me bein"ere, if you please, sir. It's priwate business, so to speak."

With the consul's assurances, he left the office, staggering a little as he went.

Once out in the open air, he paused to mop his face with a handkerchief. Then he leaned against the building, staring at his taxi with unseeing eyes. Despite the stiff salt breeze that swept the city, he was white as a sheet.

"Lud!" he muttered, removing his hat and running his fingers through his gray hair. "Lud! To think o' this 'ere bobbin' up to 'it me!"

An expression of anguish wrenched his features for a swift instant.

"James Mowbray!" The words were torn from him as in a groan. "And to think as you slipped out o' me 'ands in Egypt, after all—and 'id yourself away! All these years—and 'ere I be, and 'ere you be—just like that! And me thinkin' you dead an' gone to 'ell!"

He reached out one trembling hand against the wall for support.

"It's too much! It's too much! I—I ain't what I used to be," he mumbled. "And where's that 'ere devil Sanderson—Scotchy Sanderson? Did I kill 'im in Port Said, or did 'e up an' slip away, too? Dang it! I—I can't stand it!"

He wavered, tried to step out to the taxi, and fell heavily.

They said at the hospital that it was heart failure—by no means fatal, but serious enough to warrant complete rest, a long sea voyage, no excitement. He was without friends in the city; a crippled, helpless old man who claimed to be an utter stranger. Three days later he was discharged, looking the wreck of his former self.

"There goes a man who's had some frightful shock," said the head physician, gazing after the pathetic figure. "Poor old beggar—he was mumbling something about his wife when they brought him in. And Hiram, King of Tyre! Too bad. The old chap's off his head."

The "poor old beggar," however, climbed into a taxicab and disembarked a few moments later at the main longdistance telephone office. He appeared surprisingly cheerful, and in no long while was issuing instructions to one of the operators.

"My dear, money ain't no object in this 'ere case. I want to speak wi' Cap'n Lord, o' the steam yacht *Tyrian,* now layin' in San Pedro harbor down South, and I want to speak with 'im werry quick, miss, if so be as you'll favor me a bit. This 'ere for your trouble."

The tip of a five-dollar gold piece was an amazing incident to the operator, but it obtained quick action. Inside of twenty minutes she directed Solomon to a booth.

" 'Ello!" he wheezed. "This you, Mr. Lord? Werry good. 'Ow's that 'ere new propeller an' the barnacles on 'er bottom; all ship-shape an' Bristol fashion, eh? Well, sir, you'll 'ave to get up 'ere in a mortal 'urry, and be pickin' of me up, just like that. I've been in 'ospital, I 'ave—no, no, there ain't no trouble to speak of now. Send me a wireless at the Palace 'Otel—aye, aye! And 'urry."

He hung up the receiver with a sigh of relief.

CHAPTER II

KING UNDERSTANDS CLEARLY

HIRAM KING found the run to Honolulu hugely enjoyable. The *Halcyon* was an old craft, so slow that she had not been commandeered for war purposes; but she was the very height of luxury, both inwardly and outwardly, from the rosewood paneling in the saloon to the steam steering gear on the bridge.

His job as captain, King discovered, was a sinecure—or would have been one had he so desired, for the mates were quite willing to take full charge of the ship. This was not the way of Hiram King, however. He was the skipper, he enjoyed being skipper, and he meant to be skipper in every respect. Accordingly they had covered half the run to Honolulu before he had thoroughly digested the *Halcyon* from the skipper's angle. Then, and only then, he notified Sir James Mowbray that he was ready to talk business from a business angle.

That evening he was summoned to the owner's cabin.

Mowbray was a tall, lithe man who appeared to be closer to fifty than forty. His face was long, thin, deeply lined, and yellowed by tropical fevers. A grizzled brown Vandyke beard was close-trimmed, and did not hide an undershot chin and firm mouth; the dark eyes were very deeply set. Prosperity sat well upon James Mowbray. He spoke crisply, authoritatively, as one accustomed to command and be obeyed.

"Ah, glad to see you, Captain King!" His speech was tinged with colonial freedom, lacking the usual reserve of the Briton.

"Cigarettes—no? Then your pipe, by all means. 'Pon my word, you've been making the men stand up lately, I hear!"

"That's my job," and King chuckled. The other nodded, and lighted a cigarette.

"Well, my boy, you've certainly proven that you have energy to spare; you'll do. As I told you, I wanted a man with energy; secondarily, with money to invest."

"I've not invested it yet. The securities are only in your safe temporarily."

Sir James laughed.

"All well and good. As you are aware, I'm heavily interested in the new British shipping combination. Part of my business in the Orient is to extend that combination over the various small British lines along the China and Australasia coasts. I am also purposing to whip into shape certain private investments and concessions in China, which, between ourselves, have been rather unfortunately handled by my son during the past year."

King nodded in silence. Sir James pursued the subject after an instant.

"You will, of course, appreciate the confidence, Captain King. Now, as the opening for investment which we discussed only vaguely in San Francisco."

"I'd rather hoped that I could get in on that British combine," broke in King. "Of course I've only a scant fifty thousand dollars tucked away."

"That's out of the question, my boy; the project is purely British, you know, and the subscription lists have long ago been closed. However, we shall come back to the subject in a moment. At Honolulu I expect to meet one of my business associates from Canada, who will come aboard with his niece; also my son will come aboard there. I shall proceed to China by the Pacific Mail. You, however, will take the yacht elsewhere under orders from the business partner of whom I speak—Mr. Douglas Sanderson, a prominent banker of Winnipeg and Vancouver."

Sir James paused as if expecting to counter some objection.

But Hiram King said nothing. He appeared much occupied in watching the tinge of color which his new meerschaum was gradually absorbing. King was quite willing to hear the other man to the end before making objections. This change in the owner's plans was, so far, none of his affair.

"You may know," went on Mowbray slowly, "that the Dutch colonial government has been sadly handicapped by the war, particularly as regards Java and the Celebes. In forming the Oriental shipping combination, I shall endeavor to favor them as much as possible in such respects as ports of call and so forth. This, you will understand, in an entirely legitimate fashion.

"The Dutch, in return, are opening to the capital which I control one of their closely guarded gold concessions in the Celebes. Mr. Sanderson knows that country very thoroughly, and is going there to inspect the concession; if all is as represented, we shall meet the Dutch commissioners and sign the agreements.

"It is in this concession that I would recommend your investment of funds, Captain King. You may, of course, settle the matter for yourself, but I would suggest that you go over the ground with Mr. Sanderson before deciding it. It should prove a very lucrative thing."

King smoked for a moment in silence.

"Thank you very much for the opportunity, Sir James. Provided I do go into this enterprise, what active share would I have in it? I am after work, you know; the more work to do, the more difficulties to keep me busy, the better!"

Sir James laughed.

"My dear fellow, that is precisely why I recommend you to this investment. If it goes through, we'll want a resident manager—a man of energy and one who can be trusted fully. Keep that in your mind's eye, King."

"Good! Then at Honolulu I'll turn over those securities of mine to be sold, and if Sanderson and I agree on the enterprise

I'll make you out a check and discuss stock details when the transaction with the Dutchmen is concluded."

In his own cabin, after a turn or two about the quarterdeck, Hiram King lighted his meerschaum and gazed reflectively at the smoke before undressing.

"You're an extremely clever man, Sir James Mowbray," he soliloquized to himself. "A big man in England, no doubt; he's a financial pillar and a commercial keelson—h'm! Then why the devil is he grafting? He doesn't need that concession badly enough to get it in a crooked fashion. There's only one answer. Something wrong in his blood! I'll have to look him up at Honolulu."

King knew very well that the big shipping combine was being formed with an eye to the post-bellum trade situation—the war after the war; and especially was this true in the Orient. That Mowbray should favor the Dutch colonies, in return for one of their jealously restricted gold concessions in the Celebes, was out and out graft—no less.

"But why worry about his soul?" reflected King as he turned into his bunk. "It will be a blamed fine investment, and a good deal safer just now than any shipping business."

So, without further incident, they raised the islands and slipped in to anchorage under Diamond Head.

When a man turns fifty thousand dollars, or its equivalent, into a checking account at one lick, and when he is a man highly recommended in every way he can obtain about anything he desires in the way of confidential information.

Thus Hiram King speedily became acquainted with the fashion in which James Mowbray, of South America and nowhere, had come into an unexpected title. Sanderson, his bank ascertained by cable, was a man who for the past five years had been actively identified with extensive banking operations in the northwest of Canada. His money had been made in rubber.

"Rubber!" King sat at a table in the Japanese inn and cogitated this report over a tall but innocuous drink. "And rubber comes from South America! That cinches it. Mowbray and Sanderson knew each other down there.

"Now that Mowbray's handling millions, South America is still in his blood: he can't resist the chance to graft. Must be pretty rotten inside—h'm! He'll take my fifty thousand like a shot, too, if I let him, or he'll tell Sanderson how to take it. Good! I'll give it to him. Then I'll take the Celebes concession away from 'em both. The only question is, how will Sanderson attempt to get hold of my money legally? We'll wait and see. In the meantime—"

From Waikiki, Hiram King returned to town. If he were perplexed, he showed it not at all; his rather square features were quite blank, his china-blue eyes absolutely devoid of expression. He looked much more like a meditative bank clerk on a holiday than a two-fisted captain of the merchant marine.

Alighting from the trolley car, he walked a few blocks and turned into John's Place. Here he strode directly to an obscure table, where, as if awaiting his coming, sat two men. One was the boatswain of the *Halcyon,* the other a seaman, also from the yacht.

"Well?" said King curtly, as he came to the table and seated himself. "Yes or no?"

"Yes it is, cap'n," answered the boatswain, albeit a trifle sheepishly. "She's a wonnerful fine berth, she is, but—well, sir, it's poor men we are."

"Rather wise men just at present," said King dryly. From his pocket he took a small canvas bag and counted out five hundred dollars in gold. He pushed it toward them. "There's your advance. Get aboard the *Shoshen Maru* immediately—she sails at midnight—and before Diamond Head's out of sight her purser will give you the other five hundred. Your passages are paid to Nagasaki. Here are the tickets."

He handed them two ticket envelopes, and rose.

"Good night, lads, and good luck! Keep out of sight for a few months. Good luck!"

"Same to you, sir," they responded.

Hiram King strode away from John's place and made his way to the water front. It was only nine in the evening, and the great harbor was alive with lights. Instead of proceeding to where the *Halcyon's* launch awaited him, however, King called up a boatman and was presently on his way from shore.

Following his directions, the boatman took him alongside of a dingy little fore-and-aft schooner that stunk abominably of copra and other things indescribably. King sniffed as they came to leeward of her, and grinned.

"Sheer off, down there!" growled a voice.

"All right, Marcos!" sang out King. "I'm coming aboard."

He bade the boatman wait, and a moment later took a seat in the little cabin of the schooner. Her master, a big, square-jawed Peruvian, faced him with inquiring gaze.

"A lighter came off to-night with some monstrous big packing cases, sir," said Marcos in perfect English. "I supposed you had sent them."

"Yes." King nodded as he puffed at his pipe. "Yes, Marcos, I ordered them before leaving San Francisco. It's a wireless outfit. Are you operator enough to install it?"

"*Si, señor.* If I am not, then I have picked up a man who can; he was assistant operator at one of the island stations and was fired for drinking. Once at sea—"

"Very good, Marcos. Pull up your hook as soon as you can get papers for Macassar in the Celebes. Go there and wait for orders from me; if they come by wireless, they'll be in our regular cable code. If I'm there ahead of you, I'll leave a letter with the American consul."

"*Si, señor.*"

"About six bells to-morrow afternoon put ashore Mimms and Grimsen. I want Mimms to ship as A.B., Grimsen as quartermaster, aboard the *Halcyon;* see that they're provided with two automatics each. I'll send our launch ashore for 'em."

"*Si servase, señor,*" returned Marcos apologetically. "I hate to lose that Grimsen. I had to fire my second mate because he tried to knife me, and without Grimsen—"

"Oh, you'll get him back before a great while, Marcos. In the meantime, ship some one here." King rose. "Need any money? No? Then—see you at Macassar maybe."

"Hasta luego," and Marcos showed his white teeth in a smile as they struck hands.

King returned to shore, then sought the yacht's launch and went aboard.

On the following day arrived Douglas Sanderson and his niece via the Oriental line from Vancouver, while from the westward Horace Mowbray was due in another twenty-four hours. Sir James had discovered the desertion of his two men, and had willingly assented when King proposed to fill their places. Accordingly Grimsen and Mimms came aboard as scheduled.

King was busied with this and other matters through the afternoon, and he did not meet the new guests until dinner that evening. When he did meet them, it was with a certain sense of shock.

Sanderson was a huge hawk of a man, with a large, rangy figure tokening great strength, vulpine eyes and features, and a straggly red mustache; he inspected King with a sniff as they shook hands, and King, taking an instant aversion to the man, was very polite. But—

Hiram King had the pleasure of taking Norma Douglas in to dinner.

He could not understand it. King did not regard Mowbray and Sanderson as financiers, as great men; he regarded them simply as men, and held them in none too high esteem from what he had fathomed of their characters. How, then, did Norma Douglas come within the arc of their lives? It seemed incredible!

Before the dinner was over he had learned the answer, from piecing together what was said. Norma, an orphan, had come out to Canada, and her uncle three years previously; her mother had been the sister of Douglas Sanderson; her life in Canada had largely stripped away her Scotch reserve.

To King she was as a dream. He found her not beautiful in the accepted sense of the term, but sensible, practical, and vibrant with the essence of youth; she could not be more than twenty-two, he considered. She retained her rosy, old-country cheeks, and beneath her curling tendrils of brown hair lay eyes of a deep violet blue, thoughtful, alert, merry.

When Hiram King turned in that night he dreamed of a woman's face for the first time in his life.

He did not stand watches here in port, and was awakened early the next morning by the new quartermaster. Grimsen, who quietly entered the cabin, closed the door, and touched King on the forehead. Grimsen was a Danish-French product of Australasia, knew the island seas like a book, and spoke every tongue under heaven correctly, except English, which he spoke after no fashion except his own.

"What is it?" demanded King, sitting up and staring at his visitor.

"Wale, sir, I hafe not know," answered Grimsen hesitantly. "You look through the port, mebbe you see that *Tyrian*."

Knowing his man well, King asked no questions, but obeyed. Off the port quarter he made out the gray shape of the yacht *Tyrian*. She had dropped anchor only a few hours after the *Halcyon,* and King at the time had admired her fast lines and generally efficient air.

"She is of Singapore," went on Grimsen ferociously, "and she hafe the English flag, sir. But I hafe look her up, and she hafe no registry. Yah! And yesterday late, when the big Scot man and his pretty girl hafe come aboard, there was a man on her bridge watching us through glasses. Yah! He is up there now, if you hafe want to see him."

Thus did Grimsen come to the point after his own fashion. King dived to his desk and secured his binoculars. Returning to the port, he focused upon the bridge of the *Tyrian*. A moment later he rubbed the large end of the glasses against his pajamas and looked again. Then he turned to Grimsen, his blue eyes a trifle wider than usual, his voice expressionless.

"Very good, Grimsen. Keep your eye peeled as usual; I'll look into this fellow."

Grimsen departed. Left alone, King once more looked through his glasses at the bridge of the other yacht; then he sank down on the edge of his bunk, staring at nothing. In his eyes was helpless perplexity.

"It's absolutely incredible!" he murmured dazedly. "Yet it's true. No one could ever mistake that dumpy little figure with its stiff walk—and the face! And the clay pipe! Yes, it's the man I met in San Francisco—the man who broke my meerschaum— *my* man of the St. Francis Hotel who refused to drink with me!

"Yet—was I so mistaken in him, after all? I must have been. What is he doing aboard that yacht? He's watching this ship, and—and that day, when I mentioned the name of Mowbray, he turned white and left me. I wonder, now! I must find out about this; there's something in the wind—something outside my calculations; Grimsen must make inquiries."

He dressed hurriedly and went on deck. Fifteen minutes later Grimsen went ashore in the launch, which immediately returned to the yacht.

Horace Mowbray arrived that morning, and came over to the *Halcyon* as soon as he was clear of quarantine. His complexion, like that of his father, was swarthily sallow, but where the father's eyes were deeply and authoritatively commanding those of the son were weakly arrogant and cruel; where the father's mouth was thin and cold that of the son was loose, selfishly obstinate. He made it quite clear that he regarded King and the other shipmen as servants pure and simple.

That afternoon, after a prolonged conference with his son, Sir James summoned King.

"I'm going ashore in an hour, Captain King. You'd better

come with me, and clear for Macassar, getting off before dark, if possible. I'll keep in touch with you by wireless."

"Very good, sir."

Sanderson was with Mowbray. As he turned to leave, King caught the harsh voice of the Scot-Canadian lifted in utter indifference to his proximity.

"It should be arranged before we reach Macassar, James; the boy is willing—ye could see it in his eye when he met her. I'll work on the lassie, never fear—"

The rest was lost. King stood for a moment in the companionway, his face white as he realized the import of those words. They meant to match Horace Mowbray and Norma Douglas— these two kestrel hawks meant to combine title and fortunes!

"Damn!" said King. The man Mimms was cleaning brasswork; he raised his head and stared in utter astonishment at his skipper. It was the first time any one, to the knowledge of Mimms, had heard Hiram King use that word or any other of its kind.

Grimsen had not returned when King took Sir James and his suit cases ashore. By the time King was clear of the harbor master the afternoon was two-thirds gone. Returning to the *Halcyon*, King was greeted by his first mate.

"Mr. Grimsen came aboard a half hour ago, sir, in shocking state. He said that he had been hit by an automobile—huh! Pack o' fools he must think us! If I don't know what kind of a smash a slung shot makes."

"Where is he? In his cabin? Very well," broke in King. "We pull out immediately. You will take the bridge and get up the anchor; I'll be along in a moment."

Making his way to Grimsen's cabin, King entered without ceremony, and found the quartermaster calmly washing and plastering a very badly cut head.

"Yes, sir—slung shot it was," he admitted, with a wry grin, to King's question. "Come near to hafe make me coffin bait, yah! A chink stevedore—walks up to me and hafe hit me without a word. I put him in the hospital."

"And the *Tyrian?*"

"About her I hafe find nothing at all. But she is owned by a man named John Solomon, and it was him what we hafe seen this morning on her bridge. That is all."

"What kind of a crew?"

"American officers, sir; Chinese crew."

"Oh! Chinese!"

King looked at his quartermaster, who met his quiet gaze with a slow wink. Nodding to himself, his lips a little compressed, King went on deck and took the bridge.

That queer little man named Solomon, who seemed to be keeping an eye on the harbor from his bridge, and who had a Chinese crew—why had he sent one of his men to blackjack Grimsen?

"The logical answer," reflected Hiram King to himself as he took the yacht out of the harbor, "is that he knew Grimsen was my man, saw him go ashore, and tried to lay him up. But such a supposition is impossible of credit; this fellow Solomon is only a washy-eyed cockney. No, by thunder, or he wouldn't own that yacht!

"Confound it, the man has me puzzled!"

CHAPTER III

VOX EX MACHINA

FOR THREE days after leaving Honolulu, Captain King held the *Halcyon* two points off her course—for an excellent reason; it gave the yacht a nastier roll, and Horace Mowbray was an extremely sick young man.

The crew was English, all except the cook, who was a Chinaman, Ling Woo by name. The first mate had a partially paralyzed hand, the second had a bad heart—and so forth; none of the men were disabled, but each was individually useless to the English navy, hence their signatures on the yacht's papers. Having by this time firmly impressed upon them that he and none other was skipper, Hiram King eased off on his watches and saw a good deal of Miss Norma Douglas.

On the third afternoon out, he passed through the saloon and encountered the girl, who was opening up a case of new records which Sir James had ordered aboard at Honolulu—American records which fitted the big, old-fashioned English cylinder phonograph installed in a corner of the saloon.

"Come and help me, Captain King!" she called gayly. "That is, if you can stand this tinned music. Uncle is taking his siesta, I've read all my novels, and now I'm going to investigate these records; Sir James Mowbray told me that he'd ordered some of the finest obtainable, and I'm wild to hear them."

"Very gladly, Miss Douglas. You'll not find me a skilled musician, but I'll try and master the technique of *this* instrument."

The records had not been disturbed since they had been

fetched aboard, on the last day in port. King opened up the corrugated board case, while Miss Douglas made room in the rosewood cabinet for the new pieces. Then, when the last of the cylinders had been unpacked and set on the floor, and the steward had taken away the debris, they went over the titles.

"What are these?" With a puzzled frown, the girl picked up two of the blue cases which bore no printed inscription, but instead had been penciled "Special." "Oh, good! Let us begin our concert with the unexpected, Captain King. Don't you love surprises?"

"I do," and King smiled a little as he took from its cotton-sheathed case one of the brownish-gray wax cylinders. A moment later he had adjusted it and started the machine.

Gaining permission to smoke, King began to fill his pipe while the needle scratched over the first of the record. Then suddenly his fingers paused in their employment.

"Thank you werry much, sir!" exclaimed a voice from the big horn—a voice that made King's blue eyes open a trifle wider. "If you'll be so good as to wait a jiffy, I'll 'ave me old pipe lit up, then I can tell me story, shipshape an' Bristol fashion."

That voice pierced King like a knife. It was the voice of the little man whom he had met at the St. Francis in San Francisco—the wheezy, unmistakable voice of the little cockney who owned the *Tyrian*—the voice of John Solomon! There could be no error.

"I wonder who's talking!" exclaimed Norma Douglas, her eyes sparkling with excitement. "My! Doesn't it sound interesting?"

"Very," agreed King. He was thunderstruck with amazement, but did not show it. After a brief period of scratches, the wheezy voice took up an abrupt speech:

> "It 'appened in Port Said, a matter o' goin' on thirty year back, where I'd taken up me business o' ship chandlering and 'ad made a fair start. I'd been an' got married, too.
> "Well, sir, one time I 'ad to go to Alexandria on werry important business, just like that. There was two men in Port

Said, British, they was, and they 'ad 'appened to learn by accident, like, as 'ow I kept a bit o' money and jewelry in the safe
in me shop. I'd give 'em both a lift at odd times, not expectin'
to be repaid; 'cause why, charity is its own reward.

"Howsomever, them 'ere men repaid me. While I was up an'
gone, they went an' broke into me shop and cracked me safe.
Me wife 'ad a baby at the time, and thinkin' she 'eard a noise,
she up and discovered them 'ere men, and, what's more, she
recognized them. But before she could call for 'elp, they 'ad
caught 'er.

"What did them 'ere men, as was be'olden to me for 'elp,
do then? Why, sir, they put that poor 'elpless woman an' baby
down aboard a Levantine lugger, and they went and 'ired the
Greek skipper to land 'em up the Syrian coast, so they could
get out o' the way wi' their loot afore I got after 'em for the
crime.

"Well, sir, that 'ere was the last 'eard o' me poor wife, 'cause
why, that there danged Levantine went down with all 'ands in
a squall off Corfu—"

The voice broke off short in a wheezy choke. Then, as King
rose, thinking the record was finished, it said a few words more:

"But I'm a-goin' to tell you about them 'ere two men—"

This was the end. King checked the machine and removed
the record, then turned to face Norma Douglas. Inwardly he
was white-hot with excitement, but no hint of this was visible
in his face as he spoke:

"Shall we put on that other 'special' record? I fancy it's a
continuation of this one, but it seems a bit tragic."

"Oh, do put it on!" cried the girl eagerly. "I think it's a wonderful story. And did you hear the awful pathos in that man's voice?
It sounds almost as if it were real; there may be some huge joke at
the end, of course, yet whoever is talking must be a very magnificent actor. And the cockney brogue is marvelously done."

"Perhaps it is real," said King soberly as he put on the second
cylinder.

For a moment they sat in silence; then suddenly the wheezy voice of Solomon abruptly cut in upon them, but now there was a new note, a terrible note, in his tone:

"Them 'ere two men was the actual murderers of me family. I found out about it, I gathered me friends, and I went after 'em. One was killed down in Egypt—or I thought as 'ow 'e was. The other was killed in Suez—or so me men told me.

"But now, twenty-odd year afterward, I 'ave just found that them two men, both on 'em, is still alive. It come to me quick an' sudden, and the shock of it put me in 'ospital—it did that!

"They knowed me, them 'ere two men. All these years they'd been 'iding from me justice—'iding in the wilds o' South America. But now—now I'm goin' to do as I've been done by, an' worse! I'm a-goin' to make life a merry 'ell for them 'ere two men; I'm a-goin' to put the livin' fear o' John Solomon into 'em afore I kill 'em! I am that. Mebbe as 'ow you'd like to know their names? Just a minute, sir, till I get this 'ere pipe lit; I ain't as young as I might be, and me 'ands is a bit trembly, so to speak."

The voice broke off, and for a space only the scratch of the needle filled the saloon.

"He—he seems to have a strong sense of the dramatic pause," said Miss Douglas, with a laugh. But her laugh rang false. Even she had been shaken by the terrible tensity of the voice which had come to them.

King sat staring at the machine, immobile, waiting. Already he had guessed what was coming. The great question in his mind was concerning the truth of this story.

Intuitively he sensed at last the explanation of Solomon's activities. He knew that against his employers and possible partners had uprisen a hideous ghost from the past. That they had in other days been guilty of gross crime was not improbable; it did not concern him in the least.

"Why, that's the end of it!" The voice of Norma Douglas broke in upon him as the needle clicked off the end of the record. "He didn't give their names, after all."

King sprang up and checked the machine. Then he turned to the girl, his blue eyes quite placid and unexcited. Why not put it to the test?

"Miss Douglas," he said quietly, "this is a very odd occurrence. You see, this is actually a true story; the man who told it is named John Solomon, and I've met him and spoken with him long enough to recognize his voice instantly. The story is probably true."

"What!" The violet eyes of the girl met his with a tragic realization in their depths. "Then what was it doing here—why did Sir James—"

"That is what I'd like to call your uncle to explain. He may know about it."

King touched an electric button. A moment later the steward bobbed in the door.

"Steward, go to Mr. Sanderson's room, and, if he is still sleeping, rouse him up. Give him my compliments, and ask if he can join us here at once."

"Yus, sir." The steward bobbed out, and was gone.

King stared down at his hand, silent for a moment. The girl's troubled look followed his eyes; then, leaning forward, she spoke as if to relieve the tension which they seemed to have sensed in unison.

"What an odd ring, Captain King! Do you mind if I look at it?"

King smiled, and twisted the ring from his finger, extending it to her.

"Certainly not, Miss Douglas. It belonged to my mother, or so I am told; she died when I was a baby. It must be old. I very seldom wear it; happened to slip it on to-day."

"It certainly looks old—and it's really beautiful!" said the girl quietly.

The ring was large—more a man's ring than a woman's—and

had a large square gold bezel. Upon this was a deeply incised square, with diagonal lines running from corner to corner; the incisions had been filled with black enamel.

A moment later, as the great figure of Sanderson filled the starboard door, Norma Douglas handed back the ring to its owner. King dropped it into his vest pocket and rose.

"Sorry to have disturbed you, Mr. Sanderson," he said apologetically, "but Miss Douglas found a very queer phonograph record among a lot that Sir James sent aboard us at Honolulu. She thought you might know something about it."

"Uh-huh!" Sanderson dropped into a chair and pulled forth a cigar. "Let's hear it."

King repeated the second cylinder, and, sitting down, placidly resumed his pipe.

For all his money, the banker was a rough man, the corners of his soul unpolished. As the first words of that second cylinder wheezed out upon the room, Sanderson let fall a smothered oath. His eyes went to King, a lurid flame shooting in their depths, but the skipper was so obviously innocent of purpose that Sanderson stared back to the machine.

Slowly, as he listened, the vulpine features of the man grew harsher, whiter, more pronounced. His powerful fingers tightened; he did not know that the cigar in his hand had crumpled to powder, unlit. Then came fear into his face.

Although seeming to gaze, wide-eyed, at the machine, Hiram King observed these things, and he knew that he had guessed aright. The two men of the story were Sanderson and Mowbray.

There came the slow, interminable rasp as the voice of Solomon ceased. Sanderson was leaning forward now, beads of sweat standing out on his forehead. Suddenly he sprang to his feet, rushed forward, and with a smashing blow of his fist struck the wax record into a thousand fragments. The suspense of awaiting the names had broken him.

"Damn it!" He whirled, catlike for all his size, his face

convulsed. "We thought he was dead four years ago. Mowbray had heard about it."

He paused, realizing what he was saying. Norma Douglas had come to her feet, and was staring at him, her face ghastly white.

"Uncle!" she broke out. "Uncle—what do you mean? Not—not that you and Sir James—I knew you had been in Egypt—"

The eyes of Sanderson leaped from her to King. In that moment King knew how dangerous was this man, for Sanderson straightway collected himself and forced a smile.

"Yes," he said, his harsh voice cold as ice. "Yes, my dear. I am sorry that this happening arose in such a fashion, Captain King—"

"I beg your pardon, sir." King bowed slightly and turned to the door. "I regret that I was present. If you will allow me to forget the entire matter—"

"Not at all!" exclaimed Sanderson imperatively. "Stop, sir! Norma, you need not stare at me so—quite needless, lass. Sit down and I'll tell you about it."

They obeyed. Sanderson also seated himself, and drew another cigar from his pocket. But his fingers trembled as he lighted it.

"How that cursed thing came aboard I don't know," he said, with apparent frankness. "Probably Mowbray framed it up; it's like one of his devilish jokes. This fellow Solomon is a real person, by the way; Mowbray and I knew him when we were in South America. He's a lunatic, harmless enough. Mowbray and I were—were instrumental in having him confined in an asylum, and he swore eternal hatred against us. We heard some years ago that he was dead. The poor fellow was quite off his head. He's dead now and out of the way."

Norma drew a deep breath as she gazed at him.

"Then—then this story, uncle, is true?"

"Is utterly absurd, lass." Sanderson forced a rough laugh. "No doubt Mowbray fixed up that cylinder; it's like him. And I'll admit that when I heard the name of John Solomon I was hit for a moment. You see, he was an infernal clever fellow; many

lunatics are. He followed us for two or three years. Well, he's
dead now and out of harm's reach, so I'll not say more against
him. That's all."

King excused himself and went to the bridge.

Pacing up and down in the keen sea wind, he threshed out
the affair. That Sanderson had lied like a trooper he knew very
well. That the story which the phonograph had told was true in
every word he believed indubitably.

Yet, what of it? It was not his concern. His duty to his owners
was obvious.

"It's a curious situation," he reflected, dismissing the story
entirely. "Here I've been preparing to be trimmed financially by
Mowbray and Sanderson—and to trim them if my suspicion
is right. Now Solomon comes on the scene; it's quite plain that
he spoke the truth in that record, that he is after Mowbray and
Sanderson himself with deadly intent.

"Well! It's quite possible they'll be so badly scared that they'll
run straight with me. In that case my duty is to stand by them;
a twenty-year-old crime has nothing to do with it. H'm! It's a
queer world."

An hour later he heard the wireless crackling, and stepped
into the office. The operator glanced up with a smile.

"Odd sort of messages to be sending, sir—eh?"

King lifted his brows in surprise. Evidently considering that
the skipper was "in" on whatever was forward, the operator held
out two messages he had written down—one a message which
had been sent by Sanderson to Sir James Mowbray, on the *Ocea-
nia* for Shanghai; the other one which had come in reply from
Mowbray.

Sanderson's message read: "Have discovered Solomon alive
and somewhere about." The answer from Mowbray was equally
curt and significant: "So have I."

King went back to his pacing across the bridge deck, chuck-
ling to himself. It was plain that Solomon had the situation
thoroughly in hand and knew that Mowbray was now off the

Halcyon and bound for China. King could imagine that Sir James Mowbray had received a far worse shock than had come to Sanderson.

"This little cockney is certainly possessed of a devil," he reflected. "How did he know that Mowbray was sending those things aboard, and how did he?—let's see! Mowbray ordered them the day we anchored, and they came aboard almost the last thing. Solomon must have been spying on every one who went ashore; yes, that's it. I'll bet a dollar he knew about my visit to the old schooner. Well, he'd better try none of his tricks on *me*."

That evening while he was dressing for dinner, King removed the ring from his pocket and slipped it on his finger, intending later to place it with his personal valuables in his desk. He had barely finished dressing when the steward knocked.

"Miss Douglas, sir, is up on the for'ard deck. She arsks, sir, if you'll be so good as to step up that wye immediate."

"Sighted a submarine?" demanded King jocularly.

"I think, sir, as she wants to speak with you right off."

"Very well. Tell her I'll be along in no time."

Two minutes later King left his cabin and went forward by the port alley. Amidships, he paused at a sudden roll of the ship and threw out his hand to a stanchion for support.

As he did so there came a choking cry from behind him. He whirled, and to his utter stupefaction saw the Chinese cook standing in a doorway with a short creese half raised. The man had appeared silently, with obvious intent, but something had halted him.

King caught him by the wrist and wrung hard. The cook cried out again, and the knife fell to the deck. The man seemed possessed by inarticulate fright.

"What's the matter with you, Ling Woo?" snapped King. "Trying to murder me, were you?"

"Ling!" cried the man, pointing to King's hand. "Where you catchum ling?"

"Where I catchum ring? None of your business! Who put you up to this?"

It seemed as though a mask fell over the man's face.

"No savvy," he returned sullenly. "I catchum one piecee knife, peelum potate."

There flashed across King's mind Grimsen's report on the *Tyrian*—a Chinese crew!

"So Cap'n Solomon put you up to this, did he?" exclaimed King harshly. For some reason the old ring had saved his life, and King was not slow to appreciate the fact. "You savvy that ring, eh? You make one first chop big mistake this time, Ling Woo. March!"

He took the man by the neck, picked up the knife, and without ceremony shoved Ling Woo. Reaching the forward deck, he saw Miss Douglas standing in the bows, but paid her no attention.

"Here, you!" His voice brought the two men on watch running to him. "Stow this fellow in irons below—and watch out for him. He nearly got this knife into me. Too much opium probably. Let him go to-morrow morning. You savvy that, Ling Woo? Try any more of such work, and overboard you go!"

"I savvy heap plenty," mumbled the abashed cook as he was seized by the two men. "I catchum much solly, cap'n."

"You'd better be sorry!"

King laughed shortly and strode forward to meet the gaze of Miss Douglas.

"What's happened?" she cried, staring at the receding figures. "What has he done?"

"Oh, merely a breach of discipline," and King smiled. "The steward told me that you wished to speak with me, Miss Douglas."

She squared around toward him, as if suddenly remembering. King was astonished to see how hard and cold and antagonistic her face had swiftly become.

"Yes, I did, Captain King. I want an explanation from you.

When you played that record for my uncle you deliberately repeated the second cylinder, ignoring the first one. You admitted to me that you knew and had spoken with the man Solomon, although my uncle very distinctly said that he was dead.

"Now, you may fool my uncle, Captain King, but you cannot fool me! From the moment we began to play the first cylinder you were highly excited. Oh, I was watching you! And I intend to know at once the truth from your own lips. Did you bring those records aboard, as I suspect? Did you deliberately arrange to give my uncle that shock? Are you in league with this madman Solomon—are you a traitor to your employers and possible partners?"

King smiled a little. He was thinking that this girl was extraordinarily clever—a wonderful, wonderful young woman!

CHAPTER IV

HORACE LEARNS HIS PLACE

"NO, MISS DOUGLAS, I am not guilty on all counts," said King slowly. "You must understand one thing—Mr. Sanderson told you this man was dead, doubtless to allay any possible fears on your part. Solomon is not dead; he was at Honolulu when we left, and it is my belief that he sent those records aboard us.

"As for my being in league with Solomon, did you not see me send Ling Woo to be ironed a moment ago? On my way here the cook barely missed getting his creese into my back. He was sent by Solomon to murder me."

The girl shrank back, a little cry on her lips.

"It's quite true; ask Ling Woo if you wish," went on King gravely. "Now, Miss Douglas, I am naturally diffident about discussing the story told through that phonograph. I—"

She broke in quickly, hotly:

"If you are diffident about it, that means you disbelieve my uncle!"

"You naturally believe him," King evaded the point. "I am in the employ of Sir James Mowbray—at least nominally so—and I refuse to discuss the subject of his past life or that of your uncle; about it I know no more than you, and my private opinions I prefer to keep to myself.

"You ask me for my own intentions. Can you not guess? This man Solomon will hardly run across our path again, Miss Douglas; if he does so, I shall bend every energy to crush him—quite literally, I assure you. My motive is twofold, as you can see. My duty to my owners, the compellent duty of every seaman, is motive enough. On top of that, Solomon has made a dastardly attempt to murder me indirectly. Believe me, Miss Douglas, I shall sooner or later repay that attempt with big interest! I am not a man who forgets his debts. John Solomon shall bitterly regret the day when he crossed *my* path."

For a moment longer her eyes dwelt searchingly upon him, then she extended her hand.

"Thank you, Captain King. You have been very frank, and I appreciate it. Shall we go to dinner?"

King bowed assent. The incident was closed so far as he was concerned, but he knew that Norma Douglas, her very silence on the subject being tacit admittance, believed the story of John Solomon rather than that of Sanderson. No avuncular loyalty could stand against the plain evidence of the voice that had come from the machine—against the fact that Sanderson had palpably lied in his explanation.

In the days following, King saw little of her. The *Halcyon* was bearing along on her true course now, they had run into magnificent weather, and Horace Mowbray had found his sea legs. The heir to the baronetcy promptly became as a second shadow to Norma Douglas.

King was quite certain that the girl was avoiding him; he understood that she must feel a horror of the thing they had together discovered—the brand that stood upon the past life of her uncle. He was convinced that she disbelieved Sanderson entirely.

"I'm glad she takes the trouble to avoid me," he thought smilingly. "She's worried. All the while she's testing out that blessed uncle of hers, and she is finding him false. Thank Heaven she has been awakened to his true character! Yes, I'm glad she's avoiding me. If she were not, then I'd begin to grow anxious."

King had plenty of other matters to cause him inward uneasiness, if not anxiety. The ship herself was running like clockwork;

Ling Woo had been released and was conducting himself with exemplary caution—but trouble was in the air.

Sanderson was showing the effects of worry. He had developed nerves; he spoke seldom, watched everything and every one, and his huge figure was always striding somewhere about the decks, as if he feared to remain under cover. He had chewed his mustache ragged. Since that scene over the records, he had treated King with surly coldness, which at infrequent intervals became strikingly cordial warmth. Obviously the man was almost beside himself.

Horace Mowbray was, of course, entirely blind to any sinister influence beneath the surface of things. He was more Spanish-Brazilian than English, for he had never seen England until his father had been called to the baronetcy, and unless he exerted himself in the effort to be agreeable, which he seldom troubled to do, he possessed the happy faculty of being mortally offensive to all around him. He was, in short, a snob of the first water.

Being a judge neither of men nor of anything else, he mistook King's punctilious politeness for servility. From this error he was very rudely aroused one noon.

The barometer was making a headlong plunge for the cellar, and on the morning this fact was noted King prepared to take careful observations at noon with a possible typhoon in view. At five minutes before noon, Horace Mowbray made his appearance on the bridge after very evident potations. He was just in prime shape to make public the dislike which he had taken to King.

"There's—there's only one thing wrong with this ship," he announced, steadying himself against the front wall of the wheelhouse and addressing the helmsman, who happened to be Quartermaster Grimsen, through the open window with entire disregard of the fact that King stood almost at his elbow.

"Jus' one thing wrong," he hiccuped. "That's a skipper of a baronet's yacht who—who wears evening clothes—at dinner—*and* thinks his bally self better than his owners!"

Finding that no one paid any attention to him, Mowbray whirled about and clapped King heavily on the shoulder, heedless that the captain was in position to "shoot the sun."

"I—I'm addressin' you, old top!" he exclaimed thickly. "Yes, look at me all you like. I don't—don't want you to wear 'em any more, you savvy. Maybe you'd savvy pidgin English better. I've lived in China, I have—"

"You get off this bridge!" said King quietly.

Mowbray stared, then drew himself up and laughed.

"That's bloody rich, that is!" he said. "You—tellin' me get off my own bridge! Who owns this ship, old top? Who—"

"Get off inside of thirty seconds or I put you off!" said King placidly. "You're interfering with important duty, sir."

"Interfere nothin'!" responded Mowbray, again clapping the captain on the shoulder. "Go ahead with duty, but don't wear 'em any more, I tell you. Here, take your eyes away from that bally thing—look at me, will you! Don't you know I'm owner—"

"It hafe one minute to noon, sir," said Grimsen stolidly.

An instant later young Mowbray found himself seized by neck and arm, run across the ladder, hustled down, and flung to the deck below, where he rolled into the scuppers. King returned to his post and made his observation.

Before he had quite finished, Sanderson's huge figure arose on the ladder, waited until King had done, then approached with lowering gaze.

"What's this, Captain King? Mr. Mowbray is telling me you insulted him, threw him off the bridge, and so forth. What's the meaning of it?"

King faced him with a calm gaze.

"Why, sir, it means that I'm captain of this ship. When I'm making observations to determine our exact position, with a hurricane in prospect, I can't have any half-drunken fellow up here interfering with my work. If I were you, I'd cut off his liquor."

Sanderson's vulpine features turned livid.

"Do you realize, sir, that—that this is a gentleman's ship? That you are only—"

"That I am in command of her—yes," said King, his blue eyes very level. For a long moment Sanderson glared at him, then forced a smile.

"You're right; aye, ye have the right of it, cap'n!" he growled half amiably. "The cub was up to his eyes; that's the truth. You're right."

With this, he turned about and stamped away below again.

King turned, and met the stolid gaze of Grimsen across the wheel. They looked at each other silently, unwinking, as though between them were passing some occult message. The hard, sea-worn face of Grimsen slowly cracked into a queer smile.

"Yah! When we hafe to shoot that man, sir, it will be like shooting a gorilla—six bullets will not stop him! Eight bells, sir, and past."

"Make it so," said King, as the mate and another quartermaster came up to change watches.

Carefully and consistently King had, except at dinner, kept from mess until Sanderson, his niece, and Mowbray had left the table. He now went to his room and wrote out a wireless message regarding the price of copra and shell in the islands, addressing it to Captain Marcos, of the schooner *El Rey*, bound for Macassar from Honolulu. Sending it to the wireless operator for immediate dispatch, he went down to mess and encountered Sanderson just leaving.

"By the way, cap'n," said the big Scot, halting him, "would ye mind havin' a bit o' talk after lunch? I had a wireless from Sir James this morning, relayed from Manila, and we may change our plans a bit. Also, I don't suppose Mowbray told you about the concession arrangements?"

"Nothing definite, sir. Yes, I'll join you right after mess."

Forty minutes later King found Sanderson in the smoking room, alone and settled down to fill his pipe. Sanderson eyed him keenly; then spoke abruptly:

"Mowbray wirelesses, captain, that there's been some hitch in the ship-combine affair, and that for the present he's not going to take it up."

"Then the Dutch concession automatically lapses?"

"No. That goes through in any case, for Mowbray's an influential chap, d'ye see? The point is he's met a man aboard his *Oceanic* ship—the very man he wants to take hold of his interests in China. Name's Ralph Carter. Mowbray has engaged him to pull things into shape there, while Mowbray himself will come direct to Macassar to meet us."

While speaking, Sanderson produced a number of papers.

"You know the Gulf of Boni, just across Celebes from Macassar?"

King nodded in silence.

"I imagine the concession lie up that way; can't tell till we meet the commissioners at Macassar. Now, if the thing looks good to us, here's the way Mowbray and I talked it over. We want to buy the concession—"

"Buy it?" broke in King. "I thought it was an outright concession."

Sanderson eyed him savagely.

"You did? Why?"

"Sir James said as much. A *quid pro quo*—you understand."

Sanderson looked as if he wanted to curse. Then he smiled in a tigerish fashion. It was plain that he read no danger in the wide blue eyes of the young man facing him in the serious, earnest face.

"Oh, that's a bit of all right, too," he made response. "But we have to pay a nominal purchase price. Well, then! We buy the concession, Mowbray and I; then we issue stock, at dollar for dollar of the purchase price; then you buy as much of the stock as you wish at par, and remain on the spot as general manager. You can get the gold out, my boy; Mowbray has told me of your devilish energy. Good thing, I say. Blasted good thing."

"That seems very fair of you," said King, a hint of gratitude in his voice.

"It is. It's downright generous," assented Sanderson. "I told Mowbray so, but he laughed. 'What of it,' said he. 'Men like ourselves can afford to be generous.' He likes you, King. With Mowbray behind you you can go far, lad."

"It's very good of you, sir," said King humbly. "Of course I don't know much about business; I'll appreciate your guidance. And now another matter, if you please—this about the man John Solomon."

Sanderson started, as if the name had been a whip that flecked him on the raw.

"Eh, man? What the devil d'ye mean by that?"

"You know well enough," returned King placidly. "I met the man in San Francisco a few days before we sailed; had a little run-in on my own account. Later he tried to have me murdered. So, you see, I know that you lied to Miss Douglas the other day. I think she knows it, too. However, no matter—the point is, sir, that in this fight against Solomon I'm with you to the finish, and I'll whip him."

The face of Sanderson was suddenly gray, drawn, haggard; the man showed the awful nervous strain under which he had been laboring. Then he breathed a deep sigh and leaned back in his chair.

"All right, King; I don't mind saying I'm glad you're in with us. Tried to murder ye?"

King nodded.

"That's his way, damn him!" went on the other man heavily. "Dog you like a hound of hell, he will; he's a snake—you can't catch him except when he's ready to strike, and then if you miss your stroke he's got you!"

"He has a yacht—a fast one, the *Tyrian*," said King, his tone reflective. "She lay close to us in Honolulu. One of his men tried to kill Grimsen that day ashore. And that's how Solomon managed to send those records aboard us; he was watching us closely."

Sanderson's gaunt face assumed a more ghastly hue.

"Is that—the truth?"

"Yes." King smiled slightly. "But we'll get him, sir, this trip. I've got a few plans laid myself. If he shows up at Macassar or elsewhere—I'll get him before he strikes."

He rose and departed, leaving Sanderson staring at vacancy from somber eyes, a man who saw uprisen before him a dread specter from dead years.

Once in his own cabin, however, King's lip curled in scorn.

"The confounded crook!" he muttered. "They think I'm merely a sailor—sell me all the stock I want, and then squeeze me out! We'll see about that, Mr. Sanderson. Cursed fools, when they could have my utmost help merely by playing fair!"

That night the *Halcyon* ran into a heavy blow that continued for three days and grew heavier each day, until she was rolling and spinning through a smother of smashing surges that kept her decks awash.

Not a fast ship at best, she made up none of her lost time in the blow. Meanwhile, however, her wireless was working hard. The afternoon of his talk with Sanderson, King sought the wireless cubby and handed the operator a message to Captain Marcos, of the *El Rey*.

"H'm! 'Buy copra up the Gulf on Boni,'" said the operator, a young chap who had lost an eye at Ypres. "What's this *El Rey*, sir—a windjammer?"

"A trading ship in which I have an interest," returned King. "She's somewhere back of us, I imagine."

Sanderson and Mowbray were corresponding heavily, but King was too busy with his work to pay any attention to the messages until the third afternoon of the gale. Then, as watches were being changed at eight bells, the wireless operator beckoned King back into the wind-lashed cubby of a cabin.

"See here, sir," said the operator anxiously when the door had closed them in with the apparatus, "if you don't mind my asking, do you happen to know anything about this man John Solomon? Of course the name has been figuring in code messages between Mr. Sanderson and Sir James Mowbray, but I've a better reason for asking."

King dropped into a chair and lighted his meerschaum. "I know all about him," he responded slowly. "Why?"

"Well," and the operator looked nervous, "I just got in a brute of a message, sir, and wasn't sure just what to do with it. If it's a rotten fake, then well and good; if not, it seems to me the authorities should be called in. Here it is, Captain King. There was no code about it, either."

He picked up a paper and handed it to King, whose eyes widened slightly as he read the amazing message thereon:

> DOUGLAS SANDERSON, ESQUIRE, *Steam Yacht "Halcyon"*
>
> You may hope to catch sight of me within a few hours, if you look sharp. About the time you see me, another man will die aboard your ship. Look out for yourself! You will never escape from me the second time. John Solomon.

"Another man!" King smiled a little at the wording. By this time, he reflected, Solomon supposed him dead, murdered by the Chinese cook. Or had Solomon intercepted the messages to Captain Marcos? Well, no matter; they had been in private code. The words "another man" were open to double interpretation.

"What d'you think of it, sir? Should we notify the nearest British commissioner—"

"Not a bit of it, my dear chap. This would seem a maniacal thing to send by wireless, subject to picking up by any ship, but Mr. Solomon is no maniac. He's about as wise as his namesake, the king of the Jews. How far had that message traveled?"

"There's the very point, sir!" exclaimed the operator. "It was hard to guess at; I could just barely catch the message. Yet I'd swear it hadn't come far. It sounded to me very much as if the sender had been within a radius of fifty miles, but had sent the message so weakly that it would reach us and would not be picked up by any of the land stations."

"That's about it." King nodded, and returned the paper. "Well, you'd better deliver it to Mr. Sanderson, and keep your head shut about it."

"Trust me, sir. Thank you very much."

So another man was to be killed! Who? How? By whom? Ling Woo was biding quiescent. Was there still another of Solomon's agents aboard?

King was more worried than he cared to admit, for in this message he perceived much below the surface. Solomon, in his faster craft, could have overhauled the *Halcyon* at any time she left Honolulu, but had not done so. Now he was probably within fifty miles, and was seemingly preparing to give Sanderson a sight of his cockney person; at the same time, evidently by a plan coordinated long since, Ling Woo or another agent aboard the *Halcyon* was to commit murder.

"I said he was possessed by an infernal genius, and he is," reflected King. "He's going about it slowly—and deliberately to break down the nerve of Sanderson and Mowbray; he's doing it with an absolute disregard of human life, and, upon my word, I'd do the same thing were I in his place, with the awful grievance he has! Yet he's tried to enmesh me—and that's enough. I'll show that beggar a few things!"

King betook himself to the cabin of Grimsen, who was off watch.

"You've been knocking around the China Seas, Grimsen," he said. "Know any one by the name of Ralph Carter? Ever hear the name?"

"No, nefer. But Mimms tells me, sir, he hafe last night caught that yellow cook grinding up one of those sleefe knifes what the chinks throw athwart a man."

"So?" King frowned. "H'm! Somebody's due to be murdered aboard here before very long, Grimsen, and I shouldn't wonder if that chink is going to be responsible—or thinks he is. You tell Mimms to watch him pretty sharp. I don't want any one murdered if we can help it."

"Why not trice up the chink, sir?"

"I'm not at all sure he's the one. You keep a sharp eye out for yourself, too."

Grimsen smiled his hard, slow smile, saying nothing.

But with all their forewarning, all their watching, King and Grimsen could not prevent the hand of fate from falling.

AT EIGHT bells of the morning watch—or, lands-man's time, eight a.m.—Grimsen and the mate, he of the partially paralyzed hand, were descending the port ladder from the bridge. Sanderson was striding up and down on the bridge, keenly nervous; King had placed a man aloft to keep watch for any sign of the *Tyrian*.

Just as the two officers reached the deck, the lookout hailed that a smoke was coming up astern. Grimsen whirled as if to go up to the bridge. With his motion there came a singing flash of light—a knife, razor keen, that shaved under his arm and buried itself in the heart of the mate. The latter was dead before he touched the deck planks.

Two minutes later King was on the scene, gazing at Mimms, who held in his grip the writhing figure of Ling Woo.

"I was half a minute too late, sir," said Mimms in humble apology. "I was watchin' him sharp, and seen him duck up for'ard to the saloon. I sneaks after him—but Lord! 'Fore I could see what was up, the yeller devil had flung that knife, all o' twenty foot, sir, and was duckin' back below. Then I got him—too late."

"Call all hands," said King. "Grimsen, reeve a block to that yard for'ard."

Over the dead body of the mate, he gazed into the mortally frightened eyes of Sanderson. Solomon had fulfilled his threat in frightful earnest; the mate had died at the very moment the

Tyrian had been sighted. She was now overhauling them at a good rate.

"What—what do you mean to do?" demanded Sanderson awkwardly.

"Hang him."

"But—my heavens, man! You can't do that! It isn't legal!"

King's placid blue eyes checked the words.

"In half an hour, Mr. Sanderson, the *Tyrian* will be running past us. I intend to give John Solomon a message that he'll understand, blast him! I trust that you'll keep Miss Douglas below, out of sight for the present."

Sanderson nodded, and after a helpless gesture stamped off. King turned to face the crew assembling on the fore deck.

"My lads," he said quietly, "some time ago this Chinaman tried to murder me. He has now murdered a better man—and more by accident than anything else, since he was trying to get his knife into Mr. Grimsen.

"The parties who have hired this devil to do his murderous work are aboard that craft that's overhauling us. When they pass they'll see what we think of them and their friends. Mr. Grimsen is now reeving a block and tackle to the fore yardarm. Draw lots for six men to tail on the rope. Mimms, take that friend of yours for'ard and bend a line around his neck."

In the cold, savage justice of this there was something that appealed to the men, their murdered officer at their feet. Ling Woo submitted with imperturbable calm to the fate he saw coming. While the men were removing the mate's body, King walked forward to the murderer and held out his hand, on which shone the ring of old yellow gold.

"Tell me what that ring is, Ling Woo," he said, "and we'll not hang you."

A brief look of scorn flitted over the yellow features.

"I savvy you heap plenty now," returned the Celestial. "You catchum ling one piecee steal, eh? You not savvy—one first chop fool, cap'n!"

"You'll tell?"

"No! Go hellee."

King took himself to the bridge. The *Tyrian* was coming up fast, and through the glasses he could recognize her without trouble. The second mate, looking a bit pale, came to King's side.

"If you'll pardon me, sir, we really ought to turn this chap over to authority."

"I am authority," said King coldly. "There's more to all this than you yet know, Mr. Fortescue. By the way, you will now become mate; Quartermaster Grimsen has mate's papers and will be second mate, pending the O.K. of Sir James Mowbray."

"Very good, sir."

The mate withdrew to the wheelhouse. King turned to the foredeck below, standing alone at the break of the bridge, and lifted his hand.

"Ling Woo, will you confess who hired you to commit murder aboard this ship?"

The Celestial looked up, then spat on the deck.

"Go hellee!"

King signed to Grimsen; a low order, and the men tailed on the rope.

When, twenty minutes later, the *Tyrian* drew up abreast and half a mile distant, Sanderson had not reappeared. King, watching through his binoculars, could discern on the bridge of the other yacht the stumpy figure of John Solomon. A smile curved his lips as he saw the little cockney shake a fist toward them.

"Cut away the body, Mr. Grimsen," he said, addressing the men below. "Bos'n, at six bells pipe all hands to burial service. Pipe below!"

King did not see Norma Douglas until after the mate's body had been committed to the deep and the men dismissed. Then, as he turned toward his own cabin, King saw her standing between Sanderson and Horace Mowbray, silent witnesses of the funeral. He touched his cap as he passed, but from the girl's eyes he caught a flash of mingled anger and loathing—a glance that astonished and puzzled him. However, he passed on in silence, and set to work writing up the rough log of the morning's events. The *Tyrian* had swirled past and was hull down to the southwest, evidently bound on the same course as the *Halcyon*.

"This will hold Solomon for a while," reflected King grimly. "I'd like to know why the sight of that ring saved my life. Evidently Ling Woo had orders to get me or Grimsen; that infernal little cockney must have figured out that I was an obstacle to his plans. Come in!"

A knock had sounded. The door opened, and Mimms appeared.

"Well, Mimms?"

"Why, sir, you know that lame fellow in the port watch, Nast? He'd been to Mesopotamia with the Royal Naval Reserve men; got his limp there. When the *Tyrian* went past he recognized her right off, and I got him talking."

"Good! What luck?"

"Quite a bit, sir, if it's true. He says she was on government service in the Red Sea and those waters, under another name then. I mentioned the name John Solomon, and he bit at it proper. Says the guy is a funny little cockney; don't look worth a cuss, but is known all over Egypt and them parts as the one what put over the Arab revolution—stands big with the Britishers, sir. That's all."

"And quite enough." At King's nod, Mimms departed abruptly. King picked up his pipe and lighted it. "So this is what we're up against, eh?" he soliloquized. "And this explains why the hitch developed in the plans of Sir James. I'll bet a dollar Solomon worked it to get Mowbray down to Macassar—to get us all together in one place. Then he'll strike. How? There's no telling. He's out to put Mowbray and Sanderson through an education in hell; so much is plain. I said he had a genius. Well, I've won the first round. By the time we've managed our business at Macassar and pull back into the Gulf of Boni, the *El Rey* will

be on the spot also. If I can't outguess his deviltry and beat him
to it, my name's not Hiram King!"

With which self-confident assertion he set to work and
finished his log, putting down the happenings of the morning
succinctly and truthfully.

Knowing the terrible motive and purpose of John Solomon,
King guessed that for the present they would hear no more
from the cockney, who had doubtless gone on to Macassar to
sow further seeds of vengeance. Solomon wanted no swift, keen
revenge; he wanted to make Mowbray and Sanderson suffer,
and he was doing it. King quite discounted both men as aids. It
would be a battle of wits between himself and Solomon; a brutal,
merciless fight, with the lives of men as pawns, until one or the
other had wiped his opponent from the board. And King did
not intend to be so eliminated, without bloody protest.

For several days thereafter, King saw almost nothing of
Norma Douglas. From what little he did see it was forcibly
borne in upon him that for some reason she was thoroughly
aroused against him; twice she cut him dead upon the deck, and,
ignorant of how he had offended, King accepted her attitude
with his ever-placid demeanor.

Horace Mowbray had made no secret of his antagonism
to King, but was rarely in the skipper's way; Sanderson, daily
growing more gaunt and vulpine of aspect, tramped the deck
in solitude for hours at a time. No further word had come from
Mowbray.

Such a situation is intolerable on shipboard, and nervous
anxiety hovered over the *Halcyon* like a tangible force. The trouble, however, was cleared up so far as King was concerned by the
curious agency of the ship's cat—a huge, fuzzy, tortoise-shell
feline, who had a propensity for stealing and secreting objects
of a supposedly catty virtue.

Thus, one afternoon, King was spreading the awnings on the
after deck when a titter among the men caused him to observe

the cat, trying to sneak down the after companionway with a long white silk stocking between her teeth and trailing after her.

King rescued the stocking, and hailed the steward, who was passing:

"Jem, does this belong to your wife?"

"No, sir. Oh, it's that blarsted cat, again! I saw 'er prowlin' around while I was cleanin' up Miss Douglas' cabin; the missus is a bit under the weather this afternoon, sir."

The stewardess being ill, one man was as good as another in this emergency. King went forward, thinking to replace the stocking whence it had come without discovery. But as he came to the cabin of Norma Douglas, the girl herself appeared in the doorway. One glance at what King was holding, and her face crimsoned.

"I—er—the ship's cat is a thief, Miss Douglas," stammered King. "I came to—to return this stocking."

"Thank you," she said coldly, and took the silk from his hand. Without further word, she turned and was about to shut the door when King intervened hastily:

"Please, Miss Douglas—one minute!"

She turned again, her violet-blue eyes darkening ominously. "Well?"

"The situation aboard us, Miss Douglas, is rapidly becoming unbearable," said King quietly, his eyes squarely on hers. "It's a thing that must be settled one way or another. I'm aware that in some way I've offended you; how, I do not know. I wish to remove the offense, if it is possible. I'm ignorant of how I have offended, and I've been innocent of any desire to offend."

Her cold gaze did not warm to his awkwardly expressed thought.

"You should know very well," she said evenly. "I don't think a discussion—"

"I do, however," retorted King. "I know nothing about it, except that you are obviously angered at me. Why? Be just to me, at least."

"Just! You are a fine person to talk of justice!" Fire flashed in her eyes. "After you picked that poor Chinaman for a victim, without any cause—because you had a grudge against him, knew that he was in the employ of Solomon, you pounced on him and—and *hung* him! Murdered him brutally."

King's eyes widened.

"But, my dear Miss Douglas, he murdered the mate!"

"You don't know what he did!" she flashed. "You had absolutely no reason to think so. The moment the mate was killed you went down to the galley and seized that poor man, and five minutes later you had murdered him."

"Oh, that's a very interesting story!" King's blue eyes twinkled. "If you'll excuse me a moment, until I can go to my cabin, I'll be very pleased to prove that this version of the affair is entirely without foundation."

He left her abruptly, and five minutes later returned and knocked at her door.

"Here, Miss Douglas," he said, when she opened to his knock, "is the rough log of the yacht. Here is the entry of the day in question. I wish that you'd be good enough to read it then to question the seaman Mimms. You will realize that the log is my official report of the happenings of the voyage; it is the same as testimony under oath. Thank you, Miss Douglas."

King went up to the bridge, pondering the amazing version of the story as betrayed by the girl. Who had been responsible for that version? Not Sanderson, at least, the canny Scot was no such fool, and to give Miss Douglas such a tale was a fool's trick.

The afternoon was closing, when the steward appeared on the bridge, telling King that Miss Douglas would like to speak with him in the music room. King went below at once. When he stood before the girl he saw that she had been crying.

"I'm sorry, Captain King," she said, holding out to him the log book. "I can't say how sorry I am—"

"Please don't." King smiled as he spoke. "You no longer regard me as a brute?"

"At least, I think you executed justice," she countered. "It is not my province to pass judgment on how you manage this ship, Captain King. You probably had reasons—"

"I had. Let me tell you about them, please. You're an extraordinarily capable woman, Miss Douglas, and you may as well understand the situation now; it has to be faced."

Quietly and without concealment he laid before her the absolute truth, as he viewed it, regarding John Solomon, and his own position in the matter. He kept back nothing except his suspicions anent the schemes of Sanderson and Sir James to secure his fifty thousand.

"Thus, you see," he concluded, while her eyes gravely searched him, "I am a partner in this Celebes enterprise; also I have taken upon myself the task of blocking John Solomon in his threatened vengeance.

"Speaking confidentially, Miss Douglas, you must face the truth. Perhaps you idolize your uncle; well and good! But you heard the story on the phonograph, and you must know that your uncle is in mortal fear at this moment. So, I doubt not, is Sir James Mowbray."

"And you stand between them—and Solomon?" The roses had faded from her cheeks.

"Yes. The sooner Mr. Sanderson ceases his attempts at evasion, realizes that you cannot be deceived as to the situation, the better. We can't tell what is going to come of all this, Miss Douglas, unless your uncle and Sir James decide to throw up the Celebes affair and run away—then I think you had better leave the ship at Macassar.

"If they decide to stick and fight it out, as I hope they will do, the result is not going to be peaceful. That's frank! We don't know where it will lead us. It will most certainly be unpleasant for you."

He paused, for a slow smile was curving her lips.

"You're very much mistaken if you think I shall run away, Captain King. I agree with you that the ethics of—of what happened in Port Said years ago need not be discussed now. You are acting from your sense of duty, as well as from personal antagonism to Solomon; I am also acting from duty. My uncle has been very good to me, and I intend to stand by him; right or wrong, he is my uncle, the only relative I have in the world. You understand?"

"Perfectly. And I congratulate you on—"

"Wait! I've done you an injustice, Captain King. Now let me do you what I think to be an act of justice in reparation. You spoke of investing fifty thousand dollars." The girl paused for a moment. In her face King read that she had something in mind that was hard for her to say. She continued slowly:

"From one or two remarks I have heard, sir, I have some reason to believe that—that certain parties intend to—to take your money away from you. I would not breathe such a thing unless I were very certain of what I am saying."

She paused again. King leaned forward earnestly.

"I know how it hurts you to tell me this, Miss Douglas. Believe me, I deeply appreciate your action in telling me. I was already aware of the fact, however."

Her eyes, watching him, widened in amazement.

"What! You knew—and you said nothing—"

King laughed.

"My dear Miss Douglas, I usually do say nothing. However, I will say this: When a man has fought hard to get fifty thousand dollars in the bank, he is going to fight a hundred times as hard to prevent that money being taken away from him. So, if—"

A swift gleam of warning in the girl's eyes caused King to break off and glance up. In the doorway he saw the figure of Horace Mowbray.

The young man gazed at the two with a slowly insolent stare.

"Upon my word!" he said, his voice touched with liquor. "Captain King, why aren't you on the bridge?"

King flushed.

"What is that to you, sir?"

"What is it to me?" Mowbray took a step forward, passion flooding into his eyes. King rose. "What is it to me? Aren't you drawing my money?"

King bowed slightly to the girl.

"If you'll excuse me, Miss Douglas, I'll see that everything's right above," he said calmly. Mowbray laughed in ugly fashion.

"More right above than below, eh what?" he sneered. "I'm a bit surprised at you, Norma, demeaning yourself to meet this sailor in private—"

The words ended in a choking squeal of fright, as King's hand closed about the younger man's neck. Mowbray plunged forward to his knees, striving desperately but vainly to tear free the hand that had gripped into his flesh. Miss Douglas darted forward with a cry of alarm.

"I'll not hurt him, Miss Douglas. Stand aside, please!" King chuckled a little. "Now, my dear Mr. Mowbray, we're ready to hear you speak up like a gentleman. Unless you desire to have a very stiff neck in the morning, you'll apologize at once to Miss Douglas—a heartfelt apology, and no pretense. Out with it!"

With a moan of anguish as King's grip tightened. Horace Mowbray apologized.

CHAPTER VI

MACASSAR

I T WAS late afternoon, and long past the siesta hour, when the *Halcyon* dropped anchor within Macassar Bay, off the long, flat iron go-downs and whitewashed houses of the town. Off to the east ran into the sky the high backbone of mountains that is the spinal column of Celebes.

From the harbor officials, even before casting anchor, King had learned that not only had the *Tyrian* not recently visited Macassar, but such a ship was wholly unknown. So, conflict with Solomon removed from possibility for the present, King drew a breath of relief. Macassar, he thought, would be a heavenly spot in which to further his acquaintance with Norma Douglas.

Sanderson came and joined him on the bridge after pratique had been settled and the Dutch officials had gone.

"Young Mowbray wants to go ashore to the hotel, Captain King. I think we'll go, too; it'll give Norma a bit of a change. Sir James should arrive in a couple of days. Will you come with us?"

"Not I, thanks." King called down to Fortescue, and ordered the steam launch unshipped. "I'll probably spend daytimes ashore, but there are too many things to attend to here aboard ship to permit my absence. You expect to meet the Dutch commissioners here?"

"Yes—after Sir James arrives. They may be here already, but the deal must go through with him personally, d'ye understand?"

King nodded.

"You'd better take Grimsen as guide, sir. The hotel's next door to the governor's residence—down that broad street to the left."

"Oh!" Sanderson gave him a quick glance. "You've been here before?"

King nodded, without other response.

Not until the following morning did he go ashore. Scenery aside, the place was novel and pleasing; there was always something new to be seen in Macassar, and it was five years since he had previously been here as mate of a tramp trader.

The wide streets, their lamps hung from the boughs of shade trees, the tiled roofs and gables of the Dutch buildings and barracks, the piratical natives, the huge walls of old Fort Rotterdam—these things fascinated King and held him sauntering about the streets. And over in the east were the forested mountains, mute testimony that only a few miles away from the ramparts of Macassar was rank savagery, unpenetrated for three hundred years; headhunting and killing of men, unglimpsed rivers, bluish haze that concealed primeval man.

In the bazaars he came upon Horace Mowbray and Norma Douglas.

To the severely trained Scotch girl, broadened as she had been by the influences of western Canada, the sights of Macassar came as a distinct shock. It was hard for her to meet, without blushing, the entirely naked children and the half-naked native women, to say nothing of the brown men who lacked all self-consciousness. Horace Mowbray, on the other hand, was frankly bored by his surroundings; but not too bored to greet King with a scowling anger.

"My, it's good to see your clean American face!" exclaimed the girl as King shook hands. "We'd begun to feel as if we'd been submerged in a sea of brown and yellow men here; even the Dutch have been turned saffron!"

"Yes, they get that fever stuff over in Java, and get it badly," said King. "There's no fever here, however; the whole island is wonderfully healthy."

"Coming back to the hotel, Norma?" put in Mowbray with an assumed yawn. "I told your uncle we'd be along."

"Oh, don't wait for me, then," said the girl coolly. "Run along, by all means. Captain King will see me back, I hope."

"Delighted, Miss Douglas!" And King smiled.

Mowbray could not help recognizing his pointed dismissal, and swung off, scowling.

"Has he been telling any more tales about my doings?" inquired King lightly. Norma Douglas gave him a quick glance.

"He? I never said he had been telling anything!"

"You didn't need to," chuckled King. "I guessed quickly enough where the story about my murdering Ling Woo came from. Well, have you seen the museum on the *plein*—what we'd call the square?"

"I don't like museums," and she grimaced, "when we can enjoy this wonderful open air."

"Good! Would you like to drive over to Goa—say this afternoon? That's a historical old place, and you can have tea with the king or his mother."

"Perhaps. We'll have to see what my uncle is planning, however."

They strolled back to the hotel for luncheon. Sanderson greeted them in surly fashion, and King sensed with malicious satisfaction that his presence was by no means agreeable. Horace Mowbray had not returned, and did not show up for another twenty minutes.

Sanderson set down his foot firmly upon any proposed excursion until after Mowbray, senior, arrived; the packet was expected on the following morning, and he had already wirelessed that he was coming aboard her. So, it proved, were the commissioners.

"We'll settle matters, d'ye see," said Sanderson; "then we'll go look at the concession and prove up the Dutchmen's reports on it. But until Sir James shows up, do all of ye bide close to home. I've too much on my mind to be worried by your catching fevers or getting lost or maybe having some nigger run amuck and stick a knife into Horace or the skipper. Eh, King?"

"Quite right, sir," assented King gravely. "Not to mention poisonous snakes and insects and the possibility of our being kidnaped by bandits."

"Exactly," said Sanderson. His niece gave King a twinkling smile.

Finding the atmosphere deliberately unfriendly to his cherished hopes of showing Macassar to Norma Douglas, King departed after luncheon by himself.

Pipe alight, he strolled through the Arab quarter, then passed on to the kampongs outside the town proper, where a great proportion of the city's inhabitants lived. Suburbanites these, dwelling in houses raised above the ground on poles, neat with matting and nipa thatch and carven woods, huge trees everywhere.

Now it chanced that, entirely by accident, King paused before one of these houses to knock out and refill his pipe. Yet not wholly by accident, in a secondary sense; for the figure of a very handsomely clad old Arab, sitting on the stoop and gravely smoking a big water pipe, had caught his eye.

An instant later he regretted his too openly evident curiosity and admiration for the picture made—for in the midst of his operation he saw the stately old Arab rise, looking down at him very hard, and stride forward. King was tempted to turn away, but his natural disinclination to shirk possible trouble retained him where he stood.

Six feet away, the old Arab halted, his glittering eyes swept King from head to foot, and then, just as the American expected some sharp rebuke for his curiosity, the old Arab smiled and extended his hand, speaking in guttural English.

"I have been expecting you, effendi!"

"The devil you have!" thought King as he shook hands. Aloud, however, he said nothing of the sort. "Expecting me, my friend? You know me, then?"

"Do you not bear the token of our master Suleiman, effendi? Enter, for the house of our master is yours to enjoy. The message may be delivered later."

The word "Suleiman" shot through King like a lightning flash. As he spoke, the Arab had lightly touched the gold ring with the black design, which King was wearing, and then turned toward the house behind. King followed, his mind working with the speed of light.

"Suleiman"—could that have any connection with John Solomon? He remembered what Mimms had reported of Solomon's reputed activities in Arabia; perhaps the man was as strongly connected with the Arabs of these seas as with the Chinese. And the ring, the ring which had struck amazement and fear to the very soul of Ling Woo! That ring was "the token," then!

King followed his guide into the house. The old Arab clapped his hands, and two more Arabs appeared with low salaams, receiving orders in a tongue strange to the American. Here King realized full well that he was literally over a volcano—a single word might betray the mistake which had been made, and it would mean his death or worse.

Even yet he was not certain that his conjectures were correct, however.

The interior of the house left him speechless with amazement. It was furnished like a veritable palace, and was hung with rugs and tapestries which a king might have envied. The American sank back upon silken cushions of a divan, opposite the old Arab, and neither man spoke again until the servants had fetched in small gold cups of such coffee as King had seldom tasted. Then King made an effort to throw off the spell.

"I am Captain Hiram King," he said slowly, wondering if the name would arouse any hostility, "of the yacht *Halcyon*, now in harbor."

The old Arab merely interrogated him with keenly smiling eyes.

"I am Yusuf ibn Ali, effendi. If you bring orders from our master, let them be obeyed."

This was an indirect method of putting a blunt question.

King, however, settled back among the cushions, and with the wondrous aroma of that coffee lingering upon his palate drew forth his pipe. He shook his head when the Arab motioned toward ready cigarettes, and sat silent for a moment, puffing at his pipe. He had to think hard and fast, and did it.

"I do not bring orders; I give them," he said at last.

"That is true, effendi. One knows a man among other men."

"I have come hither from Honolulu, where I last saw Solomon," went on King, with ambiguous truth. "I await my master's coming—possibly within a day or two. Before Solomon comes I may have to depart again. Therefore, Yusuf ibn Ali, tell me what has been done that I may know where to look for help in case of need."

The old Arab jerked his head to denote satisfaction, and King smiled to himself. What a wonder of coincidence was this! Or was it coincidence, after all? It was hard to decide. At least, thought the American, he was well on the track of Solomon's secrets.

He was brought up with a round turn, however, at the Arab's reply;

"Effendi, who am I to know what Suleiman has done? Ask of the wind whither it would blow, or of the ocean whither it runs its course. When Suleiman, on whom be the blessing of Allah, lays a net and a snare, no man knows thereof."

"But you were expecting me? You had orders for me?"

"Effendi, when any guest comes wearing the ring of Suleiman, him we welcome as a brother. I have no orders. This is the house of Suleiman, and it is yours."

King comprehended at last. He had stumbled upon the headquarters, or one of the headquarters, of Solomon's activity, but it promised to do him little good. He would learn nothing here, it seemed.

"You don't know where the *Tyrian* is now, Yusuf?"

"No, effendi. We expect the master when he comes, and not until then."

Realizing that further effort at discovery would be dangerous in the extreme, King rose and took his cap.

"Then for the present I shall bid you farewell, Yusuf. I am glad to have met you."

"Effendi, your presence reflects light and beauty upon this poor habitation!"

King strode away, breathing more freely once he had left the place behind.

He was quick to realize that this apparent stroke of fortune was very likely to prove misfortune. That lucky ring would serve him no more. Once Solomon learned of his visit to Yusuf ibn Ali, the little cockney would take prompt measures to warn all his men against King. Unless there were some way of using the old Arab to immediate advantage—

And the ring—what did the graven symbol upon its face mean?

With this query agitating his thoughts, the American found himself back in the town proper. He paused at sight of a large Dutch trading house, and, at a sudden inward prompting, entered the place and sought out the proprietor, who proved to speak English.

"I am in search of information," said King frankly, handing over his ring. "I wish you would inform me about this curio; more particularly about the design in black."

The Dutchman inspected the ring, took out an enlarging glass, and inspected it anew.

"What iss diss scratching on de inside? Oh, it is Arabic! But it iss worn away. De name of de maker, perhaps."

"Mere pin scratches, I always thought," returned King. "But the seal itself—do you happen to know anything about it?"

The Dutchman returned the ring with a smile. Yes, he knew all about it—did he not trade with the Arabs?

The design of a square with diagonal lines from corner to corner was as old as the Arab race, and was also found all over the Oriental world, under the more or less mythical name of the Seal of Solomon. According to Arab legend, this symbol had been the seal of the great king, by which he dominated the powers of good and evil spirits. That was all.

With this information, King thanked his informant and departed. The mystery was solved. Solomon, no doubt taking advantage of the prestige which his name alone would give him among Moslems, had turned that particular symbol to his own uses. The mistake of his henchmen was quite natural.

King had always cherished a faint hope that the ring might prove some clew to his own identity, perhaps through the half-obliterated scratches on the inner side. This hope was now dissipated.

The symbol was a common one, to be found on everything produced in the Eastern world, from rugs to jewelry. The ring was of an old-fashioned design, and would now be impossible to trace back to any dealer; especially as it must have been bought to have been found on the body of King's mother, a good twenty-five years ago. The symbol therefore meant nothing at all, except as it had been taken up and used by Solomon, probably of late years.

"Well, what matter?" thought King as he strolled on past the trading go-downs and dropped into the warm beach sand, watching the harbor. "My present name's as good as that of any other man, and maybe I've made it a better one than most. Still, it would be fine to discover some one in the world who might care a hang whether I lived or died."

He sighed a little, and thought of Norma Douglas.

Grimsen and a portion of the crew were on shore leave that afternoon. Growing tired of his lazy idling, and deciding that he had better collect the men, King rose after a time and strolled back toward the wharves, watching the native fishing boats that filled the harbor, and the *Halcyon* swinging with the tide to her anchor chains.

"Interesting beggars, these brown Bugis!" he soliloquized. "Finest seamen to be had, and a devilish lot of pirates at heart, trading all over the archipelago in those little craft. Yet they make good soldiers. Up at the barracks those boys look trim and alert."

He broke off suddenly, hearing his name called in a low voice: "Cap'n King!"

Behind him was a nondescript white man dressed in tatters, and filthily dirty—a beach comber, who inspected him inquiringly after speaking.

"That's my name," said King curtly, thinking he was to be asked for the price of a drink or two. To his surprise, however, the other held out a note, and then waited. The note was folded over, and had been sealed with wax, and the seal was the Seal of Solomon.

King handed the man a coin, watched him slouch off, then tore open the missive. It proved to be couched in French, was addressed to him, and was signed by Yusuf ibn Ali. The contents was entirely to the point:

> Word has just been brought to me that two men have been hired with gold to murder you. They are soldiers of the native army here. The man who hired them was he who registered at the hotel as Horace Mowbray. If you need help, call upon us. In the name of Allah, the Merciful!

Smiling to himself, King tore up the note. So Solomon's men were now serving him by virtue of that ring! And Horace Mowbray—

"Talk about intrigues!" muttered King as he turned toward the wide street leading to the hotel. "I'm in the thick of it right enough. Well, my friend Horace, what you need is a good trimming, but the time or place is not yet. H'm! I wonder where Grimsen is?"

Unable to see anything of his mate, he turned into the hotel and passed to the bar. Here, as he expected, he found Horace Mowbray seated at a table, drinking. Without regarding the scowl that greeted him, King dropped into a chair and leaned over the table, his blue eyes suddenly keen and cold.

"Well, Sir, I'm not dead yet!"

"Eh?" Mowbray started and turned pale. "What—what the deuce d'you mean?"

"You know cursed well," and now King smiled in a fashion that drove uneasy fear into the dark eyes facing him. "You've hired two soldiers to murder me, sir. Unless you want to be hauled up before the governor to be sent to prison on the charge, I'd advise you to hustle out and rescind your orders. I'm not sparing you because I love you, Mowbray, but because your father is my owner. Now move—and move cursed sharp, unless you want to be very unhappy before long."

Mowbray rose, staring at him from a ghastly face.

"You—you're a devil!" he mouthed the words feebly. "How—how—"

"You hustle along and find your assassins," snapped King. "If you try any trick like this again, you'll go the way Ling Woo went. Jump, you pup—jump!"

Horace Mowbray turned and fled incontinently.

Five minutes later King returned to the street and once more took up his course toward the water front. Barely had he reached the European offices near the wharves, however, when he caught sight of Grimsen and Mimms hurrying toward him; they greeted him with a wave of the arm, and King saw that both men were highly excited.

"We've got it, Sir!" exclaimed Mimms sharply as he joined them. "By the hokey, we've got it! And we've blasted well got him, too!"

"Who?" King's eyes rested placidly upon them. "What's the row?"

"That Solomon," said Grimsen, with his slow, hard smile.

"He's here, sir. And we hafe got him for the taking. Where can we talk?"

"Right here in the street; best place of any," said King, his eyes widening. "Out with it! You don't mean that he's here in Macassar?"

"He will be pretty quick," and Mimms chuckled delightedly. "Lordy! It's rich!"

CHAPTER VII

THE SNARING OF SOLOMON

THE MAN Mimms was an odd genius, as King had more than once discovered in other days.

Left aboard the *Halcyon,* Mimms had occupied himself by borrowing the skipper's fine German binoculars and going aloft without particular intent. During the course of the afternoon his attention had become fastened on a native fishing boat which had come in from the south and was very leisurely approaching the harbor.

The attention of Mimms had quickened into lively interest when, while the craft was still some distance at sea, he had made out a white man sitting in her. Later the white man had disappeared, presumably under the matting cabin in her stern. But not before Mimms, through the powerful binoculars, had recognized the passenger—or thought that he had.

King listened in silence while Grimsen explained what he thought was the situation; then, with a nod of assent, King recapitulated and enlarged it.

"Like enough, lads; it's getting well on to sunset now, and they'll come in after dark. Solomon wants to get ashore here, but wants to keep his presence secret from us. Yes, it sounds pretty well, Grimsen.

"He either met that craft at sea and sent the *Tyrian* on to Surabaya, or else he came in her from Surabaya; probably the latter, for these Bugis are fiendishly clever at navigation. Solomon must be a navigator himself, too. Well, there's no great

hurry until dark. Let me tell you what I discovered this afternoon."

So, as they passed down toward the waiting launch, he told
them of the ring and the Arab and of Horace Mowbray's futile
and cowardly endeavor.

At the launch, they found the shoreleave men already waiting, and they went out to the yacht at once. From her bridge,
Mimms pointed out the fishing boat with her matting sail flap-
ping idly, lying two miles out and apparently waiting for dark
before coming in. No white passenger was visible aboard her,
and her crew consisted of four Bugis.

"All right." King closed the glasses. "Grimsen, keep your eye
on her, and have the launch ready. We'll mess right away, and
go out to her just at dark. Call me if she changes her position to
any extent; she may not land at the town itself."

Knowing that he himself was probably under surveillance by
the men of Yusuf ibn Ali ashore, King made his plan accordingly,
laughing to himself at thought of what lay ahead.

With the set of sun, an offshore breeze sprang up, increasing
steadily. The fishing boat had stripped down her matting sail,
and her crew had put out sweeps. Having discerned this much
before the red ball of the sun slipped down under the western
ocean rim, King pocketed an automatic and got into the launch
with Mimms and Grimsen, just as the swift twilight of the tropics fell and threatened at each instant to drop into night.

The steam launch purred almost silently over the quiet waters
of the bay, her lights unlit. Grimsen, who spoke Dutch, was in
the bow, with a boat hook. King scarce knew what he expected.
From his first meeting with Solomon he would have taken the
man to be a helpless little old chap, quite harmless. But the
American was now nerved for anything; the Bugis might turn
out to be British soldiers or Virginia darkies in disguise; Solomon might suddenly produce a machine gun or a gas bomb—
anything!

"I guess the little devil has got square on my nerves, after all." And King laughed harshly.

The engine died into silence. Ahead of them loomed the bulk of the fishing craft, long sweeps out on either side. One of the native boatmen cried out shrilly as the launch rushed down at them.

Grimsen answered the cry with threatening Dutch and made fast his boat hook.

"Take care of 'em!" King leaped over the rail as he spoke. "Wait for me."

Automatic in one hand, electric torch in the other, he flung himself forward to the opening beneath the hood of matting— the semicircular cabin roof. As he reached it and snapped on his light, the glow struck full upon the head of Solomon, emerging.

"Back with you!" snapped King, moving the torch so as to show his automatic. "Back!"

He followed the retreating figure, and found himself facing the other man in a bare little cubby, furnished with only a few mats. King stuck the torch in the framework of the roof, and the two men stared at each other.

"Glad to meet you again, Mr. Solomon!"

"Oh, it's you! Dang it!" Solomon's hand went to his pocket. The automatic snapped up, but Solomon only produced pipe and a palmful of tobacco. "Cap'n Hiram King, ain't it?" inquired the little man, glancing up. The two stood eye to eye.

King was freshly amazed at the aspect of his captive. Taken wholly off guard as he must have been, Solomon yet remained quite placid, quite undisturbed. With a muttered exclamation, King pocketed his weapon. The cockney was so obviously an old man, crippled, half helpless. Yet King was not deceived.

"Put your hand to your pocket again and you get a bullet."

"Dang it! 'Ow do you expect me to be lightin' of me pipe?"

"Here's a match. You may as well sit down to it."

Stiffly Solomon sat down. King, feeling somewhat ashamed

of his truculent attitude, sat down with his back to the door; from outside he caught the voice of Grimsen:

"All shipshape here, sir!" He saw Solomon cock an eye toward the electric torch.

"You needn't watch that light," said King coldly. "It's a new battery."

Solomon's expressionless gaze dwelt upon him with a sort of amazed wonder.

"Dang it, sir, are you a bloomin' mind reader? Well, well!" The pudgy little cockney sighed wheezily. "And that 'ere Ling Woo didn't 'urt you!"

"No. Until you passed us at sea you thought I had a knife in me, eh?"

Solomon nodded, and expelled a cloud of smoke. King went on evenly:

"You failed on Grimsen also. But your murderer did get to our mate—and I hanged him. Also, I've just had a very interesting session with your Macassar friend, Yusuf ibn Ali, this afternoon. In fact, he saved my life."

Solomon's face did not change, but the wonder in his eyes deepened.

"And 'ow did you get on to 'im, sir, if I may ask? 'Oo told you—"

"Mind reading did it," and King laughed grimly. "Don't you wish you knew? But you don't. And you're not going to see Yusuf in a hurry, either."

The cockney gazed at him, as inscrutable as a Buddha.

"You're by way o' bein' a werry remarkable man, Cap'n King, if I may make so bold. Did you get them 'ere gramophone records I sent aboard you at Honolulu?"

King took out his pipe and slowly filled it, not responding until he had trailed a match across his heel and touched it to the tobacco.

"Yes, they came—and performed their mission." King leaned

forward. "Solomon, was that the true story about your family, I mean? Is that the only reason you're dogging Sanderson and Mowbray now?"

A sudden agitation passed across the expressionless face as a breath of wind ruffles the calm surface of a mountain lake.

"Ain't it reason enough?" exclaimed Solomon bitterly. "Yes, sir, a true story it is. They—they—but I can't talk of it, Mr. King. Are you an American, sir, if I may ask? There was a man o' your name in the P. & O. boats years ago—"

"He was my father," returned King curtly.

From the cockney broke a wheezy sigh.

"Dang it! Well, sir, you've up an' got me all shipshape, and werry sorry I am. And all along o' me growin' old and trembly in the 'ands, so to speak. As a usual thing, I'm werry quick to pick up a friend to 'elp me out 'ere and there, but this time I was took so mortal sudden by findin' out Mowbray an' Sanderson was alive that I didn't 'ave no time to get me men—only one o' me 'elpers could I get 'old of, and 'e's werry far from 'ere at this minute."

"Who's that?" demanded King, his eyes narrowing. "Ralph Carter?"

Solomon looked at him for a long moment, again with that same helpless wonder, but did not reply to the question.

"Dang it! Mr. King, sir, I'd give a mortal lot if I could 'ave a spry young man like you a-workin' with me—"

"You're a bit late with your bribery," was King's cold retort. "Nothing doing! What made you get after me and my men—you and your hired assassins?"

Solomon regarded his pipe steadily for a moment.

"Well, sir, I found out in San Francisco as you was goin' to be a 'ard nut to crack; I knowed it when I first clapped eyes on you, Mr. King."

"So you tried to have me and Grimsen murdered?"

The blue eyes struck boldly up to King, a sudden terrible anger in their depths.

"Yes. And why not? I'm a-goin' to do by them 'ere two murderers the same as they went an' done by me—only worse. You're in with 'em, workin' for 'em, fightin' for 'em. 'Ere you sit this werry blessed minute, doin' of their dirty work. You know all they've been an' done to me."

"Yes, Solomon, I'm afraid you're dead right about me," said King slowly. "Yet you are also dead wrong. I'm in with them but I can understand how you're settling a just debt, if there ever was a just debt. I'm working for them, but I am quite aware that they are only waiting the chance to legally steal my money—if they can. I'm fighting for them, but I'm fighting for myself first, Solomon; remember that. You set your assassins after me and my men; you declared war upon me, and you're going to sweat for it."

Solomon settled back, pipe between his teeth, eyes steady on King. The latter, however, was suspicious of the cockney's easy acceptance of the situation.

"Grimsen!"

"Yes, sir," came the answer instantly from outside.

"See if there isn't a set of the tide inshore. If there is, start the launch towing us out. Mr. Solomon rather hopes to drift on the beach."

Solomon chuckled wheezily, as, a moment later, they began to move through the water.

"Dang it, Mr. King! A bloody wonder; that's what you are. If I may make so bold, sir, what be you a-goin' to do with me, just like that?"

King eyed his captive reflectively.

"That's a problem, Solomon, isn't it? If I take you to the *Halcyon* and turn you over to Sanderson, you'd be murdered in two minutes—and I'm no murderer, by my own hand or by proxy. If I turn you loose without bond, I might never leave Macassar alive, and I have private reasons for not wishing to be buried here. So I'll make a bargain with you."

Solomon chuckled again, without response.

"Thus far, Solomon, we've broken pretty even," went on

King. "You've caused me some worry, and your man Ling Woo murdered my mate—for which he swung. Also, Yusuf ibn All saved my life to-day. On the whole, we're quits. Suppose I let you go free on condition that you give up your threatened vengeance on my employers?"

"There's no 'uman power can get that 'ere condition out o' me," said Solomon placidly. "What I've done 'as gone too far to be stopped, nor I wouldn't stop it if I could. What's remaining to be done—gets done, just like that, sir."

The immobility of the little cockney was amazing. King, however, merely nodded. He had expected, and could have expected, no other answer.

"Very well. What kind of a bid will you make for your freedom?"

Solomon puffed silently for a moment.

"Prowidence is a werry strange thing, Mr. King," he replied at last. "It was through you as I first 'eard about Mowbray bein' alive, and Prowidence 'as been and saved you from bein' killed. Well, sir, what do you want? Money?"

King smiled inscrutably.

"No, though I fancy you'd pay a pretty sum." For a moment he was tempted to take from his pocket the ring and try its effect on Solomon. He decided against this, however; it would not affect this strange man, whose only emotion was revenge.

"Here, Solomon, I'll make you a proposition! You keep away from Macassar while we're in port; turn around now, on the spot, and sail away whence you came. Send no more assassins aboard us, and don't molest me or my men again. In return I'll set you free now, and I'll take no further measures against you on my own account. Of course I'll do my duty by my owners if you continue after *them*."

"And you'll take my word on this 'ere bargain, sir? Why?"

"Well—I'm not sure why. But I will."

Solomon sighed.

"Werry good, sir—you're on. And if Mowbray wants your
'elp—"

"He gets it."

"It's a one-sided bargain, but I can't 'elp meself, sir."

"It might be a blamed sight better to put a bullet into you,
but I can't help myself, either, Solomon. One thing more. If you
lift a finger against Miss Douglas, then I'm on your back teeth
and toe nails. I don't know how far your mad schemes of revenge
may carry you, but—"

"I 'opes, sir, as I 'ave a proper respect for a lady—even if
Mowbray and 'is danged pal didn't 'ave in times gone by."

Without further word, King crawled back to the deck, torch
in hand.

"Pile in, lads. Let the Bugis go."

The launch purred back to the *Halcyon.* Behind her, the fishing boat, sail up, slowly heaved out toward the straits—away
from Macassar.

King briefly sketched for his two aids the compact he had
made with Solomon. In their silence he read disapproval; though
they said nothing, he could imagine the disgust in Mimms' face,
the hard smile on Grimsen's mouth.

And after he had turned in that night, King lay awake,
pondering on what he had done.

When he went out to the fishing craft he had fully intended
shooting Solomon or bringing him back a prisoner, which would
have amounted to the same thing. It was no sympathy with the
man's cause, just though it was, which had deterred his hand.
What, then, had prevented him?

King was not sure. As he had stood facing Solomon in that
low matting cabin, some inner force had restrained him; perhaps
it was no more than pity, consciousness of his own youth and
strength and power. Physically Solomon was a pathetic old man,
who looked as if the only thing that kept the spark of life in him
was his bitter craving for vengeance.

"And it was the same back there in San Francisco," thought

King. "I simply couldn't hit him, though I was impelled to do it. I couldn't lift my hand to him. And the more one sees of the fellow, the more one likes him. Confound it! I must be getting soft in the head. Or else he hypnotized me. I shouldn't have let him go, blast him!"

Hiram King lay awake far into the night, wishing that he could believe and practice the theory of Teutonic frightfulness. But he could not. He was a brave man.

Solomon fought, not with his hands, but with his wits. King realized that he must conquer the little cockney on the same ground—or else fail.

"And—I'll not fail!" he told himself grimly.

CHAPTER VIII

BLOW AND COUNTERBLOW

T HE LITTLE steamer *Mossel*, of the Koninkli-
jke Paketvaart Maatschappij, drew into Macassar and
discharged a slim load of passengers. There were no tourists
in these war times, and the Dutch were discouraging travel
between the islands of the Insulinde.

What the *Mossel's* list lacked in quantity, however, was quite
made up by quality. Two government commissioners from Batavia stepped ashore to be received by the garrison and governor
with military honors, and with them came Sir James Mowbray,
guest of honor. He looked slightly thinner than when King had
last seen him, but had none of Sanderson's evident nervousness.

Quite plainly Sir James had arranged all private affairs with
the commissioners while on the voyage. Immediately after their
reception by the governor, all three came aboard the *Halcyon*,
where cabins were assigned to the two Dutch officials.

After the immense noonday meal of the Dutch colonial,
the commissioners retired to their cabins for a needed siesta.
Norma Douglas went ashore with Horace Mowbray. Sir James
spent an hour in earnest conference with Sanderson, who took
several drinks of Scotch for the first time since the trip began.
Sanderson was not a drinking man, as a rule. Leaving his friend
and partner to liquor and gloomy prognostications, Mowbray
went to King's cabin.

"Well, sir, you're looking pretty fit!" exclaimed King in some surprise that Sir James had come to him. "I hope you find every-thing to your liking aboard?"

Sir James nodded and lighted a cigarette.

"I've had a talk with Sanderson," he said shortly. "He tells me that you're fully informed about Solomon; that he's been after you, in fact, as well as after us. Eh?"

King nodded in silence, studying the speaker. Here was none of Sanderson's coarse fiber, which had gone to pieces under the first shock. Mowbray came of good blood, and was a different sort of man. His whole spirit was one of fight.

"I'm rather glad, to tell the truth," he went on frankly. "We'll need you, King. No use going into the dead past, of course, but this beggar Solomon has it in for us. Still, two can play at that game, and I mean to get him first.

"On my way to China, and ever since I left you at Honolulu, in fact, Solomon sent me wireless, and cable messages, much the same as he sent Sanderson. However, he can effect little, for I'm going to have a talk with all the crew and make sure that anything suspicious will be taken up and reported immediately."

King smiled.

"What do you expect, Sir James? That he'll come aboard us with a pirate crew on that yacht of his?"

Mowbray shrugged.

"Who knows? I expect anything and everything, but when he strikes I'll strike back harder and quicker. That's all. I can depend on you?"

"Certainly. Quite aside from my own quarrel with him, I'm captain of your ship, and my duty is to take your orders and to protect you and your property. I mean to do it, so long as I'm in that position."

"Very good." Mowbray made a gesture as if dismissing the subject. "There's another and to me more important affair which I wish to discuss with you. It's about my son, Horace."

King's eyes widened a trifle. He puffed at his pipe without response.

"You've had a bit of trouble with him?" demanded Sir James brusquely.

"Nothing to mention, sir." King smiled. "He hired a couple of soldiers yesterday to stick a knife in me; I made him call 'em off, of course."

The baronet bit his lip and swore. Then he leaned forward earnestly.

"See here, King! I like you, and I know that I can trust you absolutely. Now, I'm not blind to the defects in Horace, yet I feel that at bottom he's thoroughly all right. He's all I have in the world, King—he's my son—and I want above everything else to be proud of him, if I can.

"Money has spoiled him; we'll not shirk that fact. What he needs is hard work, hard driving, and lots of it. For his own sake I'd like to get him away from this yacht. There's a secondary reason, too—Solomon. I don't give a hang for myself, but I'm deadly afraid that Solomon will strike at me through Horace. I wish you'd help me, King. Can't I put the boy off by himself somewhere, doing hard manual labor, in the effort to work the manhood in him to the surface?"

King nodded slowly. He despised Mowbray, utterly; he knew that with one hand the baronet was appealing to him in all sincerity, with the other hand was preparing to rob him. Yet despite this, Sir James was now in terrible earnest, and showed it plainly. King felt something akin to pity for the man. After all, Mowbray and Sanderson might change their tactics regarding that gold concession; they might yet run straight with their American partner!

"We'll have to speak frankly, Sir James," said King slowly. "From a remark made by Mr. Sanderson at Honolulu, I have been under the impression that you had arranged—er—a match between your son and Miss Douglas. His absence might affect this—"

Mowbray waved his hand.

"That is settled for the present," he returned, not without difficulty. A deep flush rose in his face. "Miss Douglas has chucked him cold—and rightly. That's another reason for my appeal to you, King. If we can bring out the boy's latent manhood, turn him into a real man, I think she might change her mind."

King's lips twisted ironically.

"Well, Sir James, you're an unusual parent in that your eyes seem to be wide open. We might not, however, agree as to methods of treatment. I've no desire to be harsh, but I honestly think that downright harshness is the best cure for what ails your son."

"Exactly!" exclaimed the baronet, frowning intently. "You're right. Go on!"

"There's nowhere you can set him ashore in these seas without giving him the chance to rot to death; it takes a pretty strong white man to withstand the tropics in every way. But here, to my mind, would be the ideal thing: I know of an old fore-and-aft schooner that beats around through the islands, trading; she's probably up the Gulf of Boni now. Her name is the *El Rey*. Her skipper is named Marcos, a Peruvian. She's got a rough crew, but Marcos keeps 'em straight as a die. If you put your son aboard her, Marcos would not only be thoroughly responsible for his safety, but would take intelligent interest in his new education. And on the *El Rey* your son would be safer from Solomon than anywhere in the world. That schooner is a close corporation, Sir James, and practically every man in her has been with Marcos for years."

"By Jove!" For a space Sir James stared at the wall ahead of him with unseeing eyes, his lips clenched, his long fingers playing with his beard. Then he drew a deep breath. "You are certain that this Captain Marcos would be answerable for the safety of Horace?"

"He will answer with his life, sir, and I'll be surety for him."

"Then I'll do it. Get away from this place to-night, if you can; the commissioners are going with us up the gulf. Can we communicate with this Marcos?"

"He has a wireless, I believe, sir. But in case Solomon's yacht happens to be about, we'd better not try to reach him until we get around in the gulf itself, and only then with weakened waves. No use tipping off Solomon, you understand."

"Better and better, King. 'Pon my word, my lad, I believe you'll best him yet!"

Sir James took his departure, but that final exclamation had told King that the man was hoping against hope, that Mowbray was bitterly afraid at heart.

So Horace had been "chucked!" It must have taken place the previous day, thought King, and he whistled cheerfully to himself as he went ashore to hurry aboard some necessary stores, in order that the yacht might pull out before dark and get well away from the dangers of the Spermunde reefs.

"There are tough times ahead for Horace," he reflected, smiling at the thought, "but Sir James is dead right about it. That's the only chance of licking the young cub into shape, and Marcos will lick him if any one can."

It never occurred to King that Solomon might have decoded the wireless messages he had sent to Marcos or that the *Tyrian* might be elsewhere than in Surabaya at the present moment.

Sir James called together the crew that afternoon while King was ashore, and laid before them as much of the situation as be thought was necessary—enough to put them in hearty accord with their owner and in hearty antagonism to Solomon. He settled their half-formed doubts and conjectures, and did it entirely without involving his own past in any manner. He showed himself, in fact, to be a much-wronged baronet and Solomon a contriving little cockney blackmailer; so naturally the men gave three cheers and swore punishment upon the cockney when they encountered him. All of which being entirely as it should be. Grimsen and Mimms cheered quite heartily with the rest.

Encountering Horace Mowbray and Miss Douglas in the bazaars, King sent them to the launch, and remained to order down a consignment of fruits. He was hastily summoned by one of his launch crew, who came panting.

"They're callin' from the ship, sir; hurry up an' come aboard! Sir James has had a stroke or something. Mr. Horace says for Gawd's sake hurry, sir!"

King ran down to the landing stage, and no sooner had he jumped in than the launch darted out from shore. Horace Mowbray was white, frightened, watching the yacht with staring eyes. King turned to Norma Douglas, and found her quite calm.

"I don't know," she responded to his unspoken question. "They shouted to get aboard, that Sir James had a stroke. You think it—it could be—"

"Solomon?" King's brows lifted. "I think nothing. Conjecture is useless."

Yet, as it proved, their alarm was needless; Sir James had merely fainted. By the time the launch came aboard he was sitting again beneath the afterdeck awnings, Sanderson with him. On the table between them lay a wireless message.

"Oh, it's nothing to conceal!" exclaimed the baronet bitterly as his partner indicated King and Miss Douglas. "Sit down, my friends. We've heard from Solomon, that's all. Horace, please leave us."

Horace, who as yet knew little or nothing of Solomon, let fall a mild oath.

"Leave you? I guess not, pater! What's this—some secret I'm not in on?" He looked from one to the other, his face suddenly inflamed with passion. "I'm a man, ain't I? Come, governor! What the devil is up?"

Sir James made a gesture of resignation.

"I'll tell you later, Horace. Well, Captain King, we've had a wireless from Solomon—indirectly. The message itself came from Hangchow, relayed from Singapore and Batavia. My business in China, my silk factories, are gone to smash; the government is in turmoil and have revoked my concessions."

He could speak no longer. His sallow face, beneath its close-trimmed beard, was livid; the blow had been a stiff one to him. Then he lifted his head with new energy.

"Get out o' this cursed harbor, King! I hate the place."

Obediently King left the group and went to the bridge. Steam was up, and presently the winch rattled as the cable came in and the anchor was catted. Imperceptibly the flat town drew away behind them, the ocean horizon widened, the treacherous coral atolls to the north fell behind; they were at sea.

After a little Norma Douglas came to the bridge and stood beside King, not speaking for a moment. It was nearly sunset— the superb sunset of the Spice Islands. To port and behind, the great mountains of Celebes towered into the sky, crimsoned in the flood of glory from the west.

"I've discovered what's happened," said the girl at last. "There's no longer any secrecy except about—about what took place in Port Said so long ago. And that will come out in time. Sir James is deathly afraid of its publication. Do you know how the Mowbray corporation in China was wrecked?"

"I've a suspicion," King returned calmly. "The man Ralph Carter."

She looked at him curiously, intently.

"What made you think so?"

"Instinct." King smiled a little. "I figured out what I would have done had I been in Solomon's place; the first big stroke was to destroy Mowbray financially. Only a big man could do that, and Solomon is a big man. I don't quite understand his scope or his power, but certainly he has tremendous influence with certain governments."

The girl nodded.

"Yes. You know, on the way to China from Honolulu, Sir James met a man named Carter; he wirelessed my uncle about it. Carter was an American, energetic and forceful; had wonderful credentials and plenty of capital himself. Sir James was glad to install him as general manager of the China business; that let him leave at once, you know, since the ship combine was postponed, and join us here."

King smiled faintly, his blue eyes inscrutable.

"And all the while Solomon was getting in his deadly and terrible work, Miss Douglas. Oh, there's no need of recapitulating it! I can see it now for I've found out a good deal about him. He's strong with England and also with China. *He* postponed that ship combine! *He* has undermined the position of Sir James in England, I'll wager anything! *He* was behind Carter, and it was Carter who wrecked the Mowbray corporation with the aid of the Chinese government—wrecked it in a fortnight and beyond repair! Am I right?"

"About Carter—yes," she said, low-voiced, staring at him. "But—the rest—how—"

King turned to her with a sudden, forceful gesture.

"Well, isn't that his game? I tell you, Miss Douglas, the man is terrible. Sir James is just finding that out; he knows that Solomon will publish the Port Said story and that England will never forget it. It will wreck Mowbray at home, ruin him utterly. And that won't be the last blow."

"What do you mean?" Her face was white.

"After all else—life! Solomon means to strike down your uncle and Sir James, to wreak a fearful vengeance to the very letter of the Mosaic law. I doubt if he can touch your uncle's interests in Canada, but, depend upon it, he means to exact his debt fully."

She was silent for a long moment, her fingers clenched hard.

"But—but you said that—that you could beat him—"

"I can, and I will!" exclaimed King. "I cannot prevent those two men down below from reaping the whirlwind of their own sowing, but I can prevent murder being done, and I mean to prevent it. That is my duty, Miss Douglas."

Watching his strong face, she drew a deep breath; then, without further speech, went below.

King turned aft to the wireless cubby, and found the operator shutting up for mess.

"One minute, if you please!" he checked the other. "I wish you'd send out that private call for the *El Rey*, Captain Marcos. We meant to get into touch with them later—but this is no time to hesitate. They're up the Gulf of Boni, and you can reach 'em easily."

The operator nodded assent, and drew on his helmet.

The crackling crash of the spark filled the darkening little cabin with weird flame; again and again the operator sent out the call.

"No answer, sir."

"Call her openly, then!" snapped King. Uneasiness was upon him; a tense anxiety, an inner feeling that something had gone amiss. Again the spark crashed and leaped and flamed, and then suddenly it ceased.

"Got her, sir."

Two minutes later the operator handed King a strip of paper, and gazed up at the skipper with curious, inquiring eyes.

> Picked up schooner *El Rey* this morning, 3° 15' 32" south, 121° 29' east. Abandoned and sinking. Cause unknown. Sank hour later. *Tyrian*, Lord Captain.

"Ask him if—if he picked up the survivors," said King slowly, and waited.

It was a shrewd blow. So this was what Solomon had been up to! The *Tyrian* had been sent around to the Gulf of Boni to meet the *El Rey*, therefore, Solomon had decoded the messages sent by King to Captain Marcos. Without consulting a chart, King knew that the position given in this message was well up at the head of the gulf, but Marcos was not the man to abandon ship when he might have run her ashore anywhere and made repairs.

"The *Tyrian* sank her," King told himself. "Oh, that devil Solomon! And I let him go free when I had him between my fists! He fooled me, the devil! He knew all the time that his men were destroying my schooner—perhaps at the very moment we were talking. Confound it, he got home a blow this time! But if Marcos is not dead, there's still hope."

He turned to the operator.

"Well, what does the *Tyrian* say?"

"Refuses to answer, sir."

King's blue eyes widened suddenly. Why not? Why not? No one aboard the *Tyrian* knew him except by name; if they had sighted him at a distance, a change of costume would fix that all right. And Solomon had not been to Macassar—would know nothing about the ring—would perhaps tonight be reaching Surabaya and sending wireless orders to the *Tyrian.*

"Look here, son!" exclaimed King savagely. "You have to work all night this night; that boat of Solomon's is up the gulf, and will be getting orders to-night. Bring me every last message you can pick up, and bring 'em the instant they come in."

"Yes, sir."

King strode back to the bridge house, a thrill with the inspiration that had come to him. He found Grimsen in charge of the deck, and snapped out swift, astounding orders.

"Grimsen, rout out all hands immediately after mess! Rig up a false smokestack, send down those spars for'ard and aft, send up canvas and change the shape of this superstructure—you know! I'll leave it in your hands. You needn't bother about details. We'll meet the *Tyrian* in Saleier Straits toward morning, and under her searchlight she'll not discover anything wrong until—it's too late. And, Grimsen!"

"Yes, sir?"

"The *Tyrian* has destroyed Cap'n Marcos and the schooner."

Grimsen's hard old face did not change for a moment as he looked into King's eyes. Then slowly a tense and bitter smile grew upon his lips.

"Yah!" he said coldly. "I hafe feel sorry for that *Tyrian.* Yah!"

CHAPTER IX

SOLOMON AT WORK

NOT FAR from the water front of Surabaya, the great seaport of Java, stood a combined shop and house, the latter with a very wide veranda.

The shop was a dingy affair, well deserving of the sign over the door: "Ship's Stores." Within, it was crowded to the ceilings with everything from anchors to saluting cannon, Manila lines to sextants. The visitor who chanced to gain admittance to the veranda beyond, with its exquisite furniture of native woods, silver-mounted, and appointments which few of the merchant princes of the isles could boast, would have been amazed; still more greatly would he have been amazed to behold the owner of this property at work.

John Solomon, who did not sell enough ship's stores to buy his tobacco, was here at home with his Arab servants, and not far away, just across the city streets, dwelt his Chinese friends. Because of Surabaya's heat, the little cockney lived on his verandas.

Here, something like a week after the *Halcyon* had left Macassar, John Solomon was at work. He wore a tarboosh cocked over one ear, wisps of grayish hair protruding from under its rim; at the opposite extreme, carpet slippers adorned his feet, one of which was a mechanical foot by the way.

Before him stood a great cabinet of dungon, or Philippine ironwood, cunningly shaped by Chinese artisans and bound with brass—far less resistant than the wood itself. Filled with odd drawers and spaces was this cabinet, fitted with crafty Chinese locks and closed with great, carven doors in front, so that no Occidental cracksman might know the mystery of those locks. Oriental craftsmen bothered not the things of John Solomon.

Now from the drawers Solomon took pen and ink and a small notebook bound in red morocco, and while he puffed contentedly at his pipe he wrote in that notebook very carefully, as though the words were precious things. His writing was small but neat, a fair scrivener's hand such as men learned in the old days before typewriters were fashioned. Presently he laid aside his pen and began to whittle tobacco from a black plug.

"This 'ere is the werry first time as I closed me accounts wi' two gentlemen," he mused, "an' set 'em away for twenty year or more, an' then opened 'em up again. But it's a werry good opening. If them 'ere cables from London would only come to-day, this 'ere anniwersary would be 'ighly memorable. And where's Mr. Lord? Why don't 'e answer no messages? Dang it! Am I really gettin' on in years, or—or is that bloke 'Iram King up to 'is tricks? I never 'opes to meet up wi' the likes o' that King again. Fair drivin' me gray 'airs into the grave, 'e is. Well," and the pudgy little man sighed wheezily, "that's neither 'ere nor there."

Solomon laid his knife and tobacco on the taboret at his side, and leaned forward. For a moment he worked at a secret catch in the cabinet; then drew back quickly as a latch clicked. The top series of drawers slid away, exposing the inner back of the cabinet.

Against this inner back were set two frames of gold overlaid with chastely wrought hair crystal. The one frame contained a portrait signed by one of the greatest masters of Europe; the other frame contained a faded photograph, from which the portrait had evidently been made. The subject of both was an extraordinarily beautiful woman dressed in the fashion of a bygone day and holding in her arms an infant. In the center and beneath the two frames were two words written in small, pigeon-blood rubies: "Mary—John."

For a space Solomon stared at the two pictures, motionless, silent. With trembling fingers he had removed his tarboosh. Slowly an unutterable longing crept into his face, usually so expressionless; his cheek muscles twitched a little, and two great tears gathered in his unwinking eyes and stood upon his face.

Softly, yet startlingly, an electric buzzer broke in upon the silence.

"There," Solomon paused, clearing his throat, "there, Mary, is the cables from London. It's great men as we're fighting to-day, Mary; rich men, powerful men! Will London be sacrificing of such men at me say-so? Will they, now? Which do they need more, Mary—the rich lord, the rich banker o' Canada, or the man John Solomon as was born in sound o' Bow Bells—your 'usband, Mary? It's yes or no, me dear."

Solomon reached up and touched a spring; the cabinet closed. Then he clapped his hands.

A white-clad Arab made his appearance and salaamed to the little cockney and handed the latter an envelope—a cablegram. He withdrew silently. For a long moment Solomon stared down at the envelope in his hand, turning it over and over, his lips compressed.

"It's yes—or no!" he whispered huskily. "Yes—or—no!"

Suddenly, savagely, he ripped open the envelope and spread out the paper before him. His fingers shook as he stared at the words of the message; it was in the naval code of the empire, but Solomon needed no code book. The message was not short:

> Have received your cabled exposé re Mowbray and Sanderson, with demand for immediate publication. Have verified from Egyptian records as you request. Note your assumption libel possibilities.
>
> Have consulted foreign office and ministry. Understand you retired government service account age and private wishes, refusing peerage or emoluments, also account being American citizen. Believe, however, your sphere of usefulness by no means ended.

Urgent need your services matter utmost importance to empire, also matter of extreme personal danger to yourself, if accepted. Realizing fully value of your past services, government agrees impossible at this time create tremendous sensation by publication of your story, unless correspondingly great benefits would be brought to government. Your resumption of service would confer this benefit.

Therefore must demand you present yourself within three months at foreign office in person, to undertake matter mentioned above. If you assent, your exposé shall be given immediate publication England and simultaneous release Canadian press. Otherwise, no.

The signature was that of a man known throughout the world as a great driving force behind the British government.

Solomon stared down at the paper for a long while, a gentle, almost wistful, smile on his aged features.

"This 'ere," he said slowly, "is the biggest compliment as I ever 'ad in me 'ole blessed life, just like that! They're square up against it; they needs me more'n they needs Mowbray an' Sanderson—that's what it is. Mowbray's China business is wrecked, and a 'ard job 'e'll 'ave to prove conspiracy on me. When this 'ere story is published 'e'll be wrecked at 'ome likewise. And Sanderson in Canada—'is bloody bankin' business will go to smash, too. A man ain't no better than 'is reputation in *that* business, I says.

"About the foreign office, now. Lud! If only me son had lived—me baby boy! If only I 'ad a son wi' the brains I 'as meself—a son as could step in and fill me shoes this werry minute!" Solomon sighed wheezily. "Well, I ain't got 'im. If only Prowidence would send me a man like that 'ere Cap'n King to be 'elping of me! But no; it ain't no use to be prayin' for what can't be 'ad, says I. And I'm werry much afraid as 'ow I'll 'ave to kill that 'ere man King."

He broke off, leaned forward, and took up his pen. With careful absorption he indited a reply to the cablegram which he had just received:

Accept your condition. Will report at foreign office for duty within time stated.

Story must be published immediately, as sent you. Assume full responsibility for any libel suits. As soon as published, communicate by wireless with Sir James Mowbray, also Sanderson, aboard yacht *Halcyon,* now in Gulf of Boni, Celebes.

Signing his name, he clapped his hands and the Arab appeared. Solomon handed him the message, with instructions to send it immediately. The Arab salaamed, and spoke:

"There is a man outside who comes from Yusuf upon thine errands. He bears a letter."

Solomon started slightly.

"Oh! So the boat has come in! Send the man in to me."

A moment later there entered a native who bowed to Solomon and extended a sealed packet.

"Master, I bear this writing from Yusuf in Macassar. I also bring you news of my own affairs."

Solomon took the paper and laid it aside; he leaned forward, his blue eyes intent upon the messenger.

"Speak of this, your affair," he said. "I ordered you to make full report upon the party from the yacht *Halcyon,* and especially of the man named King. Now speak!"

The native made a gesture, and smiled in a strange fashion.

"Master, in this letter from Yusuf is report upon the man King. For myself I have to report upon the young man who was registered at the hotel under the name of Horace Mowbray. He drank much and was a man without sense."

"Was," repeated Solomon, leaning forward. "What do you mean by that word *was?*"

Again the messenger smiled in his strange fashion, as might smile a man who knows himself to be an instrument of fate.

"Master, this young man hired two soldiers of the garrison to murder the man named King. This being discovered, the young man called off the two assassins, but being, as I say, a man of no sense, he did not pay them the wage agreed upon. Therefore, these two soldiers drew him in contact with a Chinese trader who sold him at small cost a belt—a very handsome belt made of shark skin and mounted with gold. This belt, master, attracted the young man. He did not know it had been worn by many men before him and that those who had worn it had died under the hand of Allah; that is, by the sickness which men call cholera."

Solomon leaped to his feet, staring at the messenger with sudden horror in his face. He tried to speak, but the words died on his lips.

Again the messenger smiled and spoke.

"Yes, master, it was a clever revenge. They have secrets, these Chinese, and the young man will surely die. So, perhaps, with all others aboard that ship."

Solomon's figure shivered. He made a gesture, and the messenger departed. For a long while Solomon stood staring with unseeing eyes; then, wiping the sweat from his brow, he slowly composed himself. "Cholera," he said, and repeated the word, his voice hoarse. "Cholera!"

Presently he picked up his pipe and tobacco, puffed for a moment, then from the taboret at his side took a telephone instrument. He spoke in fluent Hollandsch:

"This is Mijnheer Jan Solomon speaking. I want the governor general at Batavia—and without delay. Ring me when he is on the line."

After this amazing request, he smoked in silence, waiting. The soft buzzer sounded, and Solomon clapped his hands; the Arab entered with a letter.

"Effendi, the word has come. Also, Captain Lord is approaching; he, too, came on the packet boat."

Solomon nodded and set the letter to one side.

"Tell him to wait. I am busy."

The clay pipe was not yet smoked when the telephone rang. Solomon answered.

"Yes. I have word for your excellency," he said, "that there is an outbreak of Asiatic cholera aboard the yacht *Halcyon*, belonging to the English lord, Sir James Mowbray. She is at present in the Gulf of Boni; yes, probably at the concession of which we were speaking at our last interview, your excellency."

He listened a moment, then smiled.

"No, begging your pardon, sir, I'll take charge of this. I'd suggest that you dispatch a gunboat to patrol the outlet of the gulf in case the yacht tries to leave. You can send me a surgeon willing to undertake the case? Good! You had better get him here by special train, then, to-night. We leave at dawn. Yes, I assume full responsibility. Thank you!"

Sighing, Solomon laid down the instrument and seized his pen.

"I werry much doubt if I'll come through that 'ere cholera fight alive," he mused while he wrote. "And if I don't, the foreign office is agoin' to be disappointed. But it don't matter—now."

He finished his task, and reread the note. It was a wireless message addressed to Sir James Mowbray aboard the *Halcyon*, and read:

> Twenty-five years ago to-day you murdered my son. Your son is now dying of cholera. For the sake of others, I advise you to throw overboard your son's sharkskin belt. Within a week I shall see you myself, and our game will be ended.
>
> JOHN SOLOMON.

Solomon clapped his hands, and extended the message to the Arab who entered.

"There! Get that off immediate; the ship is up the Gulf o' Boni, and they can reach 'er easy. Send in Cap'n Lord."

A moment later Lord, a bluff British seaman, entered the screened veranda apartment. Solomon nodded to him, and tore open the letter.

"Set down, sir—one minute. H'm! Well—dang it! What d'you suppose that 'ere King 'as went an' done, Mr. Lord, sir?"

"I know what he's done to me," said Lord bitterly.

"Dang it!" exclaimed Solomon with rising choler. "Yusuf

writes from Macassar as 'ow King 'ad the gall to wisit 'im—
claimed to be my man and 'ad one o' my rings! No 'arm done
mebbe, but 'ow that 'ere man gets 'ome on me is fair terrible. I ain't
never knowed anything like it afore, Mr. Lord; in all me experience this 'ere skipper comes the nearest to knockin' of me out."

Lord surveyed the cockney with gloomy satisfaction.

"You've not heard the worst, sir," he said. "He's got the *Tyrian*,
too."

Solomon's eyes widened. He picked up his refilled pipe and
lighted it.

"Well, sir, let's 'ear 'ow it come about," he sighed. "That man is
fair possessed. 'E ain't 'uman. Dang it, if 'e don't up an' fight me
with me own weapons!"

Lord grinned sourly.

"He did this time, sir, quite literally. We had sunk that schooner *El Rey* and had marooned her crew as you commanded—"

"At the right place?" broke in Solomon.

"Yes, sir. Right where the *Halcyon* would land. We came down
the Saleier Straits at night, and just before daybreak picked up
a large craft that signaled by lights that she was disabled with
engine trouble and out of oil. I was not on deck, and unfortunately no one thought I was needed."

"The other craft," put in Solomon; "o' course she was the
'Alcyon disguised?"

"Yes, sir. The man King came aboard, under another name
and differently dressed, and no one recognized him. Then he
displayed one of your rings, or a ring with your seal on it, and
that threw every one off guard. Half a dozen men came up from
his launch, and at a signal drew weapons. They took the *Tyrian*
without firing a shot, sir, and King waked me up with a pistol
at my ear."

Solomon chuckled wheezily, appearing not a bit discomfited.

"Pirates they was, Mr. Lord. Pirates just like you. But they
didn't sink 'er?"

"No, sir. They put us in boats, and we made Goa in time to

catch the packet. Last we saw o' the *Tyrian* they had her in tow. King sent you his compliments, blast him!"

Solomon puffed for a moment in silence. Then he chuckled again.

"Well, Cap'n Lord, you and the men go aboard that 'ere power schooner *Rinsdam,* out in the 'arbor, and see as 'er engines is all shipshape. We leave at dawn, if so be as all goes right and we're agoin' to get back the *Tyrian.*"

"And I hope, sir," said Lord bluntly, "that I'll have an open chance at that blighter King."

"Mr. King," said Solomon, his face quite expressionless, "is agoin' to be a werry dead man inside of a week, cap'n."

Lord stamped away with an oath of satisfaction.

Left alone, Solomon smoked for a time in silence. Slowly there settled upon his features an expression of determination— an indomitable, indescribable look that betrayed the man's terrible inward power.

"I'll not break me cowenant with 'im," he muttered at last, knocking out his pipe. "But this 'ere thing 'as got to stop, just like that! In all me days I never seen such a man as this 'ere King. Is 'e a-goin' to spoil me plans now? No, dang it, I'll 'ave a talk with 'im and tell 'im fair that I'm a-goin' to kill 'im—and afore 'e knows what's what 'e'll be dead.

"I 'ates to do it, I does that. I ain't never 'ad a man's death on me conscience—not in cold blood, so to speak; but this 'ere is different. Stands between me and *them,* 'e does, and 'e's got to go, just like that! Where did the beggar get that 'ere ring? 'Ow did 'e find out what it was? Dang it! It's 'is own fault—and 'e's agoin' to die."

Again he clapped his hands. Again the Arab entered and salaamed.

"Come here, Muhammad! Is your rifle in order?" Solomon spoke Arabic now.

"Effendi, it is spotless as the soul of my father!"

Solomon grunted.

"You are as good a shot as you used to be, my brother?"

"Effendi!" The brown features glowed as the Arab made response. "I have shot many cartridges. I have shot birds as they flew. Three days ago I went out upon the bay, and I set ten corked bottles afloat. I withdrew my boat fifty yards, and shot at the bobbing necks of those bottles, effendi, in ten shots all were gone."

"Good!" Solomon nodded, and produced a folded paper from his pocket. "Here, Muhammad, is a tracing from a government chart. It shows the river mouth of Selangin. Do you see this island that divides the river mouth in twain?"

"Effendi, I see it."

"Upon that island are many trees, but the seaward side is bare. And in the center of the bare space there stands a house of bricks, wherein no native will dwell, that was built there by a crazy Dutch trader many years ago and is now empty. There the killing is to be done, Muhammad."

"The killing of unbelievers, effendi?"

"Of an unbeliever, Muhammad. A man who is nearly as great as I myself, and who stands between me and the work which I must do. I will describe him to you so there can be no mistake, Muhammad. He and I shall go into that house together; you must swim ashore during the night with your rifle and hide among the trees. After we go in together, you must keep sharp watch, and when this man appears at the door and takes one step outside the building you must kill. Muhammad, my life shall that day rest in your hands, and if you miss the heart of this man I shall surely die."

The Arab salaamed, and rose, smiling.

"Effendi, give order to shoot at the eye and brain," he said simply. "For the heart cannot be seen, but the eye can be seen. And whatsoever can be seen that I do not miss."

"Let it be so done," said Solomon, looking a little white.

CHAPTER X

SELANGIN RIVER

SELANGIN RIVER was a curious place; to King it held a nameless and terrible bad humor, a boding aspect, a gloomy chill as of death itself.

Yet the place was fair enough. Twelve miles upstream was the gold concession, but all thought of the concession had left the visitors now. Hereabouts no natives lived; in past days a grim Dutch trader had dwelt upon the island and had given it a bad name among the tribes, who still shunned it.

The island was midway of the river mouth, and the greater part of it, like the shores on either hand, was black with great trees and jungle growth. But about the house, solidly built of Batala brick, was a wide, open space running down to the shore; that trader had cleared away the jungle, and had sown salt and chemicals in the ground, so that no more life lay in the soil. Afterward his servants had put some of those same chemicals in his coffee, so that he died—a fitting vengeance, the natives whispered.

As was the case throughout the Celebes coasts, here was no fever or malaria. Warped up to the great mangrove roots in the east channel, and out of sight of the clearing, lay the *Halcyon* and the *Tyrian*, stem to stern.

On the second noon after capturing the *Tyrian*, and, as he hoped, leaving Solomon without a leg to stand upon, King had arrived here. To his amazement, he had found awaiting him Captain Marcos and the eleven men of the *El Rey;* marooned here to be picked up by him, as they themselves knew. The significance of this fact, showing that Solomon knew all about the concession and that he had deliberately joined the men of Marcos to those under King, was deadly. The Dutch commissioners professed entire ignorance of John Solomon—yet it was obvious that Solomon knew all about the matter in hand.

The morning after arriving, Sanderson had taken the launch and six men, and had posted off up the river with the commissioners to inspect the gold country. King, however, refused to go. Sir James Mowbray would not go, for Horace was visibly ill, and the father was worried. Norma Douglas took upon herself to act as nurse.

"If he's not on the mend by dawn to-morrow," said Sir James at mess that same evening after Sanderson's departure, "we'll strike for Batavia and the hospital, Mr. King."

"Yes, sir. And Mr. Sanderson—"

"Damn Sanderson!" broke out Sir James. "I'm thinking of my boy!"

The next morning at sunrise, King quietly entered the sick man's cabin; for a moment he talked with Miss Douglas, then his face whitened beneath its bronze.

"Call Sir James, Miss Douglas," he said quietly. "Have him wait here until I return."

Leaving her abruptly, he went on deck and sought Grimsen, who was on duty.

"Swing out a boat, Grimsen, and load it up with supplies. We're going to take young Mowbray ashore to that brick house around the point. Store in plenty of bottled water and the medicine chest and cabin stores. Leave it outside that house, and come back for us."

Grimsen looked into his eyes a moment.

"Is it that bad, sir?"

"Cholera," said King, and went aft.

In the stern, he sent a hail aboard the *Tyrian,* and two minutes later Captain Marcos appeared in the bow of the other yacht.

"Take your men ashore, Marcos," said King, "and clean out that brick house for us, will you? Make it decently habitable, if you can. Wait till I come ashore before leaving."

"At once, señor," came the answer.

King returned to the cabin without arousing Fortescue, his first officer. He knew that affairs were better left to the handling of his own men. In the sick room, he found Sir James and Miss Douglas waiting for him. The baronet was haggard.

"See here, King, we'd better pull out at once!" he broke out. "The boy is in bad shape and we've no doctor—"

"We don't need any," cut in King stonily. "I can do all a doctor can do for him, sir. I'm going to take him ashore to that brick house. He's down with cholera."

Mowbray quivered as if struck a mortal blow. From the girl broke a cry:

"Cholera! Not—not that, surely!"

"Yes." King's eyes were placid, expressionless. "You will stay aboard here, Miss Douglas; Mr. Grimsen will take you in charge and will provide you with disinfectants. If—"

"I shall go ashore, too," said the girl firmly. "It is my place—"

"Be quiet!" snapped King harshly. Then, seeing her flinch beneath his words, he took her hand in his, and his eyes softened. "Please do as I say in this. I know what is to be done; you do not. Already you have incurred too much danger."

The baronet thrust between them, and his voice came like a groan:

"King, you—you will do this?"

"Certainly," said King, surprise in his eyes. "I've been through cholera before now, and ought to be immune. I know what to do for him. We must get him ashore at once before the contagion has a chance to spread to both ships, sir."

"Then," and Mowbray drew a deep breath, "I go with you. No refusal, King. You'll need help; he's my son, and, by the Lord, I stand by him! You can't go, Norma, of course; you're a brave lassie, but this is our work. How'll we get him into a boat, King?"

"I'll attend to that."

King went to the deck and called all hands; they came, wondering.

"My lads," he said quietly, "Mr. Horace Mowbray is down with cholera. We're going to take him ashore. Have you had experience in fumigation, Mr. Fortescue?"

The first officer stammered an assent. The crew, white-faced, stared at King. Not a man but knew what those words meant.

"I'd suggest that you coöperate with Mr. Grimsen," said King to his mate, "for he's had cholera experience and knows what to do. Whether there will be any spread of the disease, men, remains to be seen. I'm going ashore with Sir James; Mr. Fortescue will be in command here. That is all. Mr. Grimsen, when you get back with that boat we'll go ashore."

"Aye, aye, sir," returned Grimsen cheerfully.

Half an hour afterward the unconscious and babbling invalid was carried down the gangway to the waiting boat. Sir James followed. King, at the gangway head, was halted by a touch on his arm, and turned to look into the brave eyes of Norma Douglas.

"I—I wanted to say good-by," said the girl, her voice steady. "You're a wonderful man, Captain King. I realize what this decision must have cost you."

King's brows lifted slightly.

"Cost me? Not a bit of it, Miss Douglas. It's the best thing to do, that's all. I may be able to save the boy's life where others could not. There's very little danger to me; I've been through it before, you know."

"That's why it's so wonderful."

In her eyes he read something that sent his pulses leaping. Wordless, he took her hand and for a moment held it; then, with a confident "au revoir," he turned to the waiting boat.

Grimsen and Marcos had done their work. The brick house, of two rooms, had been hastily but thoroughly renovated and cots with bedding installed. An old punkah in the larger of the two rooms had been patched up with wire.

King waved a cheery hand to the men from the *El Rey,* waiting at the shore in the *Tyrian's* launch. Grimsen aiding him, he lifted the stretcher which bore Horace Mowbray, and with Sir James at his elbow helped to carry the sick man to the house. There Captain Marcos awaited them, grave and imperturbable.

"You'll need some one to run the punkah, señor," said Marcos in Spanish. "I shall stay with you."

Sir James, understanding the language, glanced at him in amazement.

"You?" he answered. "You do not know this is cholera."

Marcos showed his white teeth in a smile.

"But, yes, señor. That is why I stay."

The baronet turned to King with a helpless gesture.

"Good heavens, King! What kind of men are these?"

"They are *my* men." And King smiled, not without pride. "No, Marcos, my friend, go back to the *Tyrian.* Sir James is going to stay with me; whichever of us watches can work the punkah. Thank you, Marcos. You had better come over every day with news; have the wireless man keep in touch with things outside, and you can leave the messages by that big stone at the landing. If I have any word for you, I can leave a note there also.

"Grimsen, you will take charge of the *Halcyon.* See that the disinfection is thorough and unsparing. If another case develops, bring it here at the first symptoms. Take particular care of Miss Douglas."

"Yes, sir," said Grimsen stolidly. "And if Mr. Sanderson hafe return wi' the commissioners, sir?"

"See that all are well before you allow 'em aboard."

Grimsen and Marcos shook hands and went down to their boats. A cheer from the men wavered up; the boats put out and were lost to sight around the fringing trees. Within the brick house the sick man moaned and babbled.

The exile was begun.

The two men kept ship's watches, four hours each; but at times both needed all their strength to restrain the raving sufferer. Once, even, King had to lash him to the cot for two hours, until the paroxysm was over.

Day by day they watched and fought with death, unreckoning time. In the hot hours the creaking punkah kept the dull air stirring; the nights fortunately were cool.

"We could have found no healthier place than this, except in the mountains," said King. "Thank God no one else has come down!"

The contagion had not spread—so far. But there was still time.

Day and night their endless monotony of work went on. Horace Mowbray grew steadily worse; it appeared that death might come to his relief at any moment. Sir James was as a man in hell. Those terrible days stripped from him all the falseness, all the self-consciousness of position, all the veneer—stripped him down to the naked soul.

He ceased to shave or to care for himself; his one thought was for the son who lay under the hand of death. He lived in a terrible world all his own, staring down at the face of his son, never talking, acting as if wakened from dream when King relieved him. At times, after he had slept, he cursed horribly in half a dozen tongues, muttered strange stories riven from his black youth. King came to shrink from contact with the man; yet he saw awakening in Sir James, despite all this, a strange humility of spirit, a new manhood.

The work of the place fell upon Hiram King. Himself neat as usual, he had to keep the house in order likewise, and he welcomed the work. The wireless reports came as a great relief. Twice a day, or oftener, Captain Marcos brought messages and whatever supplies were needed, leaving them by the big stone on the beach. Always Norma Douglas came in the boat. King, standing on the shore, exchanged a few words with her. It at last became certain that the two yachts were free from contagion.

And thus, one day, came the wireless message from Solomon.

King took the message to the house and read it to Sir James. The baronet heard it without a word, then laughed terribly.

"No use, King. We cannot fight that devil. He has doomed us all; somehow, somewhere, he gave my boy the cholera. Think of it! Devil's work!"

"This message," said King stonily, "would imply that he is coming here."

Sir James threw out his hands helplessly.

"It does not matter. I shall let him kill me if—if the boy dies. After all, it is a just vengeance. He told the truth. Good heavens, the thing has haunted me all my life! We did not mean to kill the woman and her baby, King; as God is my judge, we did not mean it! We put them aboard that ship—the ship went down—how were we to know?"

He stared at King, in his eyes an awful helplessness. King looked at him, unmoved, not pitying him in the least.

"And if your boy does not die, sir?"

"What!" The baronet caught his arm. "You think—there is a chance?"

"There is a chance of anything, sir. To-morrow night I think we shall know."

They took up the work again. Sanderson and the commissioners had not yet returned, nor had the launch that had taken them come back.

King remained silent through the long hours. He had found the sharkskin belt among the effects of young Mowbray, and had flung the thing into the bay. The message from Solomon had shown him, as he thought, the secret of the whole business. Sir James also had guessed the same terrible fact; namely, that John Solomon had deliberately given the cholera infection to young Mowbray.

To King this did not particularly matter; he did not blame Solomon for paying such a terrific debt of vengeance in any way possible. What did arouse him, however, what did strike to his innermost soul, was the fact that the entire crew of the yacht had been exposed to the same menace. It seemed utterly incredible that any human being could have confounded the innocent with the guilty in so frightful and promiscuous a course of revenge!

"For that," he told himself, "John Solomon shall surely die— if I live. And I intend to live. He must die if only to insure the safety of Norma Douglas from his schemes."

The day and the night passed interminably. The next day began to draw its course, and with the passing hours Horace Mowbray fell into sleep, deep and composed—almost for the first time.

"At sunset we shall know," said King gravely. "He will waken then. The tide will change about then also."

Sir James stared at him from bloodshot eyes and pawed his uneven beard with trembling fingers.

"At sunset. The tide will go out at sunset! Then he will die. They always do."

"God rules the tides," said King.

That afternoon Captain Marcos fetched a lengthy wireless message, relayed from London. There was a second one also from Solomon. King did not read them until the boat had gone and he had got back to the entrance of the house. Then he passed inside to where Sir James sat watching the sleeping man, interminably pulling the punkah wire with numbed fingers.

King handed him the long message from London. The baronet read it with vacant eyes; read of the calumny and disgrace which had been showered upon him before all the earth—and Sanderson with him; read of the true, damnably true, story which had come into the public prints like a thunderbolt; read of his blasting and shame in the world's eyes.

"It does not matter," he returned, thrusting it away and pointing to the bed. "Look! There is color in his cheeks!"

"Here is another message," said King calmly. Yet he wondered at the man before him. "It is from Solomon. He says that he will be here some time to-morrow."

Sir James seemed not to hear the words.

The afternoon dragged interminably; the temperature of Horace Mowbray began to rise slowly but surely, and promised an early return of fever. The two men hung over him in anxious suspense, bathing, fanning, lending Nature every assistance in her fight against the insidious bacilli enemy. All outside the house was forgotten by them.

And now, almost in the time of crisis, came fate upon the scene; the fate foredoomed from a thousand years, perhaps, when a Higher Hand shaped the course of that coast ere ever white men were known.

For it chanced that, as one descended the Selangin River and came to the delta island, this east channel wherein the two yachts lay bound against the towering trees was all but hidden, and the main west channel was broad and obvious. Therefore, Sanderson, returning in the launch of the *Halcyon* and taking the obvious course, came out upon the bay to find the two yachts apparently gone.

The two Dutch commissioners pointed out the other channel, but at that instant King stepped to the doorway and flung out a bucket of water, without observing the launch, which was not in the direct line of vision. Sanderson instantly turned the launch to land.

"I'll join 'em here for dinner, lads," he exclaimed to the *Halcyon's* men. "You go on to the Yacht with these gentlemen. We're no doubt havin' a family picnic here—eh, but the lassie will be cooking, too!"

He flung his great frame to land, and strode up toward the house, all ignorant of the shadow that lay thereon. The hour was close to sunset.

King came for cool water from the canvas buckets swinging outside the door, and stood face to face with Sanderson. He comprehended instantly what had happened.

"Hello, man!" cried the brawny Scot eagerly. "Where—"

"Be quiet!" snapped King as the other attempted to set him

aside and enter. "Keep your voice down! Why the devil did you come here?"

Sanderson stared at him in blank anger.

"Who're ye talkin' at, me lad?" growled he. "And what d'ye mean by—"

King made a helpless gesture.

"Oh, you came down the other channel, eh? And stopped in here. Well, you'll have to stay here, Sanderson; young Mowbray is down with cholera, and Sir James is helping me nurse him. This is a pesthouse and you've blundered into it."

He turned inside with the water. Sanderson stood in the doorway, his face suddenly livid and streaming with sweat. Cholera!

King, helping Sir James with the cool water pads, suddenly heard Sanderson running, and heard the man's voice uplifted. With a grim smile, King stuffed the wireless messages into his pocket and sped outside. He found Sanderson stumbling along the beach, calling back the launch and frantically waving his arms.

"Go along, lads; there's cholera here!" sang out King to the turning launch. He came up with Sanderson and seized the man's shoulder. Without protest, Sanderson turned and stared at him, trembling. The man was smitten to the very soul with awful fear.

"You'll have to stay here, Sanderson," said King firmly. "There's no danger, I take it; neither Sir James or I have been touched, nor any one else. I think we'll pull Horace through all right. Do you understand?"

"Yes." Sanderson essayed a shaky laugh, drew a hand across his brow, and tried to pull himself together. "Yes. I—it hit me under the belt, like. Yes. I'm not a fool, lad. I understand."

"Then you'll understand better after you've read these." And King, handing him the wireless messages, turned away. He had no mind to spare Sanderson one whit.

CHAPTER XI

SANDERSON DIES

FIVE MINUTES later King had forgotten Sanderson, and was bending over the cot of Horace Mowbray, beside Sir James.

"The fever's ebbing," whispered the baronet, tense, shivering under his terrible nerve tension, racked by the anguished suspense of the moment. "Is—is there hope?"

"There's always hope," breathed King calmly. "Yes. We've got him back into peaceful sleep; now he must be held there until he awakens naturally. I believe he'll come around. But that belt— it was horrible! We know that he bought it somewhere ashore. How Solomon managed to get it into his hands I don't know, but it's evident that Solomon had deliberately arranged the whole affair. Now, watch him, sir. All depends on how he wakens."

Intent, absorbed in the play of life and death over the gaunt features on the pillow, the two men leaned forward, a hush upon the room. The face of Sir James was drawn into a livid mask; his dark eyes burned like coal-glowing embers; he sat absolutely motionless, but his hands, resting on the bedside, were clenched like the hands of a man set in *rigor mortis*.

And upon that awful hush of dread suspense broke a hoarse, raucous voice from the doorway—the voice of Sanderson uplifted in bellowing wrath:

"James, where are ye? Did ye know this? Oh, the devilment of it! He's got us, James; he's given the story to the press! He's published us!"

As a steel wire breaks under too great tension, James Mowbray flung to his feet and cried out fearfully. King made a gesture of despair, and sat watching the sick man.

"Be quiet! Be quiet, Scotchy!" The baronet's voice was knife-edged.

"Gi' me a boat!" bellowed the other furiously. "We'll get out o' this cursed place, James! Gi' me a boat, I tell ye! We'll have the law on him; he can't have proof o' the tale, James. Let me get away from here!"

Too late King regretted his action in giving those wireless messages to Sanderson. Instead of breaking the big man's spirit, they had but roused him to maddened fury.

And the evil was done. Horace Mowbray, wakened by that hoarse scream of fury, tossed up his arms and cried out with a shrill wail. At the door, Sir James turned; he was snarling like a wild beast, and a terrible cry broke from him when he saw what had happened.

"Curse you, Scotchy! You've killed him—you've killed my boy!"

The rest was lost in the sharp, smashing crack of a pistol shot.

"Damn!" exclaimed King to himself. He was unable to see what had happened.

Leaning over, he caught the wasted figure of Horace Mowbray in his arms, held the threshing arms quiet, and forced a smile—for Mowbray had awakened and was staring up at him with a pitiful wonder, lips moving soundlessly.

"It's all right, old man," said King. "Do you hear me?"

The other nodded feebly and relaxed. His eyes closed.

Outside the doorway, Sir James Mowbray stood like a man paralyzed, a revolver in his hand, gazing at the body of Sanderson. King came to the threshold, wiping his dripping brow, and understood; he stepped forward and gripped the revolver. The baronet yielded like a man in a dream, then turned a perplexed, overstrained face.

"I—I killed him, King!" he whispered. "I was mad!"

"Hush!" said King quietly. "Hush! Go in and see your son. He is not dead; he is going to live."

Sir James tottered. His vacant eyes glimmered anew with life. A hoarse sob breaking from him, he pushed King aside and darted into the house.

The sun was down behind the western mountains. For a long while King sat gazing across the body of Sanderson at the sea, wondering at it all—wondering at the ways of fate. Sanderson was dead, killed by his partner in old crimes; yet, as surely as though the cockney had pulled trigger, this vengeance was attributable to John Solomon.

What was to come of it all? This was not the end. There would be no end while Sir James and Solomon both lived. The baronet was a broken man; his wealth, his standing, his power had been swept away like rotten twigs by the hand of John Solomon. And on the morrow was coming Solomon, implacable, terrible, far planning, to finish the task.

From an impersonal viewpoint, in a detached manner, King thoroughly admired the manner in which the little cockney had thus far accomplished his work. But as a matter of cold fact, King found himself keenly concerned in the matter; his sympathy with Solomon's wrongs was quite eliminated by his vital and personal interest in the dangers which, as a result of Solomon's acts, had enmeshed Norma Douglas.

So far as he was concerned, then, King regarded the vengeance of Solomon as action quite justified, as retribution beautifully and artistically brought about, as poetic justice handled by a past master of details. From the time those phonograph cylinders had come aboard the *Halcyon*, Solomon had gone about his business with a gradual mounting to a great climax. That climax would come with his arrival—perhaps.

"But it shan't come," said King, staring upon the swift, tropic twilight. "He passed the limit when he set the peril of cholera aboard us—when he endangered Norma. And he shall have no chance to endanger her again."

So Solomon was coming here! Then Solomon should find death awaiting him.

Having determined upon this, King left the details to await circumstances, and went inside the house. In the gathering darkness he found that Horace Mowbray had passed again into a quiet, healthful sleep—the sleep of recuperation; and Sir James, his head on the edge of the bed, was softly sobbing. The strain was gone, but it had shaken the man to bits.

King lighted the lamp, and, wordless, prepared a hypodermic syringe. He took the baronet's arm and inserted the needle, pressed down the skin bulge, and led the unresistant man to his own cot.

"You can sleep now, sir," he said calmly. "I'll attend to everything."

For the first time in a week King whistled contentedly to himself as he went about his work. Lighting his pipe, he sallied forth, and with a knife scooped out a shallow grave in the sandy loam. When the body of Sanderson had been covered from sight, King bared his head and repeated from memory the service of burial at sea. There was no hypocrisy about Hiram King; he was conscientious rather than devout, and when the last words had been said he drew a deep breath and added a brief sermon of his own.

"Providence, that's what it was. None of us is to blame— no, not even Solomon—for this thing. Sanderson had run his course, tended to the rest."

Inside the house again, he stropped his razor, found a pair of scissors in his kit, and went to the bedside of the baronet. In the other room Horace Mowbray slept soundly.

King fell to work at the features of Sir James, who lay unconscious between his hands like a waxen image. In fifteen minutes the baronet was clean-shaven. King's eyes rested for a long moment on the worn features that looked so fearfully haggard even in repose.

"That'll help you a good deal; you'll need help when you wake up to-morrow," he mused, not without a touch of pity. "You'll need to feel clean, outwardly and inwardly."

After which conclusion he took a final look at his two patients, then turned in for a bit of sleep himself.

With the sunrise came awakening, facing of issues, reconstruction. Horace Mowbray wakened sane and convalescent, but very weak. King made ready breakfast, then aroused Sir James. Leaving father and son together, he strode away from the house to the rear, and by slow degrees made his way through the trees and jungled growths toward the place where the two yachts lay moored.

Half an hour later he returned to the house.

Sir James met him at the door, and at a glance King perceived that the baronet was a changed man, but so indefinable was the change that at first King was at a loss to explain it. Sir James took his arm and motioned toward the beach.

"I want to talk with you, King."

They walked together to the strand, silent. Mowbray seemed struggling within himself, and his hollow eyes were somber. Suddenly he halted and touched his shaven face.

"You did this—last night?"

"Yes." King eyed him gravely, curiously. "You are sorry?"

The terribly lined features of the older man smiled very faintly.

"No," he answered, and paused. "No. It was a good thing. A symbol, perhaps. Listen, King! I must tell you something; but it's hard to say. Years ago I helped to commit a crime, a despicable crime; Sanderson was with me—you know all about it."

King nodded.

"That crime laid a curse upon me," went on the baronet; "upon both of us. We went to South America, and by degrees we prospered—despicably. You've read about the Putumayo rubber exposures? We were in that. We made money in rubber. Nothing was beyond us—nothing! Then we heard that Solomon was dead. Sanderson went to Canada with his money.

"I fell heir to my father's title and estate and came to England with Horace. King, I tried to change, but I could not. The horror of the curse had eaten into my soul. Although I had money and position and influence, I could not change. I—what do they say in America?—grafted. That was it. I did not need to, but I did. It was the same with Sanderson over in Canada. We could not help it. This gold concession here was graft."

Again Sir James paused, staring out at the ocean.

"I must tell you this," and his voice was low, deliberate. "We picked you up, with your ten thousand pounds. We determined to—to get it. That's my confession, King. We meant to—to rob you. We were cheats, cheats!"

He faced King defiantly, expectantly. But King only smiled a little.

"You need not have told me this, sir," he said quietly. "I had already guessed it."

Mowbray fell back a pace, slowly realizing what the words meant. His eyes dilated.

"You—you guessed it?"

"Yes. Before we left Honolulu."

"And—and all the while you stood by us? And here, without a word, you have—you have done—this?" As he spoke, Mowbray flung out a hand toward the house in tacit indication. "King, I—I never knew there could be such a man in the world!"

Mowbray turned away, tears upon his cheeks.

King tried to speak, but could not. Silently he took out his pipe and filled it. At the scratch of the match, Mowbray faced about, wondering.

"I buried Sanderson," said King.

The other shivered a little, then nodded.

"Yes. That's all I needed to complete the ruin, King. Please God, Horace can go back! I can't."

They stood for a space in silence, gazing out upon the glory of the morning ocean. Suddenly there came to them the tinkle of a bell and the churning rush of propellers. They turned to see the *Halcyon* backing from the east channel, while the launch of the *Tyrian* came streaking past her toward the landing, bearing Grimsen, Marcos, and four of the latter's men.

"What's this?" exclaimed Sir James sharply.

"Why, sir," King met his inquiring gaze with placid eyes, "I'm sending off the *Halcyon* at once with you and Mr. Horace. He'll need the sea air, and the quicker the better. Mr. Marcos and his men will remain here with me and the *Tyrian*. Fortescue can handle your yacht as far as Surabaya. Marcos is coming ashore now to give you and Mr. Horace a thorough disinfecting, also me and the house. With those two Dutch commissioners aboard, you'll have no trouble about receiving a thorough quarantining at Surabaya. I'd not be surprised if Solomon had forewarned the Dutch authorities about the cholera—but they'll get a happy surprise."

"But you!" Mowbray stared at him in blank astonishment. "Why do you not come?"

King chuckled.

"I'll come—later. You forget, sir, that Solomon announced his arrival here to-day. I shall stay and meet him. No! Not for your sake. Don't thank me! It's for the sake of Miss Douglas, I'll tell you frankly. I warned Solomon that if he imperiled her I'd get him, and I mean to do it. Now I'd suggest, sir, that we place ourselves in the hands of Marcos."

The baronet assented with a helpless gesture. But his white and shaven face had gone to a deep red.

Two hours later the purging by fire was finished. Clad in clean, fresh garments and feeling like new men, King and Mowbray stood by the landing and watched Horace Mowbray borne aboard the launch. King turned and held out his hand.

"Well, good-by, sir! You'll explain to Miss Douglas, please? I'd rather not go aboard at all; my things have all been removed to the *Tyrian*—"

He ceased in some surprise. Mowbray was facing him with head erect and blazing eyes.

"What, King! Do you think I've come so low as to let another man fight my battles? No! I can't go out into the world again after what's happened. For the boy's sake I must not. I'll stay here and meet Solomon, and that's final!"

King gazed at him a moment, and accepted his sincerity.

"All right, sir. Then we'll stay together—for I've made my plans to dispose of Solomon. I trust you'll not interfere?"

Mowbray's brows lifted.

"Not interfere? Why—"

"In other words," went on King steadily, implacably, "place yourself under my orders. Do or say nothing until I allow it. I have my own quarrel to attend to, and I have arranged the settlement. Do you assent?"

Mowbray shrugged his shoulders at length.

"As you wish," he responded curtly.

King stepped over to the boat.

"Take him aboard, Marcos," he indicated Horace Mowbray. "Then return for us. Tell Mr. Fortescue to go ahead and not wait."

The baronet leaned over his son for a space, then rose, wordless. At his gesture, the launch shot out from shore.

King searched the deck of the *Halcyon* with intent gaze, half trusting to catch some sign from Norma Douglas. Disappointment hardened within him as he realized that she was nowhere in sight; surely she had been told that they were parting here.

Yet the launch came to the gangway and was slung aboard; the yacht began to turn, and Fortescue waved and shouted farewells from the bridge, but there was no evidence of the girl. The yacht steamed out upon the horizon, lessened, and was gone, and King's eyes followed her in vain.

"What do you intend to do when Solomon arrives?" At the question, King turned to find Sir James at his elbow. The launch was awaiting them.

"Do? Oh!" King waved his hand toward the house. "Take him

in there; it depends, of course, on when he arrives and how. We know nothing about it yet. But he'll go into that house for a talk with me—and he'll not come out alive!"

"Eh, man? You'll not—"

"I'd not lift my hand against him except in a last extremity. But he shall die. It will be no more than an execution, sir."

Mowbray shivered as he met the level blue eyes.

"Upon my word, King! I—I believe that you're as bad as the rest of us, after all!"

"No. He'll know all about his execution before the event; that's justice. And I've already told you why I'm taking this hand in the game. So let's go to the *Tyrian*. Heavens! I'm anxious for a bit of real living again!"

They got into the launch without further speech, and she puttered forth to the point of land and so around to the *Tyrian*.

As they came in beside the yacht that had been Solomon's, King looked up and saw Norma Douglas awaiting them. Mowbray saw also, and groaned under his breath. The girl did not yet know that her uncle was dead, or—how he had died.

CHAPTER XII

SOLOMON COMES

NORMA DOUGLAS was merrily defiant, yet beneath her defiance and beneath her merriment King sensed a very firm determination of some kind; he was not certain just what. It puzzled him. Norma puzzled him also, and fascinated him into the bargain.

"Certainly I didn't go, sir!" she exclaimed gayly. "And I ordered them to go off without me—and they went! Wouldn't I make a good officer?"

"You would," assented King, smiling a little. "Except for the fact that I sent orders for you to go—and officers know how to obey orders."

"Well, I mutinied!" Her eyes became serious now. "They told me that you intended to stay behind with my uncle. Sir James was going to nurse Horace; but why didn't he go?"

"Same reason as yours—insubordination."

King glanced over into the launch, where the baronet still remained—unable to ascend and meet the niece of the man he had slain. The situation was impossible!

"Your things are aboard?" he asked. "You've picked out a cabin?"

"Of course."

King drew a deep breath. It must be done! The truth could not be shirked. As he turned, she leaned forward, searching his face.

"What is the matter? You look—you look so strange! And why has Sir James shaved?"

Gravely King took her hand; her fingers lay passive in his, her gaze studying him.

"My dear Miss Douglas," he said slowly, "I want you to realize something—that I am wholly at your service, that I am devoted to your interests. Oh, I am an awkward fellow at expressing what is in my heart! But I want to serve you, and I will, if you allow it. There was trouble ashore last night, Miss Douglas. Your uncle was—was hurt. Now, please go to your cabin until I call you, when we shall go ashore together; you will understand better how it happened when we are on the spot."

The color had faded from her cheeks as she listened, but her eyes did not falter.

"Hurt?" she repeated. "My uncle was hurt? And you left him ashore—oh! Tell me! Tell me quickly! He is—"

"He is sleeping," said King gravely.

She caught her breath, reading the truth in his words and face. Fear came into her eyes, fear and a swift horror of despair; then she turned from him and went below as he had ordered. King followed her with his gaze.

"A girl, face to face with death, and she did not quail!" he muttered. "Gad! I wish I could say as much about what is coming—about Solomon. He deserves it; he must die—yet for some reason the thought hangs on me like a pall. And I am old friends with death, too. Bah! It is foolishness. This cholera business has unnerved me."

He made a gesture to the baronet below, and turned away.

Why had Norma Douglas exclaimed, as she had done, about the change in the appearance of Sir James? A symbol, Mowbray himself had called it. King walked into the bows and stared down at the sluggish current of the river flowing past, pondering strange things. As he had but just confessed, the coming execution of Solomon lay heavily on him, oppressed him. Yet his resolution was like chilled steel; the cockney must die.

"It was a symbol sure enough," he reflected. "Mowbray became a new man this morning, as though the loss of his beard had indeed served some mystic purpose. What a foolish thought, what an inane idea! But there are things in the world yet not of the world which we cannot fathom. I wish I could make up my mind to murder Solomon."

He shuddered a little, and at a step turned to find Grimsen beside him.

"So we hafe been wrong!" observed the seaman, who in reality was the mate of Marcos. "We are not hafe to kill that Sanderson. Wale, I hafe a bit o' news for you, sir."

"A ship has been sighted?" King shook off his gloomy mood. "Solomon?"

Grimsen shook his head.

"No and yah, sir. But the *Halcyon* she hafe sighted one o' they Dutch gunboats, sir, on patrol down the gulf. Mebbe you will come to the wireless house?"

King nodded, and followed to the *Tyrian's* wireless, where the operator shipped by Marcos at Honolulu was listening in.

"You're getting something,"

A nod. The operator began to jot down words, then halted and glanced up with a smile.

"The Dutchmen have ordered the wireless cut out, sir. But I've got the message all shipshape. The *Halcyon* was halted by the gunboat, and at the same time made out a schooner heading north under auxiliary power—pretty slow, they said; ought to get up here late to-day."

King met the hard eyes of Grimsen, who smiled.

"Schooners that hafe auxiliary power are not wasting time on places like this, sir. Solomon, he hafe been on her, yah!"

"And he'll get here late to-day," added King musingly. "Well, Grimsen, that clinches the matter. After luncheon I'll go ashore with Miss Douglas. While we're there you and Captain Marcos had better warp the *Tyrian* out into the channel, just off the island, and anchor her. I'll stave off Solomon until morning, then get him ashore in that house as we planned. You can swim ashore before morning; better leave your rifle and some dry clothes planted among the trees today."

"And the time is when he hafe come out of the hoose?"

"Yes." King's lips clenched for a moment. "Yes. When he steps across the threshold."

Of Sir James Mowbray he saw nothing more for the time being.

Of course, reflected King, Solomon might be coming with fire and sword; might have that schooner loaded with guns and gunmen—but such a supposition was highly improbable. It was not the cockney's method of working. There would be a swift, sudden stroke, a stroke that might involve Norma Douglas and every one else if it were allowed to fall. But it should not fall. King grimly told himself.

King, Miss Douglas, and Captain Marcos lunched together alone. Although she was silent and showed traces of tears, the girl had herself well in hand; her love for Sanderson might not have been great, yet, he had been her uncle, and his death had left her alone in the world, at he ends of earth, with none of her sex beside her. And this for any girl would be a hard matter.

She was obviously in wonder at these men around her, as with King she waited at the gangway for the launch to be made ready. Captain Marcos, who boasted old blood of the Pizarro *conquis-tadores,* was in his way a gentleman, and made the fact felt. The other men were strange to the girl, from Grimsen down. Hard men were they, ruled by a hard hand, but to Norma Douglas very courteous and to Hiram King very respectful.

"They are afraid of you?" she said softly, sitting beside King in the stern of the launch after it set forth, and motioning toward the two men forward. King smiled.

"Afraid of me? No. But they have been with me or with Captain Marcos for years, and they know us. Men who go down to the sea in ships, Miss Douglas, can ill afford to make mistakes."

She understood his meaning, for her Scotch blood held knowledge of the grim sea.

And so they came to the landing in front of the clearing, and went up together to the house, while the launch returned—there were none too many men to work the *Tyrian.*

King told her what had happened and how Sanderson had come to his death. Such things came hard to him, and he was awkward in the telling, for he was thinking the while how Norma Douglas was facing the world alone and how there were in his heart words which he had rather say, had he dared or had this been the time.

But to his amazement he found her less interested in the fate of Sanderson than in himself.

"You—*you* buried him, like that?" she exclaimed slowly. "Alone, at night, after all you'd been through! And did you shave Sir James also?"

King chuckled slightly.

"Yes. There is something comical in that—something terribly comical or comically terrible, like the frightful jesting of Rigoletto. It was an impulse that made me do it. I abhorred the man as he was, Miss Douglas. It was an effort to live with him."

"Yet you saved the life of his son!"

"Yes. That was simply duty, no more. Now, Mowbray has been stripped of all he had, all his pose is gone; he is down to fundamental grips with himself, knowing that he can deceive neither himself nor any one else Well, enough of moralizing. We can manage to keep you two apart."

"Not for my sake," she broke in, her voice calm. "I cannot pretend great grief for my uncle, Captain King. Since we left Honolulu on this awful trip, I have discovered many things; Horace told me, largely unintentionally, things that—that frightened me."

King nodded. He knew then that she had discovered the marriage compact made between Mowbray and her uncle, the compact by which she was to be bartered, disposed of, mated like an insentient thing. No wonder she could not pretend great grief.

"I cannot, of course," went on the girl quietly, "pretend that I want anything more to do with the Mowbrays. But we can preserve the decencies of life until we separate. I am almost— almost glad that I did not see my uncle again. Shall we return to the yacht?"

They stood together at the landing, waiting. Grimsen came with the launch, and they went aboard.

King helped the girl up the ladder. At the deck, she stumbled, and he caught her hand—nor did he release it immediately. They stood for a long moment, looking into each other's eyes, and in the gaze of the girl King read a sudden terror, a sudden realization, a sudden great heart message.

No words passed between them. None were needed. It was a moment of revelation—one of those supremely clear, vibrant moments that occur rarely, but when they come are never forgotten. Each knew what was in the soul of the other—and each was frightened, set a-wondering, filled with a great, unbelievable joy.

Then swiftly the girl withdrew her hand, and, her face flaming, was gone. King removed his cap and gazed after her, his blue eyes like stars.

"What is this, my friend?" came the voice of Captain Marcos. King turned and looked at his friend. "What is this? What have you seen that you stand thus?"

King smiled a little, but gravely.

"I have seen heaven, Marcos."

The Peruvian's white teeth showed in a flashing smile. Marcos had seen—and understood.

"Then, my friend, let us break our rule. See, in my bag is a bottle of pisco, which I have carried these two years. By the sacred wounds, my friend, when one sees heaven, then it is one's duty to toast the angels. One little drink, my friend?"

King laughed.

"One very little one, Marcos—because we are friends."

The hours of waiting dragged interminably. Neither Mowbray nor Miss Douglas appeared. King was glad he had taken that drink. Slight as was the aguardiente in the pisco, it had helped him at a very critical moment. For, after the look he had seen in the eyes of Norma Douglas, his approaching work became very hard to do. He felt terror of it.

He was afraid—and could not tell why. Solomon was projecting some blow that would finish Sir James—and would very possibly involve Norma Douglas. King could not forgive the introduction of cholera aboard the yacht, with its frightful possibilities.

Therefore, when it was perfectly obvious that a man who had gone mad over revenge must be destroyed as a public and private menace, what was it that dragged at King's soul? What was the antipathy that gripped him? He could not tell. He swayed, pulled by various reasonings and emotions in varied directions, between consciousness that he was doing the right thing and instinct that he was doing the wrong thing.

Thus, then, in mid-afternoon, the schooner that bore Solomon was sighted.

She came on slowly, more slowly, it seemed, than she should come. King realized that for some reason Solomon had timed the arrival to take place at sunset.

And at sunset the *Rinsdam* forged in to the entrance of the west channel, two hundred yards away from the yacht, and dropped anchor. Watching her, King nodded to himself; Lord and the original crew of the *Tyrian* were in charge. Out upon her quarter-deck stepped the pudgy figure of Solomon.

"'Ello, Cap'n King!" came the hail. "We picked up the *'Alcyon* this mornin'. I 'opes as 'ow she told us right and Sir James wasn't aboard 'er?"

"He's here," responded King. "So am I."

"And werry 'appy I am to see you, sir," came the cheerful retort. "Will you 'ave a bit o' talk in the mornin'?"

"Sure," answered King. "Will you come aboard?"

Solomon chuckled visibly.

"Not me, sir! But will you come aboard 'ere?"

"No," snapped King. "I'll meet you ashore at seven bells."

"Werry good, sir. At seven bells it is, sir—at that 'ere 'ouse?"

"Yes," said King shortly.

"I've brought a doctor," went on Solomon, "if so be as you 'as need o' one, sir."

King turned away without response, his lips firmly compressed. Those final malicious words had settled matters for good and all. Solomon would die in the morning!

CHAPTER XIII

THE MEETING

A T S I X bells—seven o'clock in the morning—King descended into the yacht's launch, and found Sir James Mowbray awaiting him.

"What!" he exclaimed. "You're not going?"

"Certainly I'm going," said Mowbray, coolly imperturbable.

King gazed at him a moment, then stepped into the launch. As they darted in to the shore, he could see the *Rinsdam* lowering a boat to take Solomon ashore.

"Don't wait," King said to Marcos. "Stand by aboard the yacht—and look out for trouble."

Marcos nodded. King and Mowbray stood together for a moment on the shore, and the American smiled slightly as he turned to his owner.

"You're determined—why?"

"Because," said Mowbray steadily, "the time has come to end the whole matter. I've been fighting with myself, King, and I've reached the solution. I'll simply throw myself on Solomon's mercy and let him do what he wishes. Call it fright, weakness, whatever you like!"

King met his eyes for a long moment, then held out his hand.

"No, I'd not call it that," he said slowly. "You've been a coward in the past—and worse. Now, I think you've become a brave man, Sir James. But before you do this—and no doubt you realize as well as I the implacable nature of Solomon—give me the chance to talk with and settle matters with him."

"Your own quarrel, you mean?"

King's lips twisted.

"Yes—call it that. Further, my duty as captain of your ship."

"Very well. Shall I wait outside?"

"No. Take the little room where Horace was ill."

They walked together to the house. King did not tell Mowbray of what was going to happen; he realized that so strong was the man's mood of self-abasement, of clear renunciation, of anxiety to settle old scores by the payment of life, if need were, that Mowbray would insist on seeing Solomon first. King did not intend that the two men should meet at all. There would be no sense in it. Solomon must be killed. Mowbray, regenerated, a man born anew through the fires of remorse and suffering, must be allowed to go forth into the world again—must face the world and his past and fight for his son's sake.

Thus argued Hiram King with himself, unwitting that no man may act as arbiter of destiny with impunity or with unerring accuracy.

They came to the house and entered. The front door was gone entirely.

Within, the one door that divided the two rooms was a battered affair of red tindalo, which does not rot. It was half off its hinges, and could not be entirely closed. King walked into the inner room with the baronet, and smiled at sight of the door.

"I want your promise, sir," he said, "that you'll not come into the other room until I call you—no matter what happens."

"Eh? Oh, very well. You have my word for what it's worth," added Mowbray bitterly.

"It's worth everything, sir," answered King quietly. The other looked at him for a moment, then held out his hand.

"God bless you for that word, King! Now leave me."

King swung the door to, realizing that the baronet could hear all that passed in the adjoining room. But what matter? He would not understand—until too late!

Leaving the house, King strode down to the shore, where Solomon was disembarking from his boat. The cockney waved his rowers back, and pulled forth his pipe.

"Well, Mr. King!" he exclaimed, his blue eyes wide set. "And where did Sir James go to, if I may ask?"

King motioned toward the house.

"There are two rooms. We'll take one. He's in the other, waiting until I get through with you. Then he wants to see you himself."

"And I wants to see 'im," ejaculated Solomon, a sudden growl in his voice. "Where's Scotchy Sanderson?"

King pointed to the grave.

"Mowbray shot him."

Solomon made no comment, but stumped along. At the doorway, he paused.

"Is 'e a-waitin' to put a bullet in me?" he asked wheezily. "If 'e is—"

"No." King smiled grimly. "He's waiting for you to put a bullet in him, Solomon. Come in and I'll explain. By the way, Horace Mowbray got over the cholera all right."

Without pausing, King passed into the larger room, which was bare of furniture. Upon his hand he had the old gold ring graven with Solomon's device, but had turned the bezel inward for the present. Solomon came in after him, mopping his face with a silk handkerchief, and went to one of the two windows. He stood there cramming tobacco into his pipe and gazing at the trees. Suddenly he turned, his pudgy features devoid of expression.

"Mr. King, you say as young Mowbray got well of the cholera?"

King gave him a hard look.

"Yes, Solomon. I suppose it does hit you hard, but Mowbray and I pulled him through."

Solomon quivered.

"You again!" he cried, staring at King. "You again! Every blessed move I makes, it's you as ups and blocks me! It ain't 'uman, I says!"

"Human!" ejaculated King witheringly. "You devil, to talk of humanity! After you had the infernal cunning to send cholera aboard that yacht! Oh, I'm not thinking of myself or the other men! I'm thinking of Miss Douglas. I warned you against involving her, Solomon; I warned you. And now you'll not leave this house alive; that's flat."

Solomon took a step backward, staring at him with amazement in the blue eyes. He answered hoarsely as one who hears some incredible accusation:

"But, Mr. King, I ain't done nothing of the sort. It was not me as sent that belt aboard the yacht."

King broke in sternly:

"Don't lie about it, Solomon. He got the belt at Macassar. There is no doubt but what he got it through your scheming. You had the nerve to boast about it in that wireless message."

Solomon's eyes blazed furiously at him.

"Wait!" The little man was manifestly in a rage. "You've got me dead wrong, sir. I don't mind saying as I mean to do for the lot of them, but that there cholera ain't my way. I couldn't do it, sir. That's more'n any man could do—any white man. If so be as you want to know 'ow young Mowbray got that there belt, it was got for 'im out o' revenge by them there two sojers what 'e 'ired to murder you at Macassar. If 'e 'ad given them the wages what had been promised for the job, there would have been no trouble; but instead o' that 'e called 'em off and paid 'em nothing. Them 'ere sojers was wery angry over losing the money, so they up and steered young Mowbray against that there belt. That's 'ow it was, sir, and my men at Macassar reported the 'ole blessed thing to me, just like that."

King was staggered by this defense. The very fact that Solomon spoke of the two soldiers was evidence that the little man spoke the truth—that his agents at Macassar had indeed reported the affair to him.

King stared at the speaker, not trusting himself to answer, but Solomon continued, and in his voice was a trace of sadness:

"But you're the one as ain't goin' away from 'ere alive, sir. 'Cause why? 'Cause you've set yourself in me way, just like that! Dang it! That's just what I 'adn't figured on. 'Ow did Scotchy die, sir?"

King told him. Solomon listened calmly, puffing at his clay pipe.

"Well, that ain't so bad, sir," he said, when King had made an end. "So 'e's gone, and it was me as did for 'im in a way o' speaking. Now there's Mowbray left—and after 'im the brat. Dang it!" A sudden burst of fury filled the blue eyes. "Dang it! I'm a-goin' to wipe 'em out root and branch as the Good Book says!"

The words dully horrified King. The utter ferocity of the cockney was appalling.

"You've about gone the limit. Solomon. You may have told the truth about that cholera belt, and I hope you have told the truth. None the less, you are no more than a mad dog, biting everything in your way. I can understand your pursuit of Mowbray and Sanderson—but the innocent boy! And Miss Douglas, with the rest of us—"

"Nothin' of the kind, as I've been tellin' you!" burst in Solomon irritably. Then his aspect changed. "Mr. King, sir, will you listen to reason? You've been an' called me a devil an' such names, which ain't pleasant, but that don't matter. Look 'ere! If them two men 'ad no more'n done me 'arm, just like that, I'd think no more of it. But it wasn't me as they 'urt." The little man paused an instant, choking.

"It wasn't me, Mr. King. It was me wife, and me baby—as 'ad waved me good-by and kissed me afore I went off. 'Oo's talkin' about innocent lives now? Them 'ere two devils—that's what they was—sent them poor innocent things to death—'cause why, they was rank cowards! That's why I'm 'ounding of 'em, sir. A life for a life, says I. Is Mowbray's son more to 'im than mine was to me? All I 'ad to live for, sir, was them 'ere two lives, and they was took from me. Now, Mr. King, I'll give you one chance to live. Get out o' me way! If you don't—"

The little cockney clutched at the casing of the vanished window, coughing. He was white and weak, but his blue eyes were undaunted.

King eyed him for a space. Without warning, the man's words and aspect gripped at his heart, recalled to him the frightful wrong which had been done to Solomon in the past; he had to fight to steel himself against sympathy for the little cockney.

"Solomon, by the eternal, under any different circumstances I'd feel for you from the bottom of my soul!" he said slowly. "But as it is I can't trust you. Miss Douglas is never going to be endangered again by your mad-dog tricks! You needn't talk of killing me; that's an absurdity. You are the one to take terms, not offer them. Now I'll give you one chance for your life, and that is to get out of here, be content with the damage you've already done, and leave the Mowbrays alone."

Solomon chuckled wheezily, seeming quite unafraid.

" 'Ave you a match in your pocket, sir? Thanks werry much." He lighted his pipe very carefully, for it had gone out. "I can't take up that 'ere offer, sir. 'Cause why, me wife and baby was all as I 'ad in the world; Mowbray took 'em. 'Is son's life and 'is own is all 'e 'as left in the world, and I'm a-goin' to take *them*."

"Deadlock," said King quietly. "You have a revolver?"

The blue eyes opened a trifle. "No, sir. 'Ave you?"

"No." King laughed in sheer amusement at the tragic irony of the situation. For a moment the two men looked at each other imperturbably, each searching the other for some sign of weakness.

Then, wondering if Solomon would be amazed, King reversed the ring on his finger, took out his own pipe and tobacco, and filled the meerschaum. As he did so, the ring faced Solomon squarely, and the glitter drew the gaze of the cockney.

Solomon looked at it, and suddenly a dark flush flooded into his face. The veins in his temples stood out like cords beneath the rush of blood; his blue eyes were distended, and from his fingers fell the clay pipe.

"That—that 'ere ring!" he gasped, wheezing out the words in a terrible voice. "Is that—the one you showed me men?"

"That's it." King laughed, yet wondered at the man's emotion. He drew the ring from his finger. "Want to look at it a bit closer?"

Solomon took it in a hand that trembled visibly, and held it up to the light.

"By the three lights!" he ejaculated slowly, then lowered the ring and stared at King. His face was livid, ghastly. "Where— where did you—get that 'ere ring?"

King frowned uneasily. He could not understand the terrible emotion which was shaking Solomon, wringing him to the soul.

"It was my mother's—or so they told me. I was found as a baby in a boat at sea; the others were dead."

A frightful cry burst from Solomon. He staggered, seemed about to fall, and caught at the window for support. King took a step forward, but the other waved him away.

"No—no! Wait! It's me 'eart!" Pausing, Solomon appeared to rally himself. "I—I thought as 'ow you told me as 'Iram King was your father."

"My adopted father. It was he who found me in that boat off Malta. He took that ring from my mother's hand; there was no sign of name about the boat or its occupants, and he could never discover—"

King paused, awed by the terrible eyes of Solomon. He could not understand what madness had come upon the man, yet he felt a vague, awful fear—a blind terror that throttled the words upon his tongue.

And then before his eyes he saw a strange thing. With fingers that shook almost beyond direction of the brain, Solomon had raised the ring and was fumbling at it.

"I could take me davy on it," muttered the cockney. "You never run your thumb nail along this 'ere line?"

"No."

King leaned forward. He saw Solomon's thumb pass along the black, graven lines on the bezel; he heard a very faint click, and as some hidden spring released the bezel of the ring, the square outlined in black, flew back. Within was set a tiny miniature of a very beautiful woman.

"What!" The word broke from King. "What! How did you know—I never knew that myself! How did you—"

Solomon, by a terrible effort, drew himself up with a trace of his former calm.

"Yes, sir—'ow did I know? 'Cause why, I 'ad that 'ere ring made for me wife when we was married. When she was kidnaped to 'er death that ring was on 'er 'and—that there is 'er picture! And if—if you was—that 'ere baby—"

Solomon reeled suddenly, and fell before King could catch him.

As in a dream, King knelt and raised the gray head to his knee. His brain reeled. He realized only too well what a revelation had here taken place. He was looking down at the face of his own father!

With a cry, King started up. He must get help—water—something! So still, so silent lay Solomon!

King rushed to the doorway, panic gripping him.

CHAPTER XIV

PROVIDENCE WORKS

I N T H E doorway, King paused. He heard the voice of
Mowbray, knew that the baronet was coming toward him,
but his thought was all on relief for Solomon.

"Got a flask? Any water?" he jerked the words over his shoulder.

"No. But—"

King stepped from the shadow of the doorway into the
sunlight, minded to call up Grimsen, who was hidden among
the trees to the left of the hut with some water.

But as his muscles moved, King discerned the glint of sun
on metal among the growth to the *right* of the house. Intuition
leaped upon him; his brain worked in a flash. Who was hidden
there?—Had Solomon—his father—adopted the very plan
upon which he himself had hit? Did this explain the warnings,
the threats?

Before his foot touched the ground with that first step from
the house, King relaxed his muscles, dropped headlong. As he
fell, a rifle cracked among the trees to the right; he heard the
deadly sing of the bullet overhead, heard its dull impact behind
him.

There came a second crack, echoing the first—this time from
the left. Lying prostrate, King watched. Grimsen had shot!

From the right of the clearing floundered out a brown man,
who took a step and then plunged down. Grimsen appeared on
the left, with a wave of his hand to King.

"Got him, sir!"

King dragged himself up. He felt weak with horror—horror of himself, horror at thought of what might have happened. Father and son, planning to kill the other! For a moment he could not speak.

"Grimsen!" he found his voice at last. "Bring some water; then watch the schooner. Let no one ashore."

"Aye, aye, sir!"

King turned to the doorway, then halted, staring. Sprawled across the threshold lay the body of Sir James Mowbray, a tiny blue hole in the forehead!

The American passed a hand across his brow, and his fingers trembled. He felt dazed, bewildered, stunned by this dread sequence of tragedy. Slowly his mind grasped the situation. Mowbray had been behind him, in the doorway, when he had thrown himself down. The impact of that bullet—the bullet meant for him—

"I heard the man die!" muttered King, staring down at the body.

He pulled himself together with an effort. For once his iron self-command had been badly shaken; the ghastly irony of the whole affair was more than he could stand. Solomon had deliberately planned to kill him, as he had planned to kill Solomon. Each had failed. The cockney's assassin lay dead. But Sir James Mowbray, who had come thither to deliver himself to the justice of Solomon, had been slain by an unwitting bullet—slain by the bullet meant for King!

Thus, otherwise than he had planned, Solomon's justice and vengeance had been carried out; not by his hand, not by his aims, but by a deeper fate which no man could have foreseen.

"Providence; that's what it is!" said King aloud.

"Prowidence!" muttered a voice inside the house, like an echo. King started, his nerves jumping. Then he found Grimsen at his elbow, took the man's pocket cup of water, and went inside, stepping gingerly across the body of the baronet.

He found Solomon weakly trying to sit up, and dashed his sea water over the white face. It helped. A moment later Solomon was propped in the corner, staring at King—and past King, at the body in the doorway.

"It's me 'eart," said the cockney quietly. "Comes a bit bad at times."

He broke off, his eyes meeting those of King. Wordless, they stared at each other. At last King reached forward and picked up the gold ring, which lay upon the floor.

"These scratches on the inside—"

"Arbi, sir—Arabic. Me name an' that o' me wife—your mother, sir."

"Damn it! Don't say 'sir' to me!" cried out King, breaking under the strain. Then he laughed harshly. "You had it fixed up to murder me; your man got Mowbray instead. I had framed the same thing on you; my man killed yours. It's horrible! What if—if—"

Solomon reached up with trembling fingers and felt in his pocket for tobacco. Then he abandoned his purpose. Tears were running down his cheeks.

"Thank God!" he whispered huskily.

"My father—and I'm your son!" King said slowly. "It's wonderful; it's wonderful to think of. If only we had known that day in San Francisco—if I'd only been wearing that ring!"

"If you'd only 'ad!" repeated the other wistfully. "Prowidence it is."

"Ah, but I'm glad!" exclaimed King quickly, eagerly. "I'm glad of all that's happened, I tell you. Mowbray and Sanderson—well, somehow Providence would have worked its will on them in any case. But except for what has happened—"

Solomon's eyes widened a trifle.

"You mean that 'ere girl—Miss Douglas?"

King nodded in silence, an awkward silence that came upon them both. The two men, so strangely alike, so strangely differing, gazed at each other. The same thought was in their hearts. King was first to express it.

"You've tried to kill me; I don't know how you feel about me now."

"It's you as 'as tried to kill me, no less," said Solomon. "You've been and 'ated me all along o' Miss Douglas, you 'ave. But dang it! I've told you as I'd never 'arm a woman. Didn't I know as you wouldn't let 'er come to no 'arm? And all the time something inside o' me kep' whisperin' not to lay 'no finger on you."

He broke off, brushing sweat from his brow. King's face was very white.

"It was the same with me," he returned, low-voiced. "I could—could hardly make up my mind to it. Instinct, of course. Heavens! Think of what might have happened! Here all my life I've been praying that some day I might find my father, find some relative of my blood who might love me; I've been alone in the world always, and it's easy to fight the world, but it's hard to fight the devils of loneliness."

He choked a little, and was silent.

"You!" said Solomon. "And what o' me? I ain't 'ad nothin' to live for, 'cepting a trust in Prowidence, as 'as 'elped me a mortal lot at times. An' me goin' down to me grave, stricken in years, without nothin' ahead o' me to pull me along, so to speak."

King held out a hand, a sudden glow softening and transfiguring his face.

"Dad!" he said gently. "Let's go—together!"

Solomon came to his feet, gripping King's hand hard. Tears blinded him, blinded them both.

"Son!" he said brokenly.

CHAPTER XV

THE END

T H E Y   B U R I E D Sir James Mowbray that afternoon by
the side of Sanderson. King read the burial service, while
around stood the crews of the two ships. Norma Douglas stood
beside Solomon.

When the service was ended, Solomon stepped forward, his
gray hair fluttering in the sea breeze. Between the hands of the
dead man he laid a tiny red notebook.

"Me accounts wi' Sanderson & Mowbray—closed," he said
solemnly. "Me son 'as come back to me, James Mowbray; your
son goes free. And the Lord ha' mercy on you!"

Half an hour later, as the sun was sinking behind the western
mountains, the two ships, headed out toward Saleier Straits and
the ocean. On the after deck of the *Tyrian,* once more in charge
of Lord and his men, stood King, Solomon, and Miss Douglas. King waved farewell to Captain Marcos, who stood on the
bridge of the *Rinsdam,* fast dropping behind—the *Rindsam* a
free gift from Solomon in place of the schooner sunk by Lord.

"There goes Marcos and his motto," said King soberly. "I'll
see him again."

"His motto?" queried the girl beside him.

"Yes. *Oro en pazi, fierro en guerra*—gold in peace, iron in war.
It's his motto, come down to him from Pizarro's men, and he
lives up to it. A fine man, Marcos of Peru!"

Solomon seemed a changed man. Something had gone out

of his face; he was ten years younger. He looked now at King, and smiled proudly.

"Aye, but we can use 'im!" he said, nodding his head. "We're goin' to London, son. I 'ave to take on a bit o' work for the foreign office; no, I don't know what it is yet. Will you 'elp me at it, son? I need you."

"Will you let me, Norma, dear?" King took the girl's hand in his.

"No," she said gravely. "No; not unless—unless you'll take me, too. Are you sorry that you've got an added encumbrance—father? Are you sorry Hiram did not come to you alone?"

Solomon met her gaze, then turned away, dabbing at his eyes.

"Dang it! This 'ere breeze fair gets me," he muttered, then turned back. "Sorry?" he repeated. "No, I ain't. I'm so—so danged 'appy I feels like dancin' a 'ornpipe. I do that!"

King laughed.

"We'll stop at Surabaya long enough to get married, then. And, dad—will you give away the bride?"

Solomon pulled out a new clay pipe.

"I'll do anything you says—either of you. There's only one man as 'as ever put it over on me, fair an' proper—and that's you, 'Iram King—me son!"

"My name will be John Solomon when we reach Surabaya," said King. "But I haven't—"

"Yes, you 'ave! You're the only man as I ever met in all me mortal life as could fair lick me at me own game. I'm proud o' you, I am that! You've been an' whipped me; outguessed me from start to finish, you 'ave. And we'll use that 'ere man Marcos mebbe—them 'ere men o' yours, son."

King smiled a little.

"But you're mistaken, dad," he returned. "I didn't defeat you. After all, you accomplished what you set out to do."

"No." Solomon shook his head. "No, don't blame me for that. No, I didn't do nothin'. Everything as I planned to do went wrong, just like that. What *was* done wasn't done along o' me at all. It was Prowidence, just like that; Prowidence, I says!"

He turned and stumped away. King looked into the eyes of Norma Douglas, and drew her to him.

She smiled a little as she spoke.

"Do you know, dear, that I am altogether glad for one thing—that John Solomon really had nothing to do with the cholera belt."

King nodded.

"Yes, Norma. I felt all the time that my reasoning was wrong about him, yet I had nothing to go on except instinct. But no, it was not instinct, either; as he himself says, it was Providence. And thank Providence, I say!"

"Amen!" breathed the girl happily.

JOHN SOLOMON

CHAPTER I

HUMAN EXISTENCE consists of circles; this is an old thought and an excellent one. Circles, each impinging on the other, each consisting of the infinitely smaller circles— and somehow, somewhere, each one touched by the circle of the divine.

One of these circles, one of these larger circles comprising a phase of man's activity, centered upon the Chinatown of San Francisco. It touched the Flood Building, it touched the customs-house, it touched the wharves and the incoming ships from the world's rim. It touched, too, pallid men in jail, furtive wretches who were not in jail, and certain yellow or white men who had circles of their own from Philadelphia to Asia.

This circle was one aspect of the United States Revenue Service—a circle about which clung the sweetish reek of opium.

Upon a certain day Nathan Rannals left the Flood Building for the last time. He walked with dazed, uncertain steps towards Union Square. Without a shred of warning the blow had fallen on him. He was disgraced, dismissed the service. Already the newspapers were screaming out his story to the world.

It was a frame-up, a trap so cleverly engineered, so powerfully sprung, that Rannals had not even an inkling who was behind it. And he had walked so carefully! Every revenue agent was a marked man, as a matter of course. Behind Nathan Rannals lay five years of it—five hard, grueling years of slow advancement.

Five years in which he had thought, lived, and dreamed nothing but the service. And now—this!

Rannals sank down on a bench in the square, staring dully at vacancy. Disgrace! He did not merit it. Even his chief and his associates believed him guilty.

"These dirty devils of the dope ring!" he muttered. "They don't dare to touch a government man. So they knife him in the back and get him ousted. And it was for this that I've worked like a dog, day and night, head and hands!"

Yes; it was for this. At twenty-five Nathan Rannals saw himself an outcast, a branded man, a disgraced grafter. It was for this that he had learned Chinese, with laborious patience, until he could read and speak several dialects. It was for this that he had given himself no leisure in which to form friends outside the service. It was for this that he had refused tempting offers from exporters and commercial houses. For this!

Fortunately, he had no family to suffer from his shame and humiliation. Nor was there any to hold out to him a hand of belief, of comfort, of assurance. For this, however, Rannals cared nothing. You could see his fierce self-dependence in the set of his head, in the challenge of his gray eyes, in the aggressive thrust of his face. Even in this moment you could see that he was dazed, overwhelmed, but not broken.

An old man sank down on the bench and began carefully to whittle tobacco from a plug into an old clay pipe. He was absorbed in the task. Rannals, roused from his reverie, regarded the figure with a flash of self-contempt in his eye. He was no better off than this old bum; ambition and accomplishment in the world were no longer his. He had a few hundred dollars saved up—he could take it and bury himself somewhere. And, in the end, he would become an old man sitting on a park bench.

"It's a werry nice day, sir!" said the old man, turning toward Rannals. He showed a face which was remarkable for its lack of all expression and for its two round blue eyes that held the confiding trust of a child. He was too hale and hearty for a hophead. He might be an old seaman who had wandered uptown, was the almost subconscious analysis of Rannals.

"Werry nice day it is, as the old gent said when 'e buried 'is third." The voice was a bit wheezy. "Might I make so bold, sir, as to ask if you 'ave a match?"

Having no desire to listen to hard luck stories Rannals silently extended a box of matches and then glanced

carelessly away. Only for an instant, however. When his eye fell upon the person approaching him he straightened in his seat. "Shuffles" Beeson, as this individual was known, was an unfortunate young man with the youthful look of a degenerate—which he was—and the general appearance of a hophead, in which appearances did not lie. Shuffles remained at large because both the police and revenue men used him as a stool. Rannals believed that he double-crossed the officers as well as his own crook companions. It was entirely possible.

Shuffles came to a halt before Rannals. His head was slightly askew on his shoulders, a fact which greatly aided the effect of the lividly malicious look with which he favored Nathan Rannals. He was jeeringly exultant. His upper lip was twisted awry by an old scar.

"Won't put nobody else away for shovin' mud, will you?" he sneered. Eye and voice betrayed a vicious joy in thus taunting the formerly feared agent. "Yah! When you're broke come around to Mother Meg and git a job. She'll use you with the snowbirds. Hell of an officer now, ain't you? Let's see your star now! Yah!"

Rannals did not respond. He looked at Shuffles, unable to

feel aught but a contemptuous pity for the poor devil. Under his regard the hophead was distinctly uneasy, yet tried to carry off his bravado bravely.

"Don't know yet what hit you, hey?" snarled Shuffles. "Ain't no better'n any other man now, hey? That's fine. Don't you wish you could tell me to come along? Never again."

"Nothing of the sort, Shuffles." Rannals made a gesture of dismissal. "I'm darned sorry for you, boy, that's all. Probably you never had a square chance as a kid. Better beat it out of this part of town now, or else they might pick you up."

Even as he spoke Rannals realized how singular it was that this fellow would dare to show his face in broad daylight here— where, at best, he might slink from corner to corner under cover of darkness with his twitching cheeks hidden from sight. But Shuffles, after one nervous glance around, only laughed sneeringly.

"Don't worry about me, damn you! I got better protection than you ever had, Rannals," he uttered boastingly. "I'll go anywhere—"

His shifty eyes fell upon a burly figure approaching. Instantly Shuffles lost his voice. His hands slid from his pockets and rammed his cap over his eyes. With the action, a slip of yellow paper fell to the ground. Not seeing it, Shuffles turned and departed hastily.

Rannals, acting from instinctive habit, saw Chinese ideographs brushed on the paper and picked it up. Then he, too, perceived the approaching figure. It was that of Tom Flynn, one of the Chinatown squad, a man whom he knew as well as he knew any of the city detectives.

A slight flush overspread the features of Rannals, and he pretended to ignore the burly figure. But Flynn had seen him sitting there, and now came to a halt in front of him. Rannals looked up, bitterness hardening his eyes.

"Stand up!" ordered Flynn curtly. "Give me a look in the eye, will ye?"

Rannals rose. To his utmost astonishment, Flynn put a hand to his shoulder.

"I'm surprised at ye, Nate," and the detective spoke softly, "lettin' yourself be framed that way! There's not many believe in ye this day, my lad, but I'm one. Glad I met up with ye. If ever there's anything I can be doin' for ye sing out for Tom Flynn. Ye'll know where to find me. So long, and good luck."

Flynn passed on his way—he could not afford to be seen talking with the disgraced revenue man. Rannals sat down again, wordless. He fastened his eyes on the yellow slip of paper in his hand, blinking rapidly. He had not known tears for years. Now, in this one moment of kindliness and sympathy they came unbidden.

Slowly the blur passed from his eyes. Little by little he saw the thing at which he was looking—the slip of yellow paper. With an effort he forced himself to relax; he sat back, looked at the black ideographs, and their meaning gradually penetrated to his brain.

Interest stirred and wakened within him. He saw that this was no Cantonese scrawl, nor was it even brush work. The ideographs had been mimeographed. Further, his trained eye at once perceived that a Japanese hand had brushed the original. The subtle difference between Japanese and Chinese characters— which at bottom are identical—struck him at once. He could not read these characters at all.

Suddenly Rannals glanced up and saw that the pudgy little old man had sidled along the bench and was calmly looking over his arm at the paper.

"Hullo!" He turned and looked, smiling, at the rotund features and the blank blue eyes. "Can you read it?"

The cockney, for such his accent slowed him to be, tamped down his pipe. "Why, sir," he wheezed. "It's a mortal queer thing, but I went an' found one o' them 'ere bits o' paper me own self, just like that! Dang it, where did I put it?" He fumbled in his waistcoat pocket; then, to the amazement of Rannals, brought forth a second slip of yellow paper.

"Ah, 'ere it is! I knowed I 'ad it somewhere. I'm a-gettin' old, and a werry bad job it is, sir! An old man is all werry well in 'is place, but 'is place is limited, says I. Now, sir, see 'ow this 'ere strikes you, as the old gent said when 'e kissed the 'ousemaid."

Disregarding the words of the garrulous old cockney, Nathan Rannals stared in helpless consternation at the paper which was handed him.

This paper, like the first, was mimeographed, but this one was in Cantonese. He saw that the contents of the two slips must be identical—one intended for Japanese eyes, the other for Cantonese eyes. In other words, they were handbills for distribution.

Rannals translated the Cantonese, and startled alarm leaped into his gaze. He read, in effect, these words:

> Ten thousand dollars will be laid in the hand that removes Lui Toy.

Now, Nathan Rannals knew this Lui Toy very well—knew him for one of the wealthiest merchants in Chinatown. A fairly young man, Lui Toy was a graduate of Harvard and was an American citizen of the best type. In fact, he was a better citizen in his ideals and in his daily life than many of the whites with whom he did business. Lui Toy's idea of citizenship was not far removed from that of Socrates, who died because it was his duty as a citizen.

Ten thousand dollars was offered for the murder of Lui Toy—and why? By whom? To these queries, no answer. No tong war was under way. No private feud, however, would cause such a reward to be offered by these handbills. Something large, sinister, deadly was behind this! Japanese were concerned in it, and that was a very ominous thing.

Could the explanation be political? Lui Toy, like many of the American Chinese business men, was keenly interested in republican China. Rannals dismissed this theory, however, almost at once. The Japs were not in the business of murdering American citizens. No, this would hardly explain.

Suddenly Rannals looked up, to meet those wide eyes of baby blue. He wakened from the reverie to a recollection of the queer old man who sat beside him. The latter spoke:

"Can you read it, sir? Werry interesting you seem to find it."

"Where did you get this paper?" snapped Rannals abruptly.

"Beggin' your pardon, sir, that ain't none of your business," was the cool retort. "If so be as you could tell me what it says, why, I'd be werry much obliged."

Rannals laughed harshly. None of his business! True enough—now.

"It's a chance to make ten thousand dollars by killing an honest man," he said curtly.

The pudgy old man appeared quite unmoved by this information. Perhaps an indefinite hint of sadness came into the wide blue eyes, a slight touch of regret. It might have been the imagination of Rannals.

"And who'll pay that 'ere sum?" demanded the other, placidly puffing at his pipe. "Is that 'ere thing on the bottom a name?"

Rannals looked again. At the bottom of each slip of paper was the same mark—three straight horizontal lines of even length, each broken in the center. He frowned, studied it, and finally spoke musingly:

"That's queer, sure enough! It must be one of the eight trigrams—this is the Kun or symbol of earth."

"What are them 'ere trigrams?" queried the little old man mildly.

"Very ancient symbols of the Chinese, formed from a straight line and a broken line—standing for the Yang and the Yin, or male and female principles of creation." Rannals answered almost mechanically. "Three straight lines, for example, stand for Chien of heaven. The eight trigrams, as they're called, form the basis of divination and are used today for lottery blanks."

"That werry interesting, sir," began the other.

Suddenly his whole manner changed. He took the pipe from his mouth, spoke very rapidly, the wheezy accents giving way to crisp, startled words:

"Dang it! Look at that 'ere couple comin' this way, sir—werry queer business, that is, and no mistake, says I!"

Nathan Rannals looked; then slowly he rose to his feet.

Two people were approaching along the graveled path. One of them was a girl, slender, long-bodied, dressed neatly but not showily. She walked with the free-poised grace of youth; her eyes held the serious gaze of a woman. Her face betrayed a singular sweetness. The manner in which she swept rapid and curious glances at the park, the buildings around it, the monument ahead, showed Rannals that she was a stranger here.

Beside her walked a man who was speaking rapidly to her, devouring her face with avid eyes. This man was "Bull" Logan. A mixture of Chinese and white, Logan was shunned by both races. He was a suave person, who served as a tout for gambling clubs and dens of vice. He had twice been tried—but acquitted—under the Mann Act.

Rannals stepped forward and lifted his hat. "I beg your pardon, madam," he said quietly. "May I ask whether you are aware that you are in the company of one of the most vicious and notorious characters in the city?"

Rannals half expected a command to mind his own affairs. He was relieved when the girl's eyes widened and she darted a rapid, startled glance at her companion.

"You!" Logan was furious. He faced Rannals with a malignant ferocity, then banished the look and put on his usual suavity. He turned to the girl.

"Miss Anderson, don't pay any heed to this crook. He is a former revenue agent who has been convicted of petty graft and dismissed from the government service. I helped to convict him, and so he has it in for me."

True enough; Logan had been concerned in the frame-up.

The girl looked from one man to the other, hesitation in her eyes. Nathan Rannals smiled.

"Suppose you permit me to accompany you?" he suggested pleasantly. "The first policeman we meet—"

"None o' that now!" snarled Logan. The mask slipped a trifle. "Beat it, and leave Miss Anderson alone."

"Mr. Logan says that he knows my brother," said the girl quietly, addressing Rannals. "He was taking me to meet him—"

"At what address?" queried Rannals.

Before Miss Anderson could reply, Bull Logan knew the game was up and threw off his mask. A vitriolic oath fell from his lips. "You'll get the limit for this, Rannals!" he said, passion in his tone. "You'll get the limit, if I have to croak you myself!"

He turned and walked rapidly away.

Rannals laughed as he met the questioning eyes of Miss Anderson. He saw that they were eyes of deep lapis, flecked with gold—rare and wonderful eyes.

"It's all right. Miss Anderson. Lucky I happened to see you; you must be a bit more careful about trusting people, I'm afraid. May I see you home?"

"Oh! Thank you—it's not necessary. I'm here at the St. Francis." The girl put out her hand. "Perhaps I was foolish, but—but you don't understand. Thank you so much!"

Rannals bowed. When he looked up the girl was walking away.

When Rannals returned to his bench it was empty. The little old cockney had vanished. For a moment Rannals stood looking about, then—he remembered.

"By George! I'd better warn Lui Toy instantly," he thought.

CHAPTER II

THE PUDGY, blue-eyed old man who waited for Miss Janet Anderson in one of the hotel parlors, was not the same in costume with the old man who had sat beside Nathan Rannals on the bench in the square.

He now wore a finely tailored broadcloth suit, and, despite his inconspicuous appearance, any careful dresser would have immediately been conscious of the details of his garb. His linen, for example, was heavy and probably handmade. His scarf was from a brocade woven under K'ien-lung. The only jewelry that he wore was a gold watch chain looped across his waistcoat. From this chain depended a gold ornament in the shape of a human eye encircled by the seventh letter of the alphabet.

As he waited—for he had arrived while Miss Anderson was at dinner—the old gentleman smoked his clay pipe with much enjoyment. He seemed quite blind to the fact that pipes are not generally tolerated in the parlors of ultra-fashionable hostelries. Strange to say, although his occupation was reported by at least five bell boys, the management paid no heed.

The pudgy little man sat and smoked, imperturbable, his face expressionless, his mild china blue eyes quite blank.

Presently a man in the uniform of a private chauffeur approached him—a young Chinaman, it proved. He stood before the old man and spoke in English:

"The message was delivered, sir."

"Werry good," said the cockney. "Where's that 'ere Mr. Rannals?"

"He has left his hotel, one frequented by many of the government agents, and has taken a room out in Post Street."

"Werry good." The cockney drew a folded paper from his pocket. "I want this 'ere note shoved under 'is door in the morning. I want 'is 'ouse watched all night. Mebbe you know that danged scoundrel I was a-speakin' about—name o' Logan?"

A fleeting smile touched the lips of the chauffeur. Who in Chinatown did not know of the half-breed Bull Logan? He assented quietly.

"I ain't sure," said the cockney, "but I 'ave a werry good notion as that 'ere bloody scoundrel is a-goin' to show up to-night to kill Mr. Rannals. If so be as 'e shows up, I want 'im taken to Chinatown and left there."

"Left there, sir?" repeated the chauffeur questioningly.

"With a knife in 'im," said the other placidly. "Just like that!"

For an instant the chauffeur gazed into those mild blue eyes—then he saluted and went his ways.

The cockney summoned a flitting bell boy and handed him a dollar, also a scrap of paper on which was written a number.

"Call up that 'ere number, me lad, and say that Mr. Solomon will be there at eight o'clock sharp."

"It's the Chinatown exchange!" observed the boy.

"So it is, me lad—werry good eyes you 'ave. Eyes is a waluable possession, but they ain't to be ill trained, as the Good Book says. You move sharp, me lad—Bristol fashion!"

The boy vanished.

Five minutes afterward, Janet Anderson appeared. She glanced around, not seeing the pudgy cockney until he rose and advanced toward her. She referred to the card in her hand.

"This is Mr. John Solomon? You called in regard to my advertisement?"

"Yes, miss. If so be as I might 'ave a few minutes—"

"We'll be able to talk quite freely here," and the girl smiled as she led the way to seats in the corner. "You know, the best place for private conversation is an open hotel lobby or parlor."

"Quite right, I says," assented Mr. Solomon wheezily. "Daylight makes the best priwacy, as the old gent said when 'e kissed the new 'ousemaid."

A moment later they were seated, inspecting each other. In the eyes of the girl was an amused interest, not unmixed with anxiety.

"Now, miss," began Solomon, "you adwertised for news o' your brother, name o' Randolph Anderson, least 'eard of in San Francisco three years back."

"You have some news of him?" Her eyes, of gold-flecked lapis, seemed black as she inspected the little man.

"I never 'eard of 'im in me life, miss," returned Solomon, "until I seen that 'ere adwertisment in the papers."

"Oh!" The girl relaxed, disappointment in her face.

"It was a werry imprudent thing, miss," went on Solomon, "for you to go and adwertise that way—that you'd be 'ere on such a date and offerin' of rewards and such. It's mortal 'ard for 'uman nature to resist temptation, I says, and 'ere you go, puttin' all kind o' temptation in the way o' bad men! Temptation is all werry well in its place, miss, but its place ain't in connection with a fine young woman like you, I says."

Miss Anderson listened to this sermon with some astonishment.

"May I inquire," she asked coldly, "if you called in order to lecture me—"

"No miss," put in Solomon apologetically. "If I might make so bold, miss, I would like werry much to be askin' of some questions. Was your father James Randolph Anderson, o' Fairfax, Wirginia?"

The girl looked startled. For a moment she met the blank blue eyes with a searching gaze. Then her features relaxed in a smile.

"Do you know, Mr. Solomon, you sound horridly impudent? But I like you. Yes, that was my father's name. What of it?"

"And was 'e in Egypt, miss, a matter o' twenty year back—no, twenty-four?"

"Yes," responded Miss Anderson.

"I thought so!" Solomon leaned back and sighed wheezily. A hint of sadness came into his pudgy features. He remained silent, his fingers playing with the watch charm; the motion drew the girl's glance to the thing. Suddenly she leaned forward.

"Why—excuse me, Mr. Solomon, but isn't that watch charm of yours very unusual? My father had one exactly like it! He said once that there were very few of them in the world—engraved gold—"

Her eyes widened, lifted to his face. One would have said that suddenly she had recognized this man whom she had never before seen. Recognition certainly lighted her gaze, startled recognition, and astonishment.

"Why—why—you must be the same man! I remember when I was a little girl, hearing him tell about his great friend John Solomon—where was it, Cairo? No, Port Said. Oh, I thought there was something familiar about that name on the card! You must be—"

"Yes, miss, I am, and werry 'appy to say so."

Solomon took the hand that was extended to him and a smile broke across the wintry blankness of his face.

"Your father, miss, was my werry good friend. When I seen that adwertisment, I thought as 'ow you might be the same family. Now, miss, did your father tell you about this 'ere watch charm?"

"Only that it was the sign of some society he had joined. He said any one having one would be a father or a brother to me—"

"You sit down, miss, and tell me all about it," said Solomon quietly. "Why you're 'ere all alone and so forth, just like that. And if so be as you don't object, I'll fill me pipe while you talk."

"I'm afraid—they don't like pipes here in the hotel—"

"What this 'otel don't like, me dear, 'as nothin' to do with the case. It's what John Solomon don't like," said the cockney with a wheezy chuckle. "If I was to up an' tell 'em to take one o' them there plush windy 'angings to your room for a bath mat, why, what 'u'd they do? They'd do it, just like that! Now, miss, let me 'ave the 'ole story, as the old gent said when 'e met the pretty girl."

Smiling at the whimsical words, her eyes fascinated by the old man, Janet Anderson watched him light his old clay pipe. Then she told him her story simply and briefly. From time to time Solomon nodded his head, but there was never a hint of expression in his blank and pudgy features.

Her father had died ten years previously, leaving a widow and two children, and little money. The boy, Randolph, was two years older than Janet; she was now twenty-one. Randolph grew up wild, impulsive, beyond the widow's control. Finally, three years previously, he had run away from home. He was last heard of in San Francisco.

When her mother died Janet was supporting herself as a trained nurse for children. Left alone in the world, with a small sum of money, the girl came to San Francisco in the desperate hope that she might personally accomplish something in the way of locating her brother.

"What you said a little while ago was right," she concluded her story. "I thought that by stopping at one of the best hotels I would be safe from all trouble. Still, some very queer people have answered my advertisement—"

John Solomon's wheezy chuckle intervened.

"Miss, you 'ave a 'ead on you," he said, leaning forward. "You're bound to 'ave a 'ead, I says, seein' as 'ow you're a nurse—above all, for children! You'll do, you will. Now, miss, I'd like werry much to know what sort o' story was told by that 'ere swab what called on you to-day—name o' Logan."

The girl's eyes widened.

"Why—how do you know about that?"

"Never you mind, miss. I know what I know, as the old gent

said when 'e fired the 'ousekeeper. Werry good thing it was, too, as Mr. Rannals took a 'and."

Janet Anderson regarded him in open astonishment, then broke into a laugh.

"This is almost like black magic, Mr. Solomon!"

"Make it John, miss—make it John, and I'll feel more comfortablelike."

"Very well—John," she responded, hesitating slightly. A perplexed expression came into her fine eyes. "I did not like the general manner of Mr. Logan when he called, but he stated that he knew my brother, who was living under an assumed name, and offered to take me where I could see the man in question for myself.

"Then came that incident in the square—you seem to know all about it. Of course, that would seem to prove conclusively that I had been wrong in accompanying Logan. Still, I cannot help feeling convinced that he was telling me the truth. I felt so at the time, and I feel so now. I actually believe that this man had some knowledge of my brother. He may have been using it as a trap for me, but at the same time—"

Solomon started slightly.

"Dang it! Why didn't I think o' that? There's a woman's 'ead for you! Mebbe you're right, miss—but no matter. I suppose you 'ave a picture o' that 'ere brother?"

In response, Miss Anderson produced a small photograph, which she had brought with her to the interview. It showed an undeniably handsome youth, the face betraying a passionate and headstrong character. For a little Solomon studied it, his face quite blank and devoid of expression. What thoughts were passing behind those mild blue eyes it was impossible to say. At length he returned the photograph, and sighed wheezily.

"Miss, I can't say nothing for certain, just like that. But I 'ave me 'opes, mind you, that I can find that 'ere brother."

"What! Here, in the city?" The girl's eyes were eager.

"Miss, I knows nothin' and I says nothin', just like that. I 'as me 'opes, that's all. I'm mortal sure as I've seen that 'ere young man somewhere. Now, miss, just 'ow far do you trust me?"

His eyes struck out, met and held the gaze of the girl. For a space she studied him, then a smile broke in her face.

"My dear John Solomon," she said quietly, "I have every reason in the world to trust you absolutely. My father—"

"Werry good," he cut in. "What's more to the point, I can trust you! You 'ave a level 'ead, miss, and there's mortal few women as can say that."

"You have a poor opinion of women in general?" And the girl smiled slightly.

Solomon leaned forward. His voice dropped to an almost inaudible tone. He was very earnest, and his earnestness impressed Janet Anderson strongly.

"Miss, I ain't in San Francisco for me 'ealth. I've been called in, so to speak, to 'andle a crew o' the most wicious and depraved and powerful criminals in the world. It's a werry bad business, miss, and for them that's associated wi' John Solomon, it's a werry dangerous business likewise. And I need all the 'elp I can get.

"You can 'elp me, miss, if so be as you will. Money ain't no object, as the old gent said when 'e 'ired the pretty 'ousemaid. You needn't 'ave no worry about money. You stay right 'ere at this 'otel, and be ready to act when so be as I needs you. I'll 'ave good and bad jobs for you; dangerous jobs, most-like—jobs that most women 'u'd turn white to think on. You won't, 'cause why, you're a nurse and you 'ave a 'ead on you.

"In return for all this, miss, I'll guarantee to find that 'ere brother if 'e is to be found in the world. Just like that."

Janet Anderson must have heard a good deal about this man from her father. She regarded him steadily, a slight smile on her lips.

"Very well," she assented calmly. "It's a bargain, John. Now tell me—you mentioned Mr. Rannals, the gentleman who intervened to-day between me and Logan. I gather that you know him? I have been reading about him in the papers."

Solomon chuckled in his wheezy fashion.

"Yes, Miss Janet, I've 'ad me eye on that young man for some time, so to speak."

"Is he really what they say—disgraced and—"

"No manner o' doubt about it, miss—'e is! But, mind you, 'e ain't guilty. That 'ere young man knowed too much, 'e did. The same gang as I'm after, they done for 'im. Done for 'im proper, miss. But that ain't neither 'ere nor there, as the old gent said when 'e buried 'is third. Mr. Rannals will be workin' for me one o' these days, I 'opes. Now, miss, it's understood between us?"

"It is," assented the girl quietly.

"Werry good." Solomon rose and shook hands. "I'll send you instructions in a day or two. I ain't rightly got any plan o' campaign laid out, so to speak. If you'll be so good as to take that 'ere adwertisement out o' the papers, I'd be obliged. You'll find some money a-waitin' for you at the 'otel desk—I want you to 'ave plenty o' fine clothes and such. That's all, miss. Good-by. About that 'ere brother, just you 'ave trust in Prowidence."

"Good-by—and thank you," answered Janet Anderson.

Solomon left the hotel.

He walked to the Post Street corner, near which a large limousine was waiting. Solomon entered the car, which started immediately as though the destination were known. The car purred to Grant Avenue, then turned to the left and went straight over the hill into Chinatown.

Ten minutes afterward Solomon was shaking hands with three Chinamen. These three were among the most influential of their race in the city. One of them was Lui Toy. They represented different tongs and guilds; all three were young men, wealthy and powerful, representative of the highest class of Chinese-American citizen. They were college graduates. One was a scientist and a physician. Among them these three men might be said to control the destinies of their race on the Pacific coast.

Yet on the heads of each of these men now lay a reward of

ten thousand dollars. Who had offered this blood money? A *hui* or syndicate whose personnel was totally unknown. What was this *hui?*

To this question John Solomon was seeking an answer.

L ATE IN the morning of the day following these events, Nathan Rannals was walking swiftly downtown. In his hand was a morning paper, whose contents overbalanced in his mind even the amazing contents of the note he had found shoved under his door that morning.

The paper told of how Bull Logan had been found dead in Dupont Street shortly after midnight with a knife in his heart. Several arrests had been made, purely on suspicion, and among them Shuffles Beeson.

"Flynn is using Shuffles as a stool—of course he had nothing to do with it," thought Rannals. "It was no tong business. Probably a private enemy did for Logan—perhaps a woman. He's no loss. And I'm out of it, out of the game!"

The realization caused him a twinge, but no more. He was already growing callous to such twinges. Consciousness of his own innocence was no great prop, yet a night's sleep had brought him around clear-brained, steadily poised. He knew that he was down, and unless he was to really go under he must start in and fight—fight to hold his own self-respect if nothing else.

"So far as ever proving my innocence is concerned," he reflected, "that's dead. The case is closed. I wouldn't go back to government work now, even if I could. Logan—well, he got his deserts, I suppose—" 'E's drinkin' bitter beer alone,' as the color sergeant said. Bitter beer! I'd certainly like to know who flavored my beer."

The craving for action, the desire to strike back at his unknown enemies, was rising strongly in him. Yet he saw no way to assuage that craving. Chinatown would laugh in its sleeve at him—now. He could effect nothing there. He was helpless.

Rannals turned into the first dairy lunch place he came to, and procured breakfast and luncheon combined. The news about Logan digested, he laid aside the paper and produced the note which had been shoved under his door. With that note had been shoved five hundred dollars in large bills, and these were in his pocket.

Rannals could not decide whether he was being bribed or employed. The note was highly enigmatic, and was liable to either interpretation. It was written in a neat scrivener's hand such as is rarely encountered in these days of typewriters and hasty correspondence. It read as follows:

> Find Shuffles Beeson. Tell him you want to meet Frederick Mordaunt. Use your head and don't lose it. Report progress to Miss Janet Anderson at the St. Francis. Destroy this.

"Miss Anderson!" murmured Rannals. "That's the name of the girl who was with Logan yesterday—the one advertising for news of a brother. Hm! Can this be on the square? I'd swear that girl was straight. And yet—"

Had she written the note? No; Rannals decided against it instantly. He smelled a keen flavor of intrigue in this affair. That girl could know nothing of Shuffles or Frederick Mordaunt. Had Tom Flynn written the note? Possibly. Tom Flynn, however, could not have sent the five hundred.

Rannals had already examined the bills carefully with an eye to a trap. They were new, crisp, unused. They were not marked—of this he was certain. He looked again at the note, with its startling suggestion of a connection between Shuffles and Frederick Mordaunt. Slowly he tore it into tiny scraps.

As Rannals knew, this Frederick Mordaunt was one who deserved that highly illusive term of "man about town." He was a handsome, wealthy man in the early fifties, and lived in an exclusive apartment house near the Fairmont, maintaining bachelor apartments. He was prominent in club and social life.

That there could be any connection between Shuffles, the mentally unsound dope runner, and the wealthy Mordaunt, whose life was an open book, was on the face of it absolutely unlikely and incredible. And yet Rannals knew that the influence of the opium circle reached out into unsuspected places. If there were any such connection, would Mordaunt be implicated in the dope ring?

"How the devil does it concern me—and Miss Anderson?" puzzled Rannals. "I'm out of the game. She can't be concerned in it. Hm! It looks to me as though somebody were trying some joke—but five hundred in cash would be a large price for a joke! One thing is sure: I'm going to take no jump in the dark."

He left the dairy lunch, and at the first drug store he sought a telephone booth. In two minutes he was speaking with Miss Anderson.

"This is Mr. Nathan Rannals—the gentleman who spoke to you and Logan yesterday," he said. "I have just received a communication telling me to investigate something and make a report to you. I want to ask whether you know anything about it—"

"Oh, yes! Mr. Solomon just called me up about it," came the girl's voice. "Yes, it's all right, Mr. Rannals!"

"And who," queried Rannals, "is Mr. Solomon?"

She was silent, as though in consternation over a mistake.

"I thought—wasn't your communication from him?"

"It was unsigned."

"It must have been from him! He said to tell you that Mr. Lui Toy would vouch for him."

"Very well. Thank you, Miss Anderson. I'm sorry to have disturbed you."

Rannals rang off and called a number in Chinatown exchange. When he obtained Lui on the wire he found that his mention of Mr. Solomon disturbed the Chinaman. Lui refused to talk, and merely said to come to the store if information were desired. From his words, Rannals conjectured that he knew the mysterious Solomon, but was afraid to say anything over the telephone.

"Who the devil is this Solomon?" he cogitated, leaving the drug store. "If Lui vouches for him, as evidently will be the case, it is all right. This has something to do with the ten thousand reward for Lui's murder—that's it! Solomon is a private detective."

For ten minutes Rannals stood on the curb, thinking swiftly. He knew that Lui Toy, frightened and suspicious of everybody, would not talk openly; yet he knew that Lui was a man above suspicion. The face of Janet Anderson impelled him to trust her. Probably, he reflected, Lui Toy had pulled him into this matter. He knew Lui very well, and Lui might suspect that Rannals had been framed.

With a snap, Rannals decided to do the very thing he had sworn not to do. He would take a leap in the dark—and see where he fell. At all events, he had not much to lose!

The side streets of Chinatown are in actual life just about as mysterious in content as they are supposed to be in stories. Contrary to accepted opinion, opium is almost unknown to the younger generation of Chinamen; there are no opium dens except in rare cases. Opium makes far too much advertisement of its own use, and the noses of revenue agents and police agents are keen. However, opium does not have to be smoked too be enjoyed. In the form of morphia, heroin, and allied extracts it becomes a brother to cocaine and gets higher prices than mere "mud."

There were two women in Chinatown who had much to do with the traffic in dope. One of them was Mother Meg, who kept a none too decent lodging house above some Chinese wholesale offices in a street near Dupont. Mother Meg was so called after a popular female who figures in the Taoist religion and who gives unhappy spirits the draft of oblivion.

This particular Mother Meg was an old harridan who grinned at every one and everything. Her grin, fawning and obsequious as it was, concealed a deadly wit and a keen cunning. At times, under the influence of her own drugs, her craft failed her and she was caught. As a rule she was far too sharp for any trap and could laugh at the officers. Shuffles Beeson lived in her house and was one of her runners.

The second woman also resided in the house of Mother Meg. Rannals knew little about her, but conjectured a good deal, and conjectures prove nothing. Mrs. Lee was her name—it might be either American or Chinese. She herself was possibly an Eurasian, for she was a marvelously beautiful woman of the statuesque type. Why she lived alone in Chinatown, what she did for a living, who her friends might be—these things were mysteries to everybody. Nobody knew anything against her, except that she lived at Mother Meg's and seemed to have plenty of money. She had never been implicated in any wrongdoing. That was exactly why Nathan Rannals had cherished secret ideas about the lady—she was too absolutely a pillar of virtue to occupy her present position.

It was early afternoon when Rannals stepped into the dirty little cubby-hole that Mother Meg dignified by the name of office. It was not one of the times when the old beldame was to be caught off guard; word of Rannals' coming had preceded him.

He found Mother Meg waiting for him—a hag whose yellowed fangs showed in her eternal grin. Derision was in her voice.

"Well, if it ain't Mr. Rannals—come to see old Mother Meg! And not on business, neither. You ain't comin' on business no more, hey? You ain't lookin' for happy dust, hey?"

Rannals ignored the taunts. "I want to speak with Shuffles. Where is he, Meg?"

The eyes of the old woman narrowed. "Shuffles is jest back from the jail," she whined. "They let him go—he didn't know nothin' about Bull's murder! It was a chink croaked Bull, I tell you—"

"Stop your drooling," commanded Rannals sharply. "I don't care anything about Logan. I suppose Shuffles hit you for some snow as soon as he got back and now he's resting up?"

"You can s'pose all you durned please," shot out Mother Meg viciously. "You ain't got no badge to flash now. Cough up what you want with him."

Rannals smiled thinly. From his pocket he took a fifty-dollar bill. His brows lifted inquiringly. But Mother Meg almost spat at him.

"Ought to know me better'n that! What you want with him?"

She would protect Shuffles obviously. For some reason she feared Rannals. Money could not bribe her.

"All right," said Rannals curtly. "I want to meet Mordaunt."

"Mordaunt!" repeated the crone, staring. "Who in hell's he?"

At this instant there was a startled cry in a woman's voice—a cry that thrilled faintly to the two. A door slammed up the hall. Mother Meg would have darted past Nathan Rannals to the hall, but he swept her back and held her by one wrist.

A slither of silk, a rush of running steps, and a voice at the door:

"Meg! You must get word at once—that fiend Solomon is here—that's why Logan—"

In the doorway stood Mrs. Lee, flushed and excited, a newspaper clutched in one hand. When her gaze fell upon Rannals, the words died upon her lips. Into her dark, glowing eyes came fear, suspicion, a flame of danger.

Nathan Rannals gave no sign of the emotion provoked in him by her words, but smiled.

"Good afternoon, Mrs. Lee. I suppose you haven't seen Shuffles around? I believe that he can direct me to—"

A snarl from Mother Meg interrupted him.

"G'wan! He's in the room. It's all right."

Rannals stepped past the wide-eyed woman at the door, and strode up the dark hall. He was smiling to himself as he went along.

Mrs. Lee had made a bad mistake in her excitement. Apparently she knew Solomon or knew of him. Had Solomon had anything to do with Logan's death? No telling—yet. To whom must Meg get word about Solomon?

"No doubt about it—I caught on to something there!" thought Rannals. "Mrs. Lee is mixed in with Meg, that's certain. Well, that's that! Now for Mr. Beeson."

Knowing the location of Shuffles' room from previous experience, Rannals tried the door, found it unlocked, and stepped into the room.

Meanwhile, in the filthy den that served Mother Meg as an office, the two women were regarding each other; Mother Meg with vicious anger, Mrs. Lee with fright and consternation.

"You done fine work with your mouth!" said Mother Meg.

"You don't—you don't understand!" The beautiful features of Mrs. Lee—for they were beautiful, despite the hints of hardness—were convulsed; the luster of the golden-pink skin had become a sickly white.

"It's this man—Solomon!" Mrs. Lee crumpled the newspaper in her hand. "I know him. He's here in town. He killed Logan. He—"

"What's that?" snapped Mother Meg. She darted forward, peered into the eyes of the other woman. "Killed Bull? How d'ye know?"

Mrs. Lee was more quiet now. "It's his sort of work, that's why."

"Who is he?"

"The devil in person." Mrs. Lee shivered slightly. "The Six Companies would give him anything, do anything for him; he's more powerful than they are. They've got him into this, I tell you! I've got to warn Mordaunt at once—"

"Steady!" Mother Meg caught her wrist and gripped it with

dirty talons. "Go slow! This Rannals he wants to find Mordaunt. Who put him wise?"

"It's a trap!" breathed Mrs. Lee. "We must—"

Mother Meg touched a button in the wall twice. Then she began to speak rapidly to Mrs. Lee. The strangely beautiful features of this Eurasian woman slowly became calm and took on their usual expression. At length she even smiled.

"All right, I'll see Mordaunt," she said. "No, Solomon has never seen me. Of course it's worth trying. But we must know where to reach him first. I'll do it."

In the room which was occupied by Shuffles Beeson, that young gentleman was sitting on the edge of his bed, fingering two fifty-dollar bills which Rannals had handed him. His expression was sullen.

"I ain't never hear of any such guy," he whined. "Who told you I did?"

"Don't lie about it," said Rannals coldly. "I'm living out near the Jap quarter—it might have been a Jap who told me."

This was purely a shot in the dark, based upon the yellow slip of paper bearing Japanese characters, which Shuffles had let fall in Union Square. Rannals was not surprised to see the shot take effect.

"Hey?" Shuffles looked up swiftly. "What d'ye know?"

"Not a thing. But I need a job with money in it—a big thing or nothing."

Shuffles nodded, yet scowled in hesitation. He was not a pretty object. The scar on his upper lip drew it back in a perpetual snarl. His head was close-cropped, the short black hairs standing up stiffly.

At this instant, a subdued buzzer in the room sounded twice—two short, sharp rings. As though this were some signal, Shuffles abandoned all hesitation. His unlovely features cleared.

"All right," he said. "You know where Mordaunt hangs out?"

Rannals nodded.

"Go up there and say you come from the Tsuroki Importing Company. That's all I can do for you."

"Thanks," said Rannals, and left the room.

Shuffles Beeson looked after him with the snarl of an animal, but did not move until the door had slammed. Then he shoved the money into his pocket.

"That's all—and that's enough!" he muttered. "So Mother Meg wanted you sent right along, hey? She knows the game, she does! And she'll put Mordaunt wise—well, it's your funeral, not mine!"

Upon leaving the place, Rannals saw neither Mother Meg nor Mrs. Lee. He cared nothing about them. He had accomplished a great thing—had established a connection from this Chinatown den to the prominent Frederick Mordaunt! Now he knew part, at least, of what the officers had for years suspected; he knew where the trail led "higher up!" And there were other trails. The Japs had something to do with this affair—

The whole thing came to him in a flash. Unfortunately it did not occur to him to report to Janet Anderson until after he had visited Mordaunt.

CHAPTER IV

Nathan Rannals, in common with the other officers, knew of the existence of a gigantic *hui*, or syndicate, engaged in smuggling opium and its derivatives. No actual member of this *hui* had ever been caught. The syndicate had existed for years in Manila, Honolulu, and on the Pacific coast. The little dope peddlers who were caught were ignorant of the *hui*. It stayed in the background, a huge and sinister force.

Now, as he toiled up the steep hill toward the Fairmont, Rannals pieced together the little threads he had just caught up, and wove them into a fabric. True, this was a fabric of conjecture only, but he felt intuitively that he had hit upon the truth.

He came to the building which he sought, a massive structure of whitestone, and entered. The palatial interior bespoke wealth and elegance. The attendants were all Japanese, as was the telephone exchange operator.

Rannals gave his name and said that he had come from the Tsuroki Importing Company to see Mr. Mordaunt. A brief wait; then he was ushered into the elevator and taken up.

Again a Jap, this time a valet who admitted him to a sumptuous apartment. The luxury of it took away the breath of Rannals; not luxury either, but sheer, stupendous blazonry of wealth, lavishly squandered on Oriental treasures. About the walls, for example, were illuminated niches, each containing some marvelous treasure of craftsmanship—a carved agate dove, a huge block of lapis carved into a Chinese scene.

The valet showed Rannals to a seat and brought him cigarettes. He was a polite, smiling little man, very talkative. His
master was busy at the moment. He, Shingoro, had been born
in this country, yes—oh, yes! No Japan for him. This very fine
country.

From the man's air Rannals conjectured that he was little of
a valet—more partner than servant, perhaps. Servants are not
garrulous, a little arrogant, almost on an equality with visitors—
no, something fishy here! When the door opened and Mordaunt
came into the room, Shingoro quietly vanished.

Rannals found himself greeted with a cordial handshake, an
impressive heartiness. This Mordaunt was ruddy, well preserved,
excellently dressed. He looked the clubman that he was. His
nose was large and heavy, and his eyes were striking—full-lid-
ded, eyes of one who commands men.

"So you're here on company business, eh?" he said. "I'm glad
to hear that, Mr. Rannals. I've read about you in the papers lately.
Too bad, my dear chap, too bad! By the way, who directed you?"

"Shuffles Beeson," answered Rannals.

"Oh, yes! Queer character, that! By the way," and this seemed
to be a favorite if not always appropriate exclamation with Mr.
Mordaunt, "by the way, what did you expect?"

Rannals smiled. When he smiled the cold sternness left his
face and men liked him.

"Anything," he responded curtly.

"So!" Mordaunt inserted a cigarette in a holder of amber and
gold. "Will five thousand a year content you?"

"Yes."

"Very good. My car is out in front. I'll take you over to
Oakland now, if you like, and the matter will be arranged. Eh?"

"Good!" Rannals thought fast and spoke faster. "Good! There's
a telephone booth downstairs. I'll run down and break a date I
had for to-night, and be waiting for you—"

He flattered himself that he carried it off excellently, for
Mordaunt nodded and rose.

"Fine! I'll be down in five minutes."

The only danger was that Mordaunt would have offered him the use of the apartment telephone. Rannals drew a quick breath of relief. Probably Mordaunt wanted to use that instrument himself—to call up some member of the gang across the bay and prepare for the arrival of the new member.

Mordaunt accompanied his visitor to the elevator and saw him off. Rannals stepped out in the lobby and went to the telephone booth which he had noted. It was a closed booth, but it did not occur to him that his message would pass over the wire of the Jap who sat at the exchange desk.

He called up Janet Anderson and got his connection.

"I'm reporting," he said briefly. "Have established a definite line between Mother Meg, Mrs. Lee, Shuffles Beeson, and one Frederick Mordaunt. Mordaunt has just engaged me at five thousand a year. I'm leaving with him now for Oakland. Got the names?"

"Yes," floated the voice of the girl, eagerness in it. "You're all right?"

"Quite, thanks. One thing more—they have received warning about Mr. Solomon, or will soon receive it. That's important."

"I'll attend to it, Mr. Rannals."

He rang off and left the booth.

He must have waited a full ten minutes before Mordaunt appeared, took him genially by the arm and walked him outside. Here a large car was waiting; the chauffeur was again a Jap. Mordaunt commanded him to the Ferry Building and they moved away.

On the way down California Street, Mordaunt was very cordial and apparently much interested in Nathan Rannals.

Traffic blocks held them up, and they drove into the Oakland slip a moment after the gates had closed. Twenty minutes to wait—it was a small matter, and Mordaunt made light of it. But upon such small matters hang destinies.

The incoming ferry arrived, and the crowd poured out. As the waiting cars were ordered aboard and started, the Jap chauffeur twisted his wheel violently—too late! The car had collided with and old Chinaman carrying two baskets slung on a pole across his shoulders. He had tried to crowd past the car, and ducked in front. The bumper sent him sprawling, and he lay motionless.

Mordaunt swore under his breath, and jumped out. The confusion was dissipated by two officers, who ordered Mordaunt's car out of the line. The old Chinaman was lifted and carried to one side. Mordaunt and his chauffeur engaged in a heated altercation with the officers.

Rannals, sitting in the car and awaiting the outcome, was suddenly aware of a man who had pulled the car door open and was staring in at him. It was the same queer little cockney whom he had met on the bench in Union Square.

"Out of 'ere, Mr. Rannals!" said the wheezy voice. "Move sharp! I'm Solomon—and a werry tight place you're in. Quick, before that 'ere Mordaunt comes back!"

The brain of Rannals had never moved so keenly, so incisively, as in this instant. Another man would have asked questions. Rannals stared into those blue eyes—and then was out of the car in a flash. The cockney seized his arm and ducked into the crowd.

Intuition? Perhaps. Better, lay it to a brain that worked without a hitch. That old Chinaman had let himself be run down— the whole thing had been framed up. Why? The answer came from the lips of Solomon:

"Dang it, that 'ere Mordaunt ain't right 'uman! 'E was wise to the 'ole ruddy game, 'e was. If you'd got across the bay with 'im you'd ha' been dead, just like that! Quick, now—in 'ere be'ind this car—"

Near the taxi stand stood a car with a purring motor. The chauffeur, who was a young Chinaman, stood by the open door. Solomon popped inside, followed by Rannals. A moment later the car was shooting up Market Street.

Solomon, panting, wiped his pudgy countenance. "Dang it! I ain't 'ad to move so quick in years!" he complained. "Werry sharp young man you are, sir, to move so lively. I knowed I 'adn't made no mistake in you."

"So you're Solomon, are you?" Rannals inspected him curiously, amusedly. "You're the detective that's in this confounded show?"

Solomon chucked complacently.

"Yes, sir. I'm the party. But I ain't the man I was, as the old gent said when 'e took 'is third. Dang it, I'm getting old! What's worse, I'm feelin' old."

"You don't act like it," said Rannals reflectively, watching this singular man. "Why, it can't be much more than three quarters of an hour since I called up Miss Anderson—"

Solomon's features were blank as ever.

"Dang it, I fair 'ad to move sharp, sir! Let's get things straight now. While you were at Mother Meg's, they warned Mordaunt—told 'im you were a-workin' for me—"

"How did they guess that?" queried Rannals sharply, completely startled.

"Guessed, that's all. Mordaunt, 'e laid a trap for you. When you went and telephoned Miss Anderson that there Jap at the board, why, 'e caught on—"

"Good Lord, man!" exclaimed the astounded Rannals. "were you there?"

John Solomon permitted himself one of his rare smiles.

"I 'ave a brain," he returned. "And I 'ave a mortal lot o' men a-workin' for me—men and women both. More'n you'd believe, mostlike, sir. So I knowed I 'ad to catch you at the ferry, else that devil 'u'd ha' done for you across the bay somehow."

"What made you think he would have killed me?" persisted Rannals.

"Mr. Rannals, them as asks questions get less'n they asks, I say." He laid a pudgy hand on the knee of Rannals and spoke in an earnest tone. "I says to you, same as to that 'ere Miss Anderson—I ain't rightly sure. Just like that. It's a sort o' instinct, or mebbe mind readin'. It's werry 'ard to give reasons, as the old gent said when 'e kissed 'is 'ousekeeper.

"And now we're in trouble, along o' that 'ere Mordaunt. I'd give five million dollars in cash this werry minute if 'e was dead. But I ain't no murderer."

"What about Bull Logan?" asked Rannals sharply.

"That 'ere was a punishment for 'is tryin' to play tricks with Miss Anderson. See 'ere! Who told you about that, me lad?"

Rannals recounted his meeting with Mrs. Lee, and that lady's words. Solomon looked gloomy, but made no comment.

Nathan Rannals found himself swept out of his depth by this astonishing man. He could not comprehend Solomon in the least. He was so busy studying the cockney that he failed to note where the car was going until it drew up before a new apartment house. A glance told him that they were somewhere in the newly built-up section of the town near the ocean, with the sand lots and dunes giving a bleak prospect. Bungalows and a few very scattered houses stood at intervals. Here was heavy fog, blanketing everything in obscurity.

"Come along," wheezed Solomon. "Dang it, I've 'urt me bad leg wi' this runnin' about. This is me 'ouse, Mr. Rannals. Lui Toy is a-waitin' for us. You talk to 'im a bit, while I'm gettin' reports from me men."

Oddly enough, nothing gave Rannals so much faith in Solomon as the fact that Lui Toy was here. He knew that Lui would not stir a foot outside his shop unless it were absolutely safe. He followed Solomon into the apartment house—and came to the realization that the entire building was occupied by Solomon.

When he entered that building Rannals gasped. He did not know what he was to learn ere long—that John Solomon had worked for years in Eastern lands and banked largely on the splendor which so impresses Orientals. He did not know that Solomon owed much of his prestige to a seemingly useless squandering of money. At all events, John Solomon had the prestige—and the power—and nothing else mattered, stage settings least of all. Perhaps, at bottom, Solomon owned a sneaking liking for such things as no other man could own.

It broke upon Rannals slowly, leaving a sort of awe. At first he was chiefly dared and blinded. The car had entered a courtyard, guarded by iron gates, and a glare of lights suddenly blazed through the fog. There were men who saluted—many Chinamen, one or two Arabs—and then a great corridor aflame with wonders.

Solomon had vanished. Rannals had found himself following a young Chinaman who wore black silk garments. The rugs underfoot were of gold bullion threads, broidered into imperial dragons; the marble walls were lighted from globes of porcelain made under Lang Yao; the sole decorations were mounted suits of imperial armor, ablaze with gems and feathers and rich silks. Such things no money could buy—only friends could give; they were not sold.

After this an elevator; the ascent to an upper floor; a series of rooms which an emperor might have envied in vain. The little treasures in Mordaunt's apartment were as baubles before the things that Rannals passed by. He could not grasp it all. The tapestries and priceless brocades, the ceiling hangings that had seen the pomp of Peking, the things of bronze and precious metals—these left him bewildered. Outdoors was foggy afternoon; here was a warm glow of light and palatial beauty.

Rannals came suddenly upon Lui Toy, sitting reading a magazine in these surroundings. The guide vanished. Lui Toy glanced up, saw Rannals, and came to his feet with extended hand. A smile lightened his broad, heavy features.

"Very glad to see you, Mr. Rannals!"

Under the honest friendliness of those dark eyes Rannals warmed.

"What's all this—a dream or a museum?" He swept his hand about. "This place wasn't furnished out of any decorator's store, Lui!"

Lui Toy broke into a laugh. "No—it was furnished by princes

and kings and—peoples. You don't know Mr. Solomon very well?"

"No. But," added Rannals dryly, "he seems to have money."

Lui chuckled. "I don't know; I suppose so. He's a very great man, Mr. Rannals. I think once, in S'anghai, he made the French give up some of China's land. Just now he's helping us."

"Us?" repeated Rannals. "The Six Families?"

"Us, ever'body. All good people," said Lui Toy vaguely.

Solomon appeared, stamping toward them with a slight limp. He was mopping his face vigorously with a red bandanna handkerchief.

"Dang it!" he broke out, stopping short and staring at them. "Dang it! I can't get hold o' Miss Anderson no-how. I'm fair stumped, I am. Mr. Rannals, I'd ha' given a mortal lot o' money if you hadn't went an' telephoned from that danged place o' Mordaunt's."

"What do you mean?" exclaimed Rannals. "Where's Miss Anderson?"

"Gone," said Solomon, and sank into a chair. "Dang it! Gone. I'm fair stumped, I am."

"You think—there's something wrong?"

"O' course there's somethin' wrong! But who done it? Not Mordaunt—'e 'as been busy. Dang it! There's more to all this than we know, says I!"

CHAPTER V

RANDOLPH ANDERSON stood before the mirror of his furnished room in Haight Street, and carefully adjusted his cravat. In the edge of the mirror were stuck two scraps of paper, and his eye was upon them rather than upon his apparel.

A knock sounded at the door. In response to his call his landlady entered.

"I heard you come in, Mr. Anderson, and brought your mail. I hope you are going to be with us a while now?"

Anderson took the letters and smiled.

"Hard to say, Mrs. Dunbar. I just got in last night from Texas, and I'll be here a few days, anyway. Perhaps I'll stick around for a while this trip."

"My, I hope you ain't gone and lost your job!" said Mrs. Dunbar, curiously poking at him from her eyes. "These is terrible times, ain't it a fact? Poor dear Mr. Hendricks, what had the next room, he lost his job and went to boot-leggin', and now he's in jail."

"Don't worry about me," and Randolph Anderson laughed. "I'll pay you up to-day for the next six months, and if I'm not here hold the room as usual. Thanks for the letters."

Mrs. Dunbar departed. Anderson locked the door after her.

He examined the letters with a cursory air, tossed them on the bed, and returned to his dresser. His gaze fastened upon the nearer of the two slips of paper. It was a newspaper clipping which related to him. It was, in effect, the advertisement inserted by his sister asking for news of him. As he read it his face took on a cynical, almost sneering, look.

The other scrap of paper bore a number of Japanese characters. It was a facsimile of that which Nathan Rannals had picked up in Union Square after Shuffles had dropped it. This one, however, differed in one particular. At the bottom of the paper were the same three lines, except that each line was not broken in the middle. Thus the character inscribed there was not identical with that inscribed on the paper found by Rannals. This was the trigram Chien.

Anderson took this paper from the mirror, tore it into tiny fragments, and threw it into his wastebasket. He took down the clipping and thrust it into his pocket. Then, lighting a cigarette, he sat on the edge of his bed and looked over his mail.

As he sat thus his face was seen to be very peculiar—not at all the face one would expect in the brother of Janet Anderson.

So black and glossy and neat was his hair that he might with justice have been suspected of wearing a wig. The black mustache adorning his upper lip was ragged, straggly, uncared for. When he sat in repose, as now, a nervous twitching possessed his left cheek. His complexion was remarkable for its waxen, yet leaden, hue. Perhaps, as his landlady believed, he was a sick man. His eyes were rather dull. On the whole, a good-looking young chap.

He tore open one of the letters. As he read the note his face changed indescribably. A flash of consuming anger lighted his eyes, and he sprang up and glanced at his watch.

"Just time to get there!" he muttered. "Does that cursed Mordaunt think I'm a dog, to be ordered around?"

He darted to his dresser. From an open drawer he produced a hypodermic outfit.

Ten minutes later he stood on the curb outside as his taxicab drew up. Anderson looked different now—more energetic of eye, more blooded of cheek. He gave the taxi driver the address of a club on Post Street and climbed into the cab.

The taxi struck down to Market, across on Van Ness to Post, and halted before the ornate portals of the club. Anderson paid the driver from a fat roll of bills, and entered.

He nodded to the attendant inside as one who knew the place well, left his hat, and went directly to the lounge room. As the hour was fairly early in the morning he found this empty except for Mordaunt, who was striding up and down.

"Ha, Anderson! Glad to see you!" exclaimed Mordaunt. "I hoped to find you in town."

"You did," said Anderson, dropping into an easy-chair. "Got in early this morning by luck. What's new?"

"Everything."

Mordaunt glanced about the place, pulled up a chair beside that of Anderson, and spoke in an almost inaudible voice:

"I'm busy as the devil, old man—there's big work on hand. I can use you steadily, if you'll consent—"

"Nothing doing," said Anderson, his voice disinterested. "I'm going to Los Angeles for a couple of days this week at least. I'm glad to pick up money, Mordaunt, but as I told you before, I don't intend to go into any steady job."

With a visible effort Mordaunt repressed the angry retort that came to his lips.

"Come, come, be sensible!" he said irritably. "You're one of the best men we have, and right now we need you badly. In fact, there's a big fight on foot, and we can't take any chances on irresponsible people—"

"Have I ever done anything irresponsible?" demanded Anderson in cool challenge. "Have I ever made a mistake, ever been suspected?"

"No, of course not. That's exactly why we need you. When I say that inside of the next week six of the eight trigrams will be here in the city you'll realize what's doing."

These words, indeed, exerted a remarkable effect upon their auditor. Anderson sat up, his eyes suddenly blazed out, and he leaned forward with a tense air.

"You mean—" He broke off, wet his lips, then nodded. "You mean—every one in this country?"

"Every one," repeated Mordaunt. His gaze darted for an instant to the doorway. He lighted a cigarette, giving Anderson one from his case. "As you know, K'en is in Honolulu and K'an in Nagazaki; thus they are out of it."

When Randolph Anderson made response his voice was curiously tremulous, uncertain. "I—you know, Mordaunt, I'm not conversant with the whole thing," he said hesitantly. "I only know one or two—"

Mordaunt laughed harshly. "My dear fellow, you're the only person who does know more than one of the Trigrams. That in itself should prove to you how valuable a man you are to us. We support you in princely fashion. We let you work when you feel like it, and at other times you disappear and enjoy yourself."

Anderson nodded. His cheeks were flushed deeply, as though by inward excitement. "Yes," he assented simply. "Yes, I know that you are Chien. I know that a Jap here in the city is Kun. And I strongly suspect that Frisbie, in Baltimore, is either Li or Tui—"

"He is Li," said Mordaunt, eying his cigarette smoke. "It was through Frisbie that you came to us, remember."

"I remember," said Anderson. For the fraction of a second a terrible light flamed in his eyes; then it was gone.

"I really summoned you because Frisbie arrives to-day—gets in on the nine-ten," said Mordaunt. "I want you to meet him, put him up here at the club, and arrange to get him a room here."

Anderson started slightly. "Still running the same old game!" he observed. "You big fellows run no risks. We're the ones who take the chances and—"

"You take no chances, as you just finished saying," and Mordaunt chuckled. "Of course, we big fellows can't afford to run the least risk. We're always in danger. If one of us should ever be suspected or nabbed—it's never happened, but it's possible—then the others must not be drawn into the net. You'll meet Frisbie, then?"

"Yes," said Anderson. Once again his eyes flashed, but his lids concealed the terrible look in them from his companion.

"Good! Now, about the fight that's on." Mordaunt glanced around, lowered his voice still further. "We've decided to wipe out the opposition of the coast Chinese to our business."

Anderson whistled. "You've taken on a big contract, then. That means you're up against the tongs and guilds, the political associations—everybody!"

"We didn't start it." Mordaunt rubbed his chin uneasily. "The fact is, they decided to wipe out our business. They've called in a fellow named Solomon, it seems. Even hear of him?"

Anderson shook his head.

"Neither did I until to-day. Mrs. Lee—you know her?"

"No. Chinese?"

"Not entirely. A charming woman, Anderson. You must meet her. She slipped me the warning. This man Solomon, it appears, is the most dangerous person we ever tackled. He has his own organization, the Six Families are of course aiding him, and he has the brain of the devil in person. It seems that he's known all over the Orient, and is rather powerful in China. That confounded republic is trying to wipe out opium, you know."

"Oh, I know all right," said Anderson, a thin smile on his lips. "The Japs are identified with our business, so the chinks naturally love us. I saw in the morning paper that Bull Logan was killed last night. Is that part of the doings?"

"Yes. War is on," rejoined Mordaunt curtly. "Under the circumstances, can we count on you?"

"More or less," said Anderson with cool nonchalance. "Does the opposition know anything about us? About the Trigrams?"

Mordaunt grunted and fished for a paper in his pocket. "Yes—something. Pure guesswork, that's all. When the row opened up I conferred with Kun—as you suspected, he's a Jap here in town. Name is Tagashi, by the way. We offered ten thousand for the death of the Chinese leaders, using the trigram for a signature. Anybody in the know would understand, of course, that the money would reach him if the work was done."

Anderson nodded, and took the paper Mordaunt handed him.

"Read that," said the latter. "It came out this morning. Offers twenty thousand for the head of each and every one of the Eight Trigrams! And it's signed John Solomon. Good Lord, Anderson, to think that such things could come off in this day and age!"

Anderson glanced up, amusement tugging at his lips.

"You started it, didn't you? Then you have no kick coming. Well?"

"We're offering fifty thousand to-day for the death of Solomon."

"Whew!" A low whistle broke from Anderson. He studied the other man curiously. "Do you mean it?"

"Damn it, of course!"

"I may take on the job." Anderson rose, shook out his clothes. "Well, I'll attend to Frisbie all right. In the meantime, give me a couple of hundred for expenses and enough happy dust to run me a while."

Mordaunt nodded. "I thought you might be running low, and brought along some stuff."

He quickly slipped a package into the hand of Anderson, who as quickly concealed it.

"Report to me here to-night, then," said Mordaunt, also rising. "If this thing pulls through all right I'll make you an offer. The first vacant Trigram goes to you!"

"Done," said Anderson, and turned away. "See you later."

When he left the apartment house Anderson went afoot to a small, medium-priced hotel in Kearny street. There he nodded to the desk clerk, asked for the key of his room, and then for mail.

"Nothing to-day, Mr. Randolph," was the reply. "Glad to see you with us again!"

He who had now become "Mr. Randolph" went to his room and was no more seen.

Just how Randolph Anderson ascertained how to reach John Solomon by telephone is not material, the point is that at seven o'clock that evening he reached him. Solomon, at the moment, was scouring the city for news of Janet Anderson without result. Probably a hundred men were actively engaged in the search, while several times that number were on the lookout.

Janet Anderson had been seen walking from her hotel, and had walked into oblivion. It may be imagined that Solomon, receiving reports every half hour from dozens of men, was a busy personage. Rannals had gone to superintend the search at the ferries. Lui Toy had abandoned an intended conference to have Chinatown scoured. Thus, when Solomon was called to the telephone, he was alone.

"This is some one you don't know," came the voice of Anderson, cool and level. "I want to see you—anywhere you say, but at once."

"What about?" demanded Solomon. "See 'ere, you 'and over your name, or I 'ang up!"

"Anderson's my name. If you want information about the Eight Trigrams, hurry."

"Werry good, sir," said Solomon promptly. "I'll send me car for you. Where to?"

Anderson named his lodging in Haight Street.

It was no part of Solomon's scheme to disclose to any Tom, Dick, and Harry the splendor and secrecy of his abode. When Randolph Anderson entered the limousine which called for him he was courteously but efficiently blindfolded by two fellow passengers. The blind was not removed until he had entered the presence of John Solomon.

Anderson blinked around. He was standing in a plain office, of which the only ornament was the priceless carpet beneath his feet. At the desk sat Solomon, puffing at a clay pipe, carpet slippers on his feet, and an old tarboosh cocked jauntily above one ear. The white hair stuck out grotesquely under the edges of the tarboosh, and the blank blue eyes took in every detail of Anderson's appearance at a glance.

"Well, sir, 'ere you be! And what can I do for you? I suppose you come on the matter o' that 'ere sister o' yours."

Anderson changed countenance. "Sister!" he repeated, staring. "What d'you mean?"

"Dang it!" observed Solomon. "Ain't you the one she's been adwertisin' for?"

"That's none of your affair," snapped Anderson, anger in his eyes.

"Right you are, sir," returned Solomon apologetically. "You made mention o' them 'ere Eight Trigrams—"

Anderson shrugged. "I don't know that you're Solomon. Prove it."

For answer the little cockney extended toward him the peculiar watch charm that he wore. A slight smile creased the blank, pudgy features.

" 'Ere you be, sir, just like that! Maybe you've 'eard your father speak o' me, sir? I see you 'ave, sir. A werry good job it is, as the old gent said when 'e buried 'is—"

The words died away, for the sight of that watch charm had effected a horrible change in Randolph Anderson.

He recognized it, no doubt of that—recognized it, remembered the name of John Solomon, exactly as his sister had done. A mortal pallor overspread his face. His left cheek twitched twice. His eyes distended. Suddenly upon the features of this man was imprinted something fearful and awful—some emotion beyond words.

"You!" he said, choking on the word. "I—I remember now— you! My father—"

Solomon ignored this display of emotion, reached for a plug of black tobacco, and began to whittle at it.

"I'm very much afraid, Mr. Anderson, as 'ow you've went and fallen into bad company, so to speak. Bad company ain't good for a young gent, as the Good Book says. Now, sir, it's true as 'ow

I was your father's friend, but I ain't your friend—yet. When I seen you yesterday I says to myself that—"

Anderson started violently.

"You didn't see me yesterday!" he cried out. "I only came back to town to-day!"

The blue eyes of Solomon lifted, lifted and dwelt upon that ghastly countenance for a long moment of silence. In those eyes were unuttered things.

"Werry good, sir," returned Solomon. "And werry sorry I am to 'ave made a mistake. Now, what was that 'ere business about the Eight Trigrams?"

Anderson forced himself to calmness by a violent effort. Solomon regarded him curiously, for the emotion which the young man fought down was pitiable; yet he fought it down, and regained his cool self-mastery.

"I understand," he said quietly, "that you are a friend to Lui Toy—and others."

"Right you are, sir," and Solomon went on whittling tobacco into his pipe.

"A price of fifty thousand dollars was placed on your head to-day."

Solomon only nodded, laid down the plug, and filled his pipe.

"This morning," went on Anderson, "I was talking with one of the men who set that price on you."

"And what," queried Solomon, "did Mr. Mordaunt 'ave to say about me?"

The eyes of Anderson widened, then narrowed.

"Oh!" he said softly. "You know a good deal, eh? I suppose you know that he's one of the Eight Trigrams?"

Solomon nodded and lighted a match. He made no further reply.

"And," pursued Anderson, "that another is due to arrive here to-night—one Frisbie?"

"No," said Solomon. "That 'ere is news, that is!"

"I am to meet Frisbie and take him to a place of safety," and now a thin, cruel smile played on the face of Anderson. "He comes from Baltimore. He is one of the six men in this country who absolutely control the drug traffic. Shall I tell you where I first met him?"

"If you please, sir," said Solomon, puffing his pipe alight.

"I don't know what you know about me, and don't care. Several years ago I ran away from home. I was a reckless, foolish young devil—and I met Frisbie. He charmed me, as an old rascal can. I thought he was a great man. He taught me—he taught me to use drugs."

Anderson halted, but Solomon made no sign.

"He fastened the morphia chain on me." Anderson's voice was now cold, inflexible, harsh. "He put me into a living hell— that was his business then. He recruited me for the drug traffic. When he got through with me I was working for the drug ring. I was shipped out here to the coast. Now I'm an important member of the trade, making big money, and trusted. Frisbie has forgotten my very existence. But—I have remembered his! And now I am to meet him to-night. He will be in my hands, alone!"

That last word "alone!" rang with a fearful exultancy. Anderson sank back in his chair, his eyes flaming terribly. John Solomon regarded him steadily for a moment.

"Well, sir?"

"I'm ready to turn him over to you—on one condition."

"Name it."

"That he be killed before another day!"

John Solomon puffed for a long while at his pipe, his pudgy face quite expressionless.

"It's a bargain, sir," he said at length. "Give that 'ere man to me for a bit o' talk to-night—and I'm your man. What's more, there's a reward o' twenty thousand—"

"I'm not in this for money," said Anderson. In those words was a frightful melancholy. In his eyes a profound despair. "You forget—I am a drug fiend. It's a bargain!"

CHAPTER VI

AT NINE-THIRTY that night Mordaunt sat in the lounge room of his club. He was both uneasy and impatient, for the train had been on time and Frisbie should have been here long since. Suddenly a sigh of relief broke from Mordaunt at sight of Anderson entering the room.

Mordaunt rose, and Randolph Anderson sauntered after him to a secluded corner.

"Well?" said Anderson coolly. "He showed up all right?"

Mordaunt started. His deadly eyes bored into Anderson.

"What—what do you mean? What happened?"

Anderson's brows lifted in surprise.

"I don't get you, Mordaunt. I was at the station to meet our friend when a man came up to me. He was a stranger. He showed a note from you, signed as usual with your Trigram, ordering me back here at once. Said he was to meet Frisbie. So I came, that's all."

Mordaunt paled, then reddened. He knew in this instant that he had received a terrible blow. It was characteristic of the man, however, that he maintained the usual secrecy which was practiced even with such trusted subordinates as Anderson.

"Very well," he said, his voice a trifle strained. "Very well—go to your rooms, and I'll reach you there tomorrow. Good night!"

Anderson nodded, and sauntered away.

Mordaunt fairly rushed to the telephone booth. He called a number in the Japanese quarter—a number which belonged to a Japanese drug store. When the response came, however, Mordaunt mentioned no name, but called for Kun. This, you recall, was the eighth Trigram—Tagashi.

"Hello, Kun?" he said after a moment. "This is Chien speaking. I have bad news for you—that devil Solomon has hit us. You know that Li was to arrive to-night? My man was side-tracked, and Li has disappeared."

"Very well," came the unimpassioned response. "Meet me at the usual place at eleven."

Mordaunt left the telephone booth.

As he returned to the lounge room he heard an attendant paging him. He beckoned the boy, and was informed that a gentleman desired to see him.

"Who is he?" demanded Mordaunt.

"He has a guest card here, sir. His name is Solomon."

Mordaunt stiffened slightly. Solomon—in person!

"Very well," he answered thickly. "Is—is any one in the card-room?"

"No, sir."

"Bring Mr. Solomon to me there."

Mordaunt sat in the cardroom, where the shaded lights illumined the green tops of empty tables. He lighted a cigar, and his nerves quieted down, tautened, tensed to the coming interview. He knew that it spelled a crisis. Perhaps his own life hung on the issue.

John Solomon entered, walking rather stiffly, and came forward to Mordaunt's table. Each man eyed the other, but in the mild gaze of Solomon there was nothing to be read. In the eyes of Mordaunt were curiosity, incredulity, challenge. Contempt, even!

"So you're Solomon!" he said in a strange voice.

"That's me, sir," responded Solomon cheerfully. "And very much alive I am, as the old gent said when 'e took 'is third. Your friend Mr. Frisbie, by the way, is a-payin' me a visit."

There was a little silence. Solomon sighed wheezily, produced his old clay pipe, and began to fill it.

"I've nothing to do with Frisbie," said Mordaunt suddenly. "Don't know him."

Solomon nodded his gray head. "O' course not, sir. My mistake entirely."

"Then what do you want to see me about?" snapped the other.

"Miss Anderson."

"Never heard of her. Who is she?"

Solomon lighted his pipe, and stretched out comfortably.

"She's a werry partic'lar friend o' mine, Mr. Mordaunt. I'd adwise you strongly to let 'er go free before noon tomorrow, 'cause why, that 'ere Frisbie might die in a 'urry, just like that! Yes, sir. You let 'er go."

Mordaunt opened his lips as though to protest, then closed them. After all, why not put his cards on the table? This little cockney was a joke.

"I'd give a good deal," he said reflectively, "to know how you learned so much."

Solomon chuckled. "I 'ave me ways, Mr. Mordaunt, same as you. We're a-fightin' each other, and I'm werry sorry to say as 'ow we've come down to primitive methods of doin' it. But that 'ere is mostly bluff, as the old gent said when 'e was sued for breach o' promise. You and me can offer rewards and all that; it's playin' the game, so to speak. I could 'ave 'ad you murdered to-night, if so be I wanted."

"That's undoubtedly true," said Mordaunt, who felt rather uncomfortable. "May I ask if you intend to do it?"

"That ain't me way, Mr. Mordaunt," said Solomon placidly. "Not unless it's necessary, which so far it ain't. O' course, if any 'arm comes to Miss Anderson—"

"She's not in my care," struck in Mordaunt hastily. "I have nothing to do with it."

"So much the worse for you, sir—and for that 'ere Frisbie."

Something about this pudgy little man had by this time got under Mordaunt's skin. His first contempt had vanished. He felt the tremendous personality behind those placid blue eyes and expressionless features. He no longer doubted that Solomon could have had him killed at any moment during the past day or two at least. The realization somehow stifled him horribly.

"What's the game?" he demanded. "What do you know? What do you want?"

Solomon smoked for a moment without response. Then he laid down his pipe, sighed, and regarded his adversary steadily.

"I'll trade you Mr. Frisbie for that 'ere Miss Anderson," he popped out.

"Nothing doing," said Mordaunt, although the refusal came hard. "It's against all the rules. If Frisbie is caught he takes the medicine."

"Werry good. Then we may count Mr. Frisbie out o' this 'ere game."

The words made Mordaunt feel very cold.

"What I know," pursued Solomon reflectively, "ain't neither 'ere nor there. But I want to know a mortal lot, Mr. Mordaunt, for one thing, I want to know everybody in this 'ere dope traffic. A complete list o' names."

"You can't get it," was the prompt retort. "Each one of us knows only the men connected with him. Each organization is separate."

"Werry good, sir. Who was it, if I may make so bold, as 'ad that 'ere Mr. Rannals kicked out o' the gov'ment serwice?"

Mordaunt shrugged. "He suspected too much, my dear sir. No member of our *hui* has ever been convicted; few have ever been suspected or caught. But that man Rannals was dangerous."

"And 'e still is." Solomon chuckled as he made reply. "Well, sir, I've been a-studyin' of you lately, as the old gent said when 'e kissed the 'ousemaid, and now I'm ready to make you an offer."

From his pocket Solomon drew a thick packet of bank notes and laid them on the table.

"This 'ere," he said, "is fifty thousand dollars. I want as 'ow you should tell me all you know, Mr. Mordaunt—just like that. Between you and me, it is. Your pals ain't a-going to know, and you'll go your way as usual. What I'm a-payin' for is information. I won't ask nothing further from you after to-night; you won't be obligated, sir, nohow.

"In return, Mr. Mordaunt, I'll save you from all consequences, so to speak. You won't 'ave nothin' to fear from me or me friend, so long as you don't do nothin' against us. But I'd adwise you, sir, to be werry strict about tellin' me the truth; 'cause why, if you don't I'm afraid you're goin' to be a werry un'appy man. Now, sir, yes or no?"

Solomon filled his pipe afresh.

Mordaunt sat in silence, his gaze fastened upon those bills of large denomination. The manner in which Solomon had led up to this amazing but matter-of-fact offer was nothing short of diabolical.

First Mordaunt had felt the chill of fear, of helplessness, pierce into him. He had never encountered such a man as this Solomon, who seemed absolutely impervious. The yellow streak deep within him was broadened and fetched to the surface. Then came the offer of protection, of money, of secrecy. There was none to know what he said here.

The hand of Mordaunt crept out, as though drawn by some power outside the man, and came slowly toward the packet of bank notes. His fingers touched them, seized on them suddenly.

"What d'you want to know?" he demanded hoarsely, stuffing the notes into his pocket. His eyes struck savagely at Solomon.

"Where Miss Anderson is now."

"In a house somewhere on Bush Street—out beyond Gough. I don't know just where."

"Jap roomin'-house district?"

"Probably."

"Besides you and Mr. Frisbie, 'ow many more Trigrams are in this country?"

"Four."

"Name 'em."

Solomon took out a little red notebook and proceeded to jot down what he now learned. As for Mordaunt, he spoke without reservation, it seemed. Having once committed himself fully, he was not the man to draw back.

Thus was made the first open disclosure of the workings of the mysterious *hui*—a syndicate long whispered of, long rumored to exist, but hitherto an impenetrable secret. This was no legal evidence, of course—Mordaunt would have balked at that—but it was a tremendous lot of information to be acquired at one blow by Solomon.

Just how Solomon got it, not Mordaunt himself quite realized. It was by a psychological combination, perhaps, more than anything else; not wholly bribery, not wholly fear. Nor did Mordaunt volunteer anything. He merely answered questions.

Of the six Trigrams in the United States, three were at this moment in San Francisco. Frisbie, representing the Li or fire symbol, might be counted off the board. Mordaunt was Chien, or heaven; Tagashi, the Jap druggist in Post Street, was Kun, or earth. The symbol of Hsun, or wind, was represented in the person of Señor Federigo Gonzales, now on his way hither from New Orleans. The Señor Gonzales was agent for most of the South American traffic.

The fifth Trigram was Chen, or thunder, represented by one Raymond Pavitt-Beasley, due to arrive in a day or so from Vancouver. The sixth, hailing from Chicago, was Charley Schwab, a gentleman of importance, who represented the Tui trigram.

These six men had waxed fat on the ruin of thousands of their fellow creatures.

When it came to his own organization Mordaunt yielded more detailed facts. It appeared that Tagashi handled the Oriental trade throughout the country. Mordaunt had for his province the Pacific coast States. He outlined his system and listed his agents; among those whom he thus betrayed was Randolph Anderson, but the name passed without comment from Solomon.

"Where does that 'ere Shuffles Beeson come in? You ain't been an' mentioned 'im," said Solomon suddenly.

"Shuffles? Bah! A pawn! He's not my man, but Tagashi's." Mordaunt began to grow sullen. "He, like all Tagashi's men, thinks I'm under their boss. It's not our policy for our men to know more than one Trigram under whom they work. Shuffles acts as go-between for me and Tagashi. Mother Meg, at whose place he lives, is my distributor."

"I see," said Solomon. "And what about that 'ere Chinaman— the Manchu?"

"What Manchu?" Mordaunt looked up suddenly.

"The one what lives out by the shore—what's 'is name, any'ow? Ch'ien-hsi, ain't it?"

Mordaunt did not respond at once. He became stiff, as though mention of that name had paralyzed all his members; his eyes gazed at Solomon almost vacantly, the eyes of a man unexpectedly and horribly stricken.

"What—how do—" he stammered incoherently, then fell silent a space.

"I can't—it's impossible to say anything about him," he said at length.

"All werry good, sir." Solomon closed his notebook with a cheerful air. The name of Mrs. Lee had not come up between them. "All werry good, and I thanks you. By tomorrow night I 'opes to wipe out your 'ole bloody crowd, Mr. Mordaunt, except for them as I wants to use later on for me own purposes. People as wants dope—new ones, that is—'as to 'ave an order signed wi' your Trigram—is that it?"

"Yes," assented Mordaunt, becoming deathly pale.

"And werry grateful to you I am, as the old gent said when 'e buried 'is third. If I was you, sir, I'd go away from 'ere and say nothin' to nobody. Let the small fry burn. You're safe enough from me, if so be as you've told me the truth."

Solomon nodded, rose, and departed.

For an instant Mordaunt sat motionless, a frightful pallor settling upon his ruddy features. Then he was up, darting to a telephone in the corner of the room. In action the man proved incredibly swift. He got the club exchange and asked for his chauffeur, who was waiting in the car outside.

In two minutes he was speaking with Shingoro, the Jap who served him in many capacities.

"Shingoro? You must move quickly. The man Solomon was here a minute ago—he is just leaving. You understand? He is a small, fat man, walks stiff-legged."

"I understand, master."

Mordaunt hung up. He wiped sweat from his features; his fingers shook terribly. It had come to him of a sudden just what he had done. The realization was horrible. He was unnerved, badly shaken. His brain was jumping, throbbing to the name of Ch'ien-hsi.

Now that he had set Shingoro on the trail of John Solomon, he repented the action—repented it as quickly as he had committed it. That had been done on impulse. However, it was done. Solomon would be dead within twenty minutes.

When Mordaunt kept his appointment with Tagashi he was forced to call a taxicab, as Shingoro had not returned. No report had come, and Mordaunt was in a fearful state. The man could keep his self-control only by a tremendous effort. Disaster peered at him from every angle—except the angle from which the actual disaster threatened.

Dismissing his cab at a corner beyond that for which he was bound, Mordaunt walked back a block to the drug store of Tagashi. He was in the Jap section of town, and the dark windows of the drug store bore only Nipponese characters. Although the place seemed shut for the night, Mordaunt walked to the door and rang the night bell; almost instantly the door was opened and he entered.

He walked straight through the half-obscured shop, opened a swinging door at the rear, and stepped into a passage. This in turn brought him to a blank door, at which he knocked in a peculiar fashion. The door opened. Mordaunt stepped into a dirty little room where Tagashi was sitting alone at a table. The table bore a bottle of rice wine and several small cups.

Tagashi looked up at his visitor, unmoving. He was a grossly fat man, this Jap, but his fat obscured his features, and his dark eyes glared out like the evil eyes of a pig. This man seldom moved. He sat ever immobile, a huge lump of flesh within which raced a brain like a machine.

"Evening," he grunted. "Si' down. What's matter?"

Mordaunt dropped into a chair, affected a calm he did not feel, and lighted a cigarette.

"Everything," he responded. "Frisbie arrived to-night. My man was decoyed, and this Solomon got Frisbie. That's when I called you up. Ten minutes afterward I had word from Solomon that Frisbie was in his hands."

"You saw him?" queried Tagashi.

In the fraction of an instant Mordaunt decided to lie.

"He was at the club—was pointed out to me there. A note was brought to me from him. When he left I put Shingoro on his trail—haven't heard yet."

Suddenly Mordaunt leaned forward, spoke with vicious rapidity: "Look here—we're getting involved. You know my man Anderson, Randolph Anderson?"

Tagashi nodded in silence.

"He's the brother of Janet Anderson. She had been advertising for him. If he finds that we've got her he'll raise hell. He's too useful a man right now for us to take any chances with."

"I'll take care of it." Tagashi put out an arm and took the bottle of wine in hand. "You didn't have any talk with Solomon?"

"No," snapped Mordaunt.

Tagashi poured wine into two of the cups.

"Too bad," he said reflectively. "To-morrow I'll have all the information this Anderson girl knows. Maybe Shingoro will get Solomon to-night—maybe not. You need a drink."

Mordaunt swallowed the wine, made a wry face, and drank more. Tagashi, however, did not drink at all. After a moment this fat man slowly heaved up his great bulk.

"You sit," he said. "I come back quick."

He left the dirty little room; like many fat men, he was light on his feet, agile. He went through another passage into another dirty little room exactly like the first. This also held a table, and at the table sat a man dealing solitaire from a dirty pack of cards. The man was Shuffles Beeson.

Tagashi halted and blinked at Shuffles, whose twisted lip curled at him in a sneer.

"He lied," said Tagashi. "Therefore he is dead. Prob'ly Solomon bribed him. That fellow is no good."

"Told you so long ago," commented Shuffles. "Hah! That stiff needed to be bumped off long ago. How'd you do it?"

Tagashi made a sign of drinking.

"There is a man named Anderson, Randolph Anderson," he said. "You have heard of him?"

Shuffles nodded.

"Bring him here to-morrow at noon—or send him. I shall use him. You may go."

Shuffles rose, stuck the cards into his pocket, pulled his cap over his eyes, and left the place.

An instant later a concealed bell tinkled twice. Tagashi turned and made his way to the drug store. There, in the obscurity, he found a Jap standing beside the telephone, who handled him the receiver. Tagashi answered into the instrument.

"Is Mr. Mordaunt there?" asked a voice.

"He not here," said Tagashi. "He gone long way off—very far." The fat man chuckled evilly as he spoke.

"This 'ere is Tagashi, ain't it? Mr. Solomon is speakin'," said the wheezy voice in the telephone. "You tell that 'ere Mordaunt as 'ow I suspected 'e was a dirty dog, just like that. And I made the plans accordin'. That's all."

Tagashi hung up the receiver and blinked into the darkness. What had happened? He wished now that he had not been quite so hasty in giving Mordaunt that death drink. What about Shingoro?

He discovered only when the morning papers appeared.

According to the papers, Shingoro had shot a man in the park during the night, and had been arrested by a motorcycle officer who happened along a moment after the shooting. The murdered man had been driven by a Chinese chauffeur, whose limousine had been hired for the evening by the victim. The young Chinaman was a perfectly respectable man, and well known. He had been engaged in Chinatown by the victim, who was a white man, to take him driving through the park. He was, of course, quite innocent in the matter.

The victim was a man named Frisbie. Nothing else was known about him.

A T TEN o'clock in the morning Randolph Anderson was sitting in his Haight Street room, intently studying a morning paper.

In that paper he found two front-page stories which, apparently unconnected, yet drew his earnest attention. One was that of the shooting in Golden Gate Park. The other story concerned Frederick Mordaunt. The clubman had been found dead in his apartments, shortly after midnight; the cause of death was supposed to be apoplexy. Anderson laid the paper aside, a thin smile on his lips.

"So they haven't discovered that the murderer Shingoro was Mordaunt's valet!" he murmured. "They never will find any connection. Probably Mordaunt's car had a fake license, same as Solomon's, while Shingoro himself won't talk. So Frisbie is ended! I wonder whether Solomon planned that out?"

Anderson was still lost in reflection when a light knock sounded at his door. He opened—to admit Nathan Rannals, whom he knew by sight.

"This is Mr. Anderson?" said Rannals. "My name is Rannals. I have called on behalf of Mr. Solomon."

"Come in, if you please," said Anderson calmly.

The two men sat down. Rannals, refusing the proffered cigarette, lighted his pipe and eyed his host with a grave frankness.

"Certain events took place last night, Mr. Anderson. From

what Mr. Solomon has told me, I understand that you are, in a way, on the inside track of things. Am I right?"

Anderson did not respond at once. He studied Rannals carefully, the suggestion of a cynical sneer in his eyes.

"You are right," he returned at length. "As to the events you mention, I probably know more of the truth than either you or Mr. Solomon. What about it?"

"I was sent to you with a message," said Rannals.

"You're working for Solomon?" snapped Anderson.

"Yes, I understand that it was partly due to you that Frisbie was caught. Whether you had anything to do with Mordaunt's death, I don't know or care."

Anderson looked dangerous—and was dangerous. He did not know how much Solomon had told Rannals, but resented anything having been told. The warped fiber of the man had retained the twin strands of shame and pride, and Randolph Anderson could not forget what he had once been.

"What's your message?" he demanded curtly.

"Solomon considers he is in your debt for the Frisbie matter, and wants to pay up. By to-night he expects to clean up the entire organization of Mordaunt from top to bottom. You are part of that organization. He intends to leave you untouched, also Mother Meg—I suppose he means to make use of her in some way."

"Thanks," drawled Anderson, fingering his mustache. "Very kind of him! But he'd have a hard job catching me with the goods. Anything else?"

"Yes," said Rannals gravely. "He wanted me to hand you this clipping."

He extended to Anderson a newspaper clipping. It was the advertisement which had been inserted in the papers by Janet Anderson. The man read it without a sign of interest, and looked up at Rannals with cold eyes.

"Well?"

"Miss Anderson—your sister—is being held a prisoner in

the Jap quarter of town. Solomon knows who has her. He has placed me in charge of securing her safety, and wants to know where you stand in the matter. Let me warn you, Mr. Anderson, that I have met your sister—and that I intend to stop at nothing to rescue her."

The deadly gravity of Rannals spoke more deeply than his words.

Anderson leaned back in his chair, searching the face of his visitor with burning eyes. Twice his lips opened, and twice he checked the words. What thoughts were rioting through his drug-twisted brain was impossible to say, but the torment in his eyes held Rannals in earnest waiting. At length words came from him—husky, jerking words.

"You know—that I am a—drug user?"

The anguish of this confession was terrible.

"I know," said Rannals gently. "Believe me, Mr. Anderson, when I say that I have had much experience with users off drugs. A man of your brain, your will power, can—"

"Stop it, for the love of heaven—stop it!" exclaimed Anderson. With an effort, he mastered himself. A faint smile appeared on his livid countenance. He sat up, once more cynically alert, once more cruelly in control of his faculties.

"You can guess that I have known you for some time, although you've not known me, Rannals," he observed coolly. "As a revenue man, of course you've been a marked person to me."

Rannals acknowledged this with a nod.

"And," pursued Anderson, lighting a fresh cigarette. "I learned very quickly what my friend Mordaunt was anxious to keep from me—that my sister had been carried off. That was why I deliberately telephoned a certain man last night and informed him that Mordaunt had sold out to Solomon. I don't know if it was true—"

"It was true," said Rannals.

A flash of surprise crossed the features of Anderson. Then it was gone.

"Very well. Mordaunt had a hand in this business of my sister, and I punished him. Frisbie was the man who changed me from a thoughtless boy into a drug fiend, a hounded and damned soul, a man without hope. And I punished him. Nor is he the last that—"

"A man such as you," began Rannals, "can do anything—"

"Stop it," snapped Anderson. "You fool, do you think I want to live in some institution all my life? No. I'm done for, and I know it. But I mean to do a few things before I give out. Now, I've done my best to find where my sister is, and I've failed. All I know is that she was abducted in order to gain from her some information about Solomon. You know who the Trigrams are?"

"I know all that Solomon knows—all that Mordaunt told last night," said Rannals.

"Good. To the Trigrams, Solomon is a mysterious person. They know little about him. They only learned something about him the day before yesterday—"

"From Mrs. Lee," said Rannals. "Yes. She warned Mordaunt. You know her?"

"No." Anderson rose to his feet and began to pace nervously up and down the rug. "The value of my sister to them is the information she can give. From Solomon's anxiety to find her I believe they greatly overrate what she knows. Now, I know that you're a straight man, Rannals. I know that you were framed and dismissed from the service. I have a high respect for you—and I'm playing square. You believe that?"

"I do," said Rannals, a slight flush rising in his cheeks.

"If I knew where my sister was I'd do anything. But I don't know. I can only suspect that she is held by a certain man. This man is a Jap. He is suspicious, bull-headed, hard to deal with. The Oriental mind is not our mind, you know."

"The man," said Rannals quietly, "is named Tagashi."

Anderson halted in his stride.

"Ah! And I am to meet Tagashi at noon."

There was silence for a moment.

"He trusts you?" queried Rannals thoughtfully.

"As much as he trusts any one."

"Very well." Rannals leaned forward. His cool poise, his quiet mien, had an immediate influence upon the nervous Anderson. "The main thing is to get your sister out of his hands without delay. That is all that matters now."

"You can't use force with him," snapped Anderson. "He's too clever and—"

"Perhaps—if I suggest a scheme that—"

There was again a short silence. It was short, yet deeply pregnant with unsaid things. These two men had clashed, had appraised each other, had finally come into a mutual trend of thought and purpose.

Now that Anderson understood the thing which was motivating Rannals he had abandoned all his first animosity. His whole attitude was changed. A feverish touch of color had tipped his cheek bones. He was eager, tingling with suppressed excitement.

"What's your scheme?" he demanded.

"Tagashi wants information," declared Rannals. "Now, I have carte blanche from Solomon to do what I like. Therefore I'll exchange myself for your sister. You arrange the matter, get her released immediately—and turn me over to Tagashi. He'd rather have me than have her, since he would figure that I could provide more information. Get me?"

Anderson stared at him, slow to credit this amazing offer. "You don't know what you say!" he returned slowly. "Tagashi would kill you—"

Rannals shrugged. "It's a gamble I may escape. Solomon may rescue me—who knows? You may help. At least I'll take the gable for the sake of saving your sister."

Anderson nodded. "It may work—it may work! Now, see here! I'll throw in with you absolutely—on one condition. Up to now you people have trailed me like the devil. I've not moved a step without being followed. Isn't that so?"

Rannals nodded. "Of course," he said simply.

"Then quit it, understand? Leave me alone, keep off my trail!"

"Agreed," said Rannals.

Anderson glanced at his watch. It was after eleven.

"All right then." He named his Kearny Street hotel. "You know the place? Be there at three this afternoon. Ask for Mr. Randolph. I'll either be there or will leave word for you at the desk. And—Rannals—you're a white man!"

"Same to you." Rannals smiled as he rose.

Left alone, Anderson darted to his dresser and took out his hypodermic outfit.

Precisely at noon Randolph Anderson entered the drug store of Tagashi. This section of the city was one which had escaped the fire and the earthquake. Consequently it held many once-fine residences which had now become built-up tenements and rooming houses.

The drug store was a little corner building, with gloomy brown structures adjoining and overshadowing it on either hand. From its rear rooms one might reach half a dozen buildings in the block by means of dark passages and subterranean corridors.

Anderson, however, was taken into that same dirty little room where Mordaunt had drunk Tagashi's rice wine the previous evening. There Tagashi was awaiting him—fat, huge, blinking. It was the first time the two men had met. Each eyed the other for an instant, then Tagashi rose and shook hands.

"I have heard of you. Mr. Anderson," he said in the fluent English he could use when he wished. He waved his guest to a seat. "Here is some good wine, if you care—"

"Thanks, I don't drink," said Anderson, seating himself.

Tagashi nodded understanding. Your true hophead has no liking for liquor.

"It was you who telephoned me last night," said Tagashi softly. "May I ask why?"

Anderson lighted a cigarette and shrugged. "Mordaunt sold

us out—or was frightened out," he said. "I can not afford to be sold out, Tagashi."

"I quite agree with you," purred the Jap, watching his visitor narrowly. "Therefore Mr. Mordaunt has—gone elsewhere. I understand that you were his most trusted helper."

Anderson smiled thinly. "I knew of you, didn't I?" he responded significantly.

"Yes. Now that I have taken over his work here. I sent for you first of all. May I inquire if you know any other Trigrams?"

"One or two," said Anderson coolly. "In fact, Mordaunt promised me the first vacant place. He did not anticipate vacating it himself—nor that Solomon would so soon put Frisbie out of the game."

A spasmodic grin contorted the fat countenance of Tagashi—a grin of pure fury.

"We will settle that dog soon!" he averred. "First, however—"

"First," said Anderson, "you and I must reach a settlement."

"A settlement?" queried the Jap. "Of what?"

"Mordaunt told me last night that my sister had been abducted and was in your hands."

This flat statement took the fat man aback. Across those huge, rounded features flitted alarm, surprise, anger. The piggish eyes glittered viciously. One of the fat hands moved slightly across the table edge.

Swift as light Anderson realized that he was in danger, and spoke rapidly:

"Listen, Tagashi! Get me right now. First, I don't want that sister of mine to know anything about me, see? If she thinks I'm dead, so much the better. But I want to get her out of here—she doesn't know anything about Solomon, anyhow.

"Second, if you turn her loose, I'll come across with some information. I know a lot that you don't. For one thing, I learned this morning that one of Solomon's assistants in this affair is Nathan Rannals. Remember him? The revenue man who was framed by Mordaunt's crowd? Well, I know how to reach him any time. If you say the word I'll turn him over to you. You have too much sense not to see the advantage in that idea."

Tagashi sat in absolute silence for perhaps two minutes.

That silence of his was ominous. Anderson knew the thoughts flitting through that machinelike brain—knew them as though they passed over a silver screen before him. That mention of his sister had made Tagashi suspect him immediately, and now the Jap was balancing in his brain whether Anderson could be trusted or not. It was a delicate question, and probably Tagashi's suspicions were perilously near the truth.

What saved Anderson was that the Jap saw in him only a member of Mordaunt's gang, who would sink or swim with the entire outfit.

"You don't want her to see you?" asked Tagashi at length. "Why?"

"Because she is a lady," said Anderson, choosing his words well. That somewhat crude method of expressing it made Tagashi understand. The fat face nodded slowly.

"And I haven't seen her for three years," went on Anderson. "She must not see me. I want to get her out of this mess, that's all. If—"

The fat hand of Tagashi waved impatiently.

"I understand; it is settled," said the Jap, blinking thoughtfully. "I agree, for we must be friends. The girl shall go unharmed when we catch Rannals. How to catch him?"

"Put some of your men to work and—"

"No!" Tagashi shook his head decidedly. "I am afraid of this devil Solomon, after what happened last night. I do nothing until the other Trigrams arrive and we have a conference. We must learn something about this Solomon at once—so far we know little. If you can bring Rannals here, all right."

Anderson frowned and fingered his ragged black mustache.

"I can fetch him here, I suppose," he conceded grudgingly. "To-night?"

Tagashi nodded. The piggish eyes glittered with an evil inspiration—how evil Anderson did not guess at the moment.

"Good. Do this, then! Tell him who you are and that you have
arranged to rescue your sister—you comprehend? Have him
telephone Solomon and get a closed car sent to the next corner
from here, at nine to-night, to receive your sister."

"Why that?" queried Anderson.

"So that you can report Solomon's telephone number to me."

"Good! And then?"

"Get Rannals here alone, on any pretext you like. I will do
the rest. You shall then see your sister sent off to Solomon—you
shall go with her, if you like."

"Nonsense! You know I don't want her to see me," snapped
Anderson. "But Rannals may be shadowed here by some of his
own men—"

"Let him be!" Tagashi grinned. "What does that matter to
me? You ought to know that Solomon can't hurt me here. So
that's all settled, is it?"

"Settled."

"Very well. Now, about yourself and—"

"Count me out for two or three days," said Anderson. "I'm off
to Los Angeles as soon as my sister is safe. I've got some private
business there which—"

"But you are working for me, young man," said Tagashi, his
voice dangerously soft.

"Don't you think it!" was the cool retort. "I'm working with
you—and on the same basis as I worked with Mordaunt, only
more so. I'm my own boss. What's more, I want a hand in the
conference of the Trigrams. I've got as good a brain as any of
you—better, when the dope is working—and I'll be worth
having. If you don't want me, just say so."

The two men regarded each other. Tagashi was imperturbable,
Anderson was cool.

"If you are as valuable to me as you were to Mordaunt—I agree," said the Jap.

"If I bring Rannals here—I'll have proved it."

"Exactly."

"Then I'll see you to-night. So long."

Anderson rose and departed. Had he looked back he might have observed a singular smile playing upon the fat lips of Tagashi—a leering smirk whose suggestion of ferocity mingled with evil craft was extraordinarily powerful.

But Anderson did not look back. Instead he was glancing ahead with eyes that saw little; a single phrase was on his mind and lips.

"He did not mention the Manchu!" was his thought. "He takes for granted that I know nothing of Ch'ien-hsi! Good."

CHAPTER VIII

HAVING SEEN Randolph Anderson during the afternoon, Nathan Rannals knew exactly what to do. It was futile to hope for any matching of strength or brains with Tagashi—just yet. The only important thing, to Rannals, was the safety of Janet Anderson. He was ready to place himself unreservedly in the hands of Tagashi to secure her safety; later would be time enough to worry about himself.

Rannals had seen to it that he would be shadowed by Solomon's men, but this would matter not a whit. Nothing short of an army could hope to search or raid that rabbit warren of Tagashi's, and even such a search would effect very little. His hope of escape would depend chiefly on Randolph Anderson.

Of Solomon, Rannals had seen nothing that day. The little cockney was an extremely busy man, arranging the blow which was even now falling in different sections of the city. Mordaunt's organization was being wiped out—not by Solomon, but by the police and other agencies. It was not Solomon's way to do his own work when he could get it done for him more expediently. Rannals felt that he had been flung overboard to sink or swim, so far as rescuing Janet Anderson was concerned, but he did not object to this.

At eight o'clock Rannals met Anderson at the corner of Post and Stockton.

"All set?" inquired Anderson.

"Sure."

"Car arranged for?"

"Yes. It'll be at the corner beyond Tagashi's store from eight-thirty until nine. That chink chauffeur is to drive it—same chap who finished Frisbie. He's clever."

Anderson looked at his companion admiringly.

"You're a cool hand, eh? Now there's one thing I want to impress on you, Rannals. My sister is to know nothing of me. Perhaps she will have to know ultimately, but I desire, if possible, to keep from her the knowledge of what I have become. It would hurt her, and it is not necessary. You understand?"

Rannals assented. "But," he added slowly, "I'm afraid—afraid it can't be kept from her forever. And I don't think your attitude is right. She's not the sort to shrink from you because of a weakness—"

"Well, no matter—you know how I stand. Come along; my car is in this block, parked."

Anderson's car was a powerful roadster, into which they climbed. Anderson drove out Post Street, and neither man spoke again. Arriving near the drug store of Tagashi, Anderson disembarked and led the way to the place. Rannals followed. The two men vanished in the store entrance.

At this point the street was dark and deserted, except for the lights of motor cars continually flashing past on the through-city route. The high houses loomed darkly, broken by occasional yellow lights in windows.

Each house was a replica of its neighbor; the porches perched twenty feet above the sidewalk; the high flights of steps were empty. These old frame structures had not been painted for years. They were gloomy in the extreme; solidly built, dour memorials to the taste of Victorian days. Long since the street lighters had come through, kindling the gas street lights from corner to corner, but the illumination was dim and poor.

Presently came a dim light near the center of the block; one of the house doors there had opened. It gave a momentary glimpse of yellow gaslight within. Two men came out and stood in the darkness of the porch, above the street. The glow of their cigarettes made two tiny red specks against the obscurity.

One of these men was Anderson. The other was Tagashi.

Below them, and near the corner of the block, a limousine had drawn in beside the curb and stood waiting. Tagashi pointed toward it.

"If you wish to change your mind, and see her—say so."

"No, thanks," returned Anderson. "I suppose you've arranged to follow that car and learn where Solomon is located?"

Tagashi grunted. The grunt might mean anything, but was a probable assent.

"Rannals suspected nothing?" he asked.

"He probably did, of course," was Anderson's cool response. "It did him no good. We were followed, but that amounts to nothing. I'll get away all right, double back here and there, go to several places. Think I'll drive down to San José and catch the night train south from there."

"Be back Saturday," said Tagashi in silkiest tone. "The conference, you know."

"Where?"

"Call me up Saturday—I'll let you know. It will not be held here in town."

"All right. Ah, there she is!"

Anderson leaned forward over the porch railing, his eyes strained on the scene below.

A door three houses away, near the corner, had opened. Two figures were descending the long flight of steps to the sidewalk—a man and a woman. The man was a short, slight figure, very deferential in manner. He was undoubtedly a Jap.

The woman appeared young, and about her shoulders and head was flung a very fine cloak of dark embroidered silk.

"I have made her a few presents," murmured the oily tone of Tagashi, "to make up for her enforced detention. Some embroideries, some jade—you understand? I thought you would appreciate the thought."

"You're whiter than I thought you were, Tagashi," said Anderson gratefully but thoughtlessly. That was a fatal error, had he known it; those words burned into the Oriental, who, like all his race, found the least hint of color distinction an insufferable insult.

But Tagashi made no response, and his broad features were invisible.

The chauffeur left his seat, opened the door of the limousine, waited. The woman—or girl—entered the car. The Jap bowed and returned up the steps. The chauffeur closed the car door, jumped to his seat, and started the limousine. Anderson drew a deep breath of relief, and relaxed his tense posture as he saw his sister whirled away down the hill. After the limousine whirred a motor cycle. This was the shadower sent by Tagashi.

"It's done!" said Anderson.

"Yes," said Tagashi. "And our friend Mr. Rannals will be well taken care of until the conference of the Trigrams Saturday night. He will then afford us some information. Now, is there anything further before you leave for the south?"

"Nothing," said Anderson. "So long!"

"So—long," repeated Tagashi, a singular inflection to the words.

Anderson passed down the steps to the sidewalk and went to his waiting car.

The limousine which had carried away Janet Anderson to safety was speeding west and south to the remarkable building which was occupied by John Solomon.

Had they been able to follow that limousine, both Randolph Anderson and Nathan Rannals would have encountered a profound shock, which would have passed into a frightful consternation.

The limousine, it is true, arrived in safety at its destination, and drew up in the courtyard to discharge its passenger. She stepped out, to be met by a politely bowing Chinaman.

"You are Missee Ande'son?" he murmured. "You come along my. Miste' Solomon, he makee wait fo' you."

With smiling acquiescence, the lady followed him to the presence of John Solomon. She was not Janet Anderson, however.

She was Mrs. Lee.

CHAPTER IX

SOLOMON'S PRIVATE office, as has been seen, was a severely plain room, with a single door. The only ornament was a very handsome carpet on the floor; it was a sixteenth-century Ispahan—a gift to Solomon from the Sherif of Mecca.

In his usual tarboosh and carpet slippers, Solomon was awaiting the arrival of Janet Anderson, whom he had ordered admitted to his presence instantly upon arrival. Despite the activity of his old clay pipe, however, Solomon was not waiting in idleness. Over his private telephone, which connected to his own exchange below, he was receiving the last of the reports anent the evening's roundup.

These reports were good. Mordaunt's entire organization was wiped out of existence, with a few exceptions. Every person implicated in the activity of the *hui* had been neatly and efficiently trapped. Even then newspaper extras were being shrilled through the city detailing what facts were known about the biggest underworld raid in history.

A buzz at the telephone, and Solomon learned that Miss Anderson was on her way to his private office. He promptly ordered all other business shelved, sat back in his chair, and began to whittle fresh tobacco from his black plug.

He was thus employed when the door opened, and Mrs. Lee entered.

Solomon—apparently without looking up—laid aside his tobacco and knife and pipe. As he did so, an awkward movement of his arm knocked over the telephone. He reached out, replaced the instrument, and came to his feet.

"Good evenin', Miss Anderson!" he began. "Werry 'appy I am—why—why—it ain't 'er at all!"

The surprise depicted upon his pudgy countenance was so overpowering as to be comical, while his blue eyes were distended in blank astonishment. But, clasping her hands together, Mrs. Lee took a step forward. Upon her beautiful features was a look utmost imploration.

"Oh, Mr. Solomon—do not be angry with me!" she exclaimed. The low, vibrant voice was athrill with emotion. It was a voice to reach the soul of a man. She had thrown back the embroidered cloak that had shaded her head, and against the rich brocade all her golden beauty was accentuated.

"Miss Anderson sent me to you," she added rapidly. "I had to reach you—it was my only chance. Give me only a few minutes—"

At this instant the door behind her opened again. A tall, swarthy man, an Arab, was framed in the opening.

Mrs. Lee darted one startled glance at him, then her eyes went to Solomon. In them was fright, pleading, a mortal anguish.

"You called, effendi?" said the Arab in his own tongue. Solomon answered in English:

"It was an accident, Yusuf. Dang it, I went an' knocked that 'ere telephone over by mistake, I did! You may go."

His eyes were blank, his face was expressionless, giving the searching gaze of Mrs. Lee no hint of anything. Because she was so intently watching his face, she failed to catch a slight gesture of his fingers. The Arab caught it, however, smiled thinly, and salaamed obediently ere he closed the door.

"Now, ma'am, if you'll be so kind as to take a chair?" said Solomon, looking rather fussed and awkward. "This 'ere is a surprise and no mistake, as the old gent said when 'e married the 'ouse-maid. You just make yourself at 'ome, ma'am."

Mrs. Lee sank into the chair he turned for her. The electric lights added to the clear beauty of the golden Eurasian skin, and there was no daylight to betray the faint harshness of her features. Instead, her limpid eyes were very tender, and in her face was something akin to the pure confidence of girlhood. Mrs. Lee was a remarkable woman.

"You know who I am, Mr. Solomon?" she asked.

Solomon, who appeared somewhat dazed, shook his head silently.

"My name is Lee," she said, watching him. The name brought nothing but another shake of the head. In his tarboosh and wisps of gray hair Solomon looked a really absurd old man. Mrs. Lee gained confidence.

"Once, and not so long ago," she said, low-voiced, "I was called Lily of Malacca."

Solomon started. It was evident that the little cockney was no actor, for this name occasioned in him a surprise, a recognition that was instant and obvious. His blue eyes widened upon her.

"Mary Sanchez!" he murmured. "The Lily o' Malacca—why, ma'am, it ain't possible! I've 'eard tell as 'ow that 'ere poor girl was dead an' gone these two year back!"

"I was Mary Sanchez," she said softly.

Now, behind these words lay a story, which Solomon had more than once heard. Yet he had never heard the same story twice.

Malacca Town is not so large a place that beauty can be hidden in it. Mary Sanchez, who had been evolved from Khmer and Portuguese and English and many other races, had been the most beautiful creature in Malaysia and points north. She was, however, Eurasian—her blood made her a prey instead of a divinity. On the China coasts, the golden beauty of an Eurasian is a bar sinister which no white man of good standing can pass over.

No one knew the truth of what happened to the Sanchez family. The accepted version was that the old man Sanchez, a disreputable half-caste, had tired to sell the girl in several quarters at once. He was a wealthy old scoundrel. Somehow he was murdered and his house burned: it was said that the Lily of Malacca had perished at the same time. The happening had made a large scandal, and several gentlemen of color, who were probably quite guiltless, went to the Andamans for life as a result.

"I'd like werry much to know 'ow you come 'ere ma'am," said Solomon wheezily.

"It's part of the story," rejoined Mrs. Lee, her beautiful eyes swimming unshed tears. "There was a trader named Tom Lee; we loved each other. My father was going to sell me to Bing Wat Low, the Chinaman who had the tin concessions at Kialapore. That—that night the house was burned, Tom Lee had come and so had Bing Wat Low. So had come—some native men. There was a fight, and my father tried to kill Tom, and Bing Wat Low killed my father by mistake—and Tom Lee carried me off and left them all fighting. Afterward no one knew just what had happened.

"Tom and I were married in Singapore," she continued, the play of emotion softening and deepening her limpid eyes. "He died two months afterward of plague; that was in Surabaya. A Dutch official seized the schooner and tried to carry me upcountry. I got away from him, and reached Batavia safely. There I met a man named Tagashi—a Jap with whom my husband had had business dealings."

A touch of rosy color came into her cheeks.

"Tagashi lent me money," she went on, "and I got away to Singapore. There he came after me. Unfortunately I had signed a chit when he lent the money to me, and in Singapore he threatened to—to give people the wrong impression—unless I helped him. I had no one to help me, no one to go to. Tagashi frightened me. There was no question of anything wrong—he wanted me to help him here in San Francisco, in the dope business. What could I do? I hoped that after I got here, to America, I could get free again.

"So I came. To all appearances I was free, traveling alone, but everything I did was watched. Spies were all around me. I dared attempt nothing. When I got here I was taken to Tagashi's place, and I have been there ever since. I have been treated well and given everything I wanted, but I have been a prisoner. Tagashi would bring men for me to talk with, and I would worm secrets from them for him. But I knew that some day it would end in disgrace and shame and dishonor—and when the chance came to-night I got away."

"Oh!" said Solomon. "To-night!"

"Yes," she said, long golden lashes veiling her eyes. "Tagashi was going to send Miss Anderson away. She was in my care, you see. We had become friends, and she knew my story. She told me to go in her place, and come to you. She said you would help me, and she could get away later on. And she said, too, that I might help you."

To this final argument Solomon nodded his head sagely. He reached for his pipe and filled it. When he had tamped it full he lighted it. Only then did he speak:

"Werry true, ma'am. That 'ere Miss Anderson, she's a good 'ead, I says. So you got away in 'er place, just like that!"

"Yes. You're not angry?"

"Angry!" exclaimed Solomon. "Angry! And what for would I be angry, miss? I'm mortal sorry for you, I am. What else did Miss Anderson say?"

Mrs. Lee drew a deep breath, and relaxed somewhat the tension that was upon her. She had expected anything but this simple, gentle old man, who had swallowed her story without a qualm.

"We talked it over, of course," she said, her eyes full on Solomon. "You see, she has been well treated and is not afraid. She thought that you might be able to use me—and I'd be glad to help you against Tagashi. I don't know just how it could be done, but she seemed certain that you could find a way."

Solomon puffed at his pipe, nodded, and turned to his telephone. He took down the receiver.

"Ask Lun Yat to step up 'ere, please."

At the name of Lun Yat the fair visitor caught her breath sharply. Her eyes stared incredulously at Solomon, who took no heed. She started to speak, checked herself, and then glanced about sharply as the door opened. A Chinaman appeared. Solomon looked up and addressed him in Cantonese. Lun Yat stolidly ignored Mrs. Lee.

"Lun Yat, you were the number-one boy in the house of Sanchez, in Malacca?"

"Yes, master," said Lun Yat.

A slow horror was creeping into the beautiful eyes of Mrs. Lee.

"Tell me what happened there the night Sanchez was killed."

"His daughter betrayed him to Tom Lee, master. Tom Lee killed him. She ran away with him. I saw it done. Later she betrayed Tom Lee to another man."

"That is all," said Solomon.

Lun Yat departed, and the door closed. The blank blue eyes of Solomon swung to the fear-wide gaze of Mrs. Lee.

"I'm werry sorry to say, ma'am," he said softly, "as 'ow I can't make use of you."

In those words there was a dreaded finality. In the silence that followed, in the expressionless face of Solomon, in his blue eyes, Mrs. Lee must have read horrible things. Her face colored deeply, then became overspread with a livid pallor.

Her fingers twisted and untwisted nervously. Suddenly she gave way—broke down completely. A low cry was wrenched from her, and she plunged forward to her knees, her hands catching at the arm of Solomon.

"Oh—I had to do it, I had to do it!" she cried incoherently, lifting her tear-wet cheeks. "Tagashi made me swear to do it! Oh, don't make me go back to him—let him think that—that I fooled you! Don't make me go back there—you don't know the hell it has been for me—you don't know what he will do when he knows I have failed!"

Solomon caught her hands in his, rose, and with a surprising display of strength lifted her back into her chair. It was gently done.

"Miss, I'm werry sorry for you," he said, and reseated himself. "Now, suppose you tells me why 'e sent you and why 'e's a-keepin' Miss Anderson?"

She checked the low, convulsive sobs that shook her bosom. Her tear-suffused face was more beautiful than ever in this moment.

"He wants to use her as a check on her brother," she responded. "He's not too sure about Anderson, and—"

"Oh, I see!" observed Solomon sagely.

"Don't make me go back to him!" she broke out again, a wail in her voice. "Oh, you don't know—"

Solomon regarded her steadily. Under those blue eyes she fell silent.

"Yes, miss, you're a-goin' back to 'im, just like that," said Solomon. "Now, you wait till I get this 'ere pipe cleaned out, and then we'll talk—"

He drew a wastebasket to him, took up his knife, and leaned forward. He was intently engaged in scraping out his clay pipe, and quite ignored the woman to one side.

Her eyes changed as she watched him—changed, narrowed, became filled with a desperate anger. She could not quite conceive just how or why she had been balked at every turn by this pudgy little cockney, and her fury mounted in a flame.

Her hands crept upward inch by inch. Solomon scraped away at his pipe, disregarding her. From her bosom she took a handkerchief, dabbed at her eyes, then thrust the scrap of lace away.

As she did so, swift as light, her hand jerked out a pistol. She fired point-black at Solomon. Two bursting reports of the automatic filled the chamber with deafening noise and acrid fumes.

From Mrs. Lee broke a terrible cry—a scream.

At the instant her fingers jerked forth the weapon a hand came over her shoulder and gripped her wrist. Another hand caught her neck from behind, holding her immovable in a vise-like grip. These hands belonged to a man who had silently appeared behind her, soundless as a shadow. He was an Arab.

John Solomon looked up at the ceiling, which had been pierced by two bullets. He laid down his pipe and looked at Mrs. Lee, whose eyeballs seemed starting from her head. Then he sighed wheezily and made a slight gesture.

The Arab, plucking away the automatic pistol, let Mrs. Lee drop into her chair. Then he vanished through the doorway as silently as he had appeared. The woman sank down, dry sobs shaking her body convulsively.

"I was a-loookiin' for that werry thing," observed Solomon sadly. "Mrs. Lee, I've met a mortal lot of actresses in me day, and I'm 'appy to congratulate you on your ability in that 'ere line. If I was you I'd quit all that 'ere weeping, 'cause why, it's makin' your nose werry red indeed. And tears don't do a bit o' good, as the old gent said when 'e kissed the 'ousemaid. What do you think is a-goin' to 'appen to you now?"

Mrs. Lee calmed herself. She was far shattered by what had happened; of a sudden all her beauty had waned and faded, and harsh lines had sprung up about her nostrils, and the golden glow of her skin had been bartered for a leaden pallor.

She looked at the man, fear in her eyes, yet she was brave enough.

"You've won," she said simply, choking down the last of her sobs. "I've done my best. I— I suppose you'll kill me now, and be done with it."

Solomon wagged his head, picked up his pipe, and filled it afresh.

"I'd be mortal sorry to 'ave to do such a thing, ma'am," he returned. "Killin' is all werry well in its place, says I, but its place ain't 'ere and now. I don't want to 'ave no truck with you just like that; none whatever!"

He stooped to the telephone and spoke into it, then he sat down and smoked. Mrs. Lee watched him, fascinated and frightened by the perfect calm of this man, sickened by the realization of how she had misjudged him, how she had played her little tricks in all futility, how he had known all the while that she was a liar and an emissary of evil.

The door opened. Solomon's Chinese chauffeur appeared.

"Take 'er back where you got 'er," said Solomon, and turned his back.

CHAPTER X

NOW IT is necessary to speak of a man who was named Ch'ien-hsi, and who lived alone with two servants in a little bungalow away out at the edge of town in the sand lots.

Certain things might be deduced from the form of the name Ch'ien-hsi. Had it been the usual form of Mandarin it would have been K'ien-hi. Its spelling, which was of the Peking dialect, showed that the gentleman had come from Peking.

Ch'ien-hsi, then, came from Peking; his features, which were sternly handsome if somewhat aflame with inner fires, showed that he was a Manchu. His two servants were likewise Manchus, and they served him with great deference. Ch'ien'hsi dressed in English fashion when he left his house, but he seldom left it. He had no visitors that any one knew of. He appeared to be a recluse. Often he might be seen walking in a tiny garden which bloomed in the sand behind his house; he would stand there gazing out across the beach out toward the fog-horizoned Pacific, as though he saw strange dragons in the heavens for the precious jewel of life.

Neighbors out there were few and far between, like the houses. The little gossip that concerned itself with Ch'ien-hsi reported that he was a Manchu prince exiled from the republic of China—although the republic supports the Manchu princes in regal style at home. Likewise rumor whispered an ugly thing—that one day he had been seen to stoop and pluck at a wandering cat, and in an instant had torn the poor creature asunder with his bare hands. But this was a bit too horrible to meet with much credence, and those who had met the man face to face deemed him a gentle soul.

There are certain things about Manchus which are not perhaps generally known. One is that Manchus are warriors and hunters pure and simple. All the Manchus in China were warriors, were maintained as warriors, and were nothing else. The Manchu princes until recent days used to go each year on great hunts in the northern steppes. It is in the blood of a Manchu to hunt, to scent blood, to prey. Without this he stagnates.

And yet this man who dwelt by the seashore certainly did not stagnate. The virile energy of his deep eyes was extraordinary.

One afternoon Ch'ien-hsi was walking in his garden, gazing as usual at the ocean breaking across the horizon.

As he walked and looked out at the sea one of the ex-bannermen came to him and saluted him respectfully.

"O Son of heaven, there is a messenger come for certain liquids. He comes from the unspeakable son of Nippon who is named Tagashi."

Ch'ien-hsi removed his gaze from the ocean and looked at his servant.

"Two vials are on my desk in the laboratory," he said. "Wrap them. Give them."

The servant departed. Ch'ien-hsi returned to his contemplation of the tumbling waves, and the gray bank of fog slowly rolling in upon the shore.

Twenty minutes later the servant again came to him—this time with a hint of excitement stirring under the impassive Mongol features.

"O son of heaven, a man is arriving! He is very sick. I think he is Hsun."

"Hsun—sick!"

Ch'ien-hsi's long, lean figure stiffened for an instant, then he strode rapidly to the house and vanished. A moment later, from the doorway, he was looking at an interesting scene.

The bungalow, of cement, was built about a patio which fronted the street. A taxicab was drawn up before the house, and its driver was assisting his fare to alight. The passenger, a man of medium height and build, wore curled black mustaches and a goatee; his ordinarily swarthy features were now ghastly pale and waxen. He gained the sidewalk and straightened up as the chauffeur set down a suit case behind him.

"Want me to help you in, sir?" asked the driver kindly.

"Thanks, no," said the fare. "I believe that a man noted down your license number as we left the railroad station. If questions are asked, forget where you brought me—or give another address."

As he spoke he handed the chauffeur a gold eagle—something rarely seen, even in California, in these latter days.

"Leave it to me, doc," said the driver, "Good luck!"

The man stood where he was until the taxicab had turned and departed. Then, leaving the suit case at the curb, he walked into the patio toward the house door. His walk was evidently a frightful agony to him; twice he halted, a spasmodic contortion seizing on his features.

The door opened, and Ch'ien-hsi appeared.

"You are safe, Señor Gonzales," he said.

At these words the visitor staggered, halted, and sank down. He was caught by the two Manchu servants, who had advanced to greet him.

This man was Señor Gonzales, of New Orleans, who represented the Hsun Trigram.

Ch'ien-hsi abandoned the doorway and hastened through the house to a small laboratory. By the time the servants had carried Gonzales hither the Manchu had opened a wall safe and laid out several little racks of tiny bottles, and was attired in surgeon's cap and apron. At his direction Gonzales, who was unconscious, was laid upon an operating table which was rolled out from the wall. The servants then began to strip the man.

It became apparent that the Manchu was a surgeon, for this laboratory of his held a good bit of surgical apparatus. None the less, it was a laboratory and a well-equipped one. The roots and dried plants which hung at one end of the chamber suggested that his researches might be made along botanical lines.

While the servants were working Ch'ien-hsi was laying out some tiny cups of eggshell porcelain. By each cup he placed one of the minute bottles from the racks. Then he turned and glanced at the operating table.

"He is not wounded?"

"Not in the body, son of heaven."

The Manchu nodded, and bent over the naked body of Gonzales. The latter was undoubtedly in a very bad way. His respiration was alarming. His stomach and chest were contorted as though some frightful spasm had seized upon his intestines.

As though they were used to this sort of business, the two servants brought out a machine and tested his blood pressure without orders. Presently they had made out a chart to which Ch'ien-hsi turned after completing his own examination. A surgeon would have admired the silent efficiency of these assistants.

Ch'ien-hsi stepped to his bottles and cups. He emptied two of the vials into two of the porcelain vessels.

"Place him in the chair," he said. "Give him these. He will die in ten minutes—first he must be made to talk."

As he said this he glanced at a clock on the wall. It was precisely four o'clock.

Gonzales was placed in an operating chair. Ch'ien-hsi stood above him as the liquids were placed on his tongue and gazed down with stern eyes. Now, of a sudden, one came to an understanding of this extraordinary man from Peking.

As he stood thus there was no pity in his eyes, no sympathy for this Gonzales whom he must have known well. Neither was there any particular interest in the victim. In fact, Ch'ien-hsi displayed only a great aloofness—a most singular aloofness. One would say that this Manchu stood apart from all the world. And he suddenly loomed larger, more sinister, as though instead of being a man he were some inhuman force, some embodied energy.

The eyes of Gonzales opened, fastened feverishly upon the gaze of the Manchu.

"What happened?" said the latter calmly, coldly.

"I—don't know." Strength came quickly into the voice of Gonzales. In his eyes was a dumb bewilderment.

"You did well to cover your trail in reaching here. You came from New Orleans in a through car? You suspect no one? Think! Was any Chinaman in the car?"

"No—wait!" The eyes of Gonzales flashed. "I was all right in San José—an hour before we got in. I remember now—an old Chinaman came aboard there. He argued with the conductor—he wanted a seat in the Pullman—"

"Describe him," said Ch'ien-hsi.

"An old man. Gray mustache and beard—thin. He carried a large bunch of flowers. Dios! All the pain is gone—it is wonderful! What have you done?"

The pain might be gone indeed, but Gonzales' face was overspread with a mortal pallor and beaded with a fine death sweat.

"The flowers!" Ch'ien-hsi pounced upon that word. "What became of them?"

Gonzales shook his head. At this moment one of the two Manchu servants made a gesture which drew the attention of Ch'ien-hsi. The man holding up the coat of Gonzales. In the lapel was a flower.

"Ah! Where did you get the flower in your coat?"

"The porter—distributed them. He said it was the custom. He gave every one a flower. That was after—the old Chinaman had disappeared—"

The stern eyes of Ch'ien-hsi gleamed in triumph.

"Clever!" he murmured. "The porter was bribed to do it. Clever!"

"What is it?" cried out Gonzales suddenly. Horror came into his staring eyes. "What is it—I feel something—"

"It is death," said Ch'ien-hsi, looking down at him.

The staring eyes widened—widened—and then suddenly closed. The body of Gonzales went limp and flaccid. Ch'ien-hsi glanced at the clock.

"Four-eleven!" he said. "I was wrong by one minute. Decidedly these errors must be stopped!" He turned to his two men. "Dispose of the body. Bring his suit case to me here. That is all for the present."

Entirely disregarding the body of the man who had so lately personified the Hsun Trigram, Ch'ien-hsi carefully disengaged the flower from the coat and took it to the laboratory bench.

The flower was a very handsome tuberose. Its naturally cloying fragrance rose quite heavily, and Ch'ien-hsi hurriedly opened the nearest window. One might have imagined that he was afraid of this perfume.

He set about an examination of the flower, which he carefully pressed open, but before doing it he wrapped a wet towel about his nostrils and mouth. For fifteen minutes he was busy with enlarging glasses and a microscope. Then he took the flower in a pair of tweezers and held it in a blow flame until it was entirely consumed. He wiped his hands and stared down at the ashes.

"Very clever," he said. "I could have done it no better myself. Hm! The man came from Chinatown in San José. Therefore he was sent by Lui Toy or his friends. So much is clear. And another Trigram is now dead. Hm! Evidently they did not know that he was bringing with him all his records and reports, or they would have tried to get them. Let us see."

He turned to the dead man's suit case, which had been brought in and opened by his two servants. It contained some clothing, a magazine, two novels in Spanish, and a small black leather manuscript case. With this case in his hand, Ch'ien-hsi went to a desk which occupied one corner of the laboratory.

He switched on the lights, for fog had come in and darkened the daylight, and sat down to examine the contents of the manuscript case. While he was engaged in this a telephone buzzer sounded. Ch'ien-hsi reached out to the instrument on his desk and responded.

"Ah, Tagashi!" he said. "Good. You received the bottles?"

"Yes," came the response. "I called up to tell you that Tui has arrived from the east, and Chen from the north. Unfortunately Hsun has not arrived from the south, and therefore we cannot hold the conference to-night as arranged."

"It can be held," said Ch'ien-hsi, his voice like cold stone. "Hsun will not arrive at all. His reports, however, are in my hands. Let me warn you urgently to take the fullest precautions to-night."

"They will be taken," answered the oily tones of Tagashi. "Is it your wish that the two prisoners be brought?"

"Yes," said Ch'ien-hsi, and hung up the receiver.

A thin, unholy smile curved his lips as he sat there reflectively. Presently he tapped a gong. A servant appeared.

"Be ready with the car immediately after dinner. We go across the bay to spend the night. Ten of the saffron bulbs in the garden are in blossom. Go and cut these buds, leaving full stems, and bring them to me here."

The servant disappeared.

CHAPTER XI

EXCEPT FOR handcuffs which closely confined his wrists, Rannals was free.

It was late Saturday afternoon, or so he figured. Since his capture he had been immured in a half-dark room. His meals had been pushed through a small aperture in the wall. He had seen no one. No questions had been asked him.

Now he was brought out, handcuffed. He emerged into a foggy afternoon, a Jap at each elbow. The street appeared deserted, except for a limousine directly across the sidewalk. To this limousine he was quickly urged. The door was opened, he was propelled inside, and then the door was closed again. It closed with a metallic clang, the sound of a turned key.

But Rannals observed nothing at first. As he entered the limousine, which was lighted by an electric bulb in the roof, he found himself face to face with a single occupant. This occupant was Janet Anderson.

"You!" he exclaimed in consternation, sinking down on the seat opposite her. "You! Why—Miss Anderson—we thought you were safe long ago! Sent back to Solomon!"

Save for a trace of anxiety in her eyes, darkening the blue to gold-specked black, Janet Anderson looked no different than when he had seen her that day in Union Square. She appeared unhurt. Her gaze held no fear—certainly no such fear as was in the face of Nathan Rannals. Yet she was indubitably surprised.

"Mr. Rannals!" she exclaimed. "I had no idea—why, you are handcuffed!"

"Exactly," said Rannals, recovering from his first astounded dismay. "I'm a prisoner. But we had arranged with Tagashi to return you to Solomon!"

The girl smiled a bit wanly.

"I knew nothing about it," she answered. "I have been kept a prisoner, but treated well enough. I have seen nobody except two Japanese women. They promised to let me go free if I told what I knew about Mr. Solomon."

"I don't think that you knew much?" queried Rannals.

"If I had I would not have told," she responded. "Who carried me off? The people against whom Solomon is fighting?"

"The dope ring," said Rannals briefly. "Hello—we're moving! Where are we?"

Sounds reached them from outside very faintly, but they caught the vibration of the engine and felt the car start into motion.

Rannals lifted his bound hands toward the windows of the car. Then he made an unpleasant discovery. The car had no windows! Instead, or on the inside of the windows, there were blank sheets of metal.

"I learned that while waiting for you," said Janet Anderson quietly. "See—there are no door handles. I was brought from the hotel in a car like this, or the same one. They said that Mr. Solomon wanted to speak to me. I started in the car door, was pulled inside, and the door slammed. No one heard me cry out."

"No one would hear," said Rannals, examining the car's interior with sinking heart. "This thing seems to have no opening anywhere, even for ventilation, but there must be an air vent. It's probably sound-proof, in any case. Where are we going?"

"I know no more than you," answered the girl.

They sat in silence a brief space, looking at each other. To Rannals it was simply appalling to discover that his own sacrifice had been in vain. He understood that Tagashi must have double-crossed him—or else Anderson had betrayed him. He inclined to the former view, however.

In such case, what had happened to Anderson?

"Tell me," said the girl. "All about it."

Rannals started. A smile broke on his lips. He liked her quiet poise, her thorough coolness at such a moment.

"It looks to me," he answered whimsically, "as though I were a badly fooled man."

Suddenly she leaned forward, touching his manacled hands with cool fingers. Her eyes regarded him with an anxious, eager light.

"My brother!" she breathed. "You know anything about him? I saw him two—no, three—days ago. They brought me to a room that had a glass door at one end. I saw my brother through that door. He was talking to a fat, hideous man, a Japanese. They told me they would send him to me if I would talk, but—"

Rannals made a gesture of despair. He saw everything crashing down now—all the structure. He would have to tell her everything. More of Tagashi's infernal craft here, more of the insidious web of intrigue and treachery and black evil! In this moment Nathan Rannals felt a profound despair, a sense of fighting against fate. His heart ached for this girl. He must tell her the truth absolutely. As he met the steady light of her eyes he knew that she would compel the truth from him. She must meet her shame and agony, she must meet it and pass above it. She must know the truth if she were to cope with lies and trickery.

So he told her of her brother, who lay gripped in a hand worse than the hand of death, and although he tried to soften the harsh truth he could not.

Now, it may be that the proud shame of Randolph Anderson had caused Rannals to exaggerate this matter in his own mind. Or perhaps he had expected this girl to learn the truth with much dramatic anguish. As a matter of fact, a person in real life seldom meets a bitter shock with any show of emotion. That is reserved for the silvery screen.

Thus Janet Anderson listened with apparent calm while Rannals told her the blunt truth—that her brother had become a drug fiend, and accomplice of the dope ring, one who preyed upon the soul of others. True, it might be that the girl paled slightly, that a slight look of hurt came into her eyes; but that was all.

Rannals went on swiftly to tell of her brother's efforts to aid her. He sketched all that had taken place in the past few days, bearing lightly upon his own share. In his words, it became evident that his intention was not to hurt, and the girl realized it.

"Listen, please," she said with a effort at calmness. "You are afraid to tell me this—just as Randolph did not want me to know. Well, do you think I am some cloistered convent flower, that I cannot face things? Nonsense! I am a woman, Mr. Rannals. Long ago I was convinced that Randolph was either dead or in jail. I was ready to face worse than this.

"And is it so terrible, after all? He takes drugs; so do millions of people. He has not led a good life; neither had St. Augustine. Oh, I don't mean to say that it doesn't hurt—it does, it does! But I am so glad to have found him that nothing else can matter now. And if he is secretly helping us and John Solomon—don't you think there's hope for the future?"

At this instant the car lurched abruptly, a sound penetrated to them; it was the roaring blast of a steamer's whistle, faintly reaching them.

"The ferry!" said Rannals. "We are going across the bay—"

The car stopped. There was no further movement. Presently the whistle reached them again, removing all doubt.

Silence again. The stillness became intolerable—the suspense of waiting bored in upon them fearfully. Twice the sound of the ferry's whistle reached them, but that meant only that they might be passing other ships.

"I want you to know," and Janet Anderson looked at him suddenly, "that I appreciate your action in exchanging yourself for me, Mr. Rannals. I do appreciate it! I thank you with all my heart—"

"Never mind, please. Ah, the engine is going!"

The car went on. Twice the lights were flashed on, twice extinguished. The smooth rapidity of motion told that they must be well away from the city out on the open highway. Rannals fancied that they might be east of Oakland on the Sacramento Boulevard, but this was sheer conjecture.

Then the lights came on, and the two prisoners realized that the car was standing still. An instant afterward the door was swung open.

"Will you please to come quiet, sar?" asked the Jap, in chauffeur's uniform, who held open the door. "Lady also, if please."

Two other shapes at the rear of the car conveyed silent warning to Rannals as he stepped out. A glance showed him that any break for liberty would be futile.

The car stood outside an open door of a large house, apparently of stucco. House and car lights brought enough of the night into illumination to apprise Rannals that trees stood all about—fruit trees.

"Where are we?" he asked the little brown man as Miss Anderson left the car.

"This house of private ranch, sar," came the answer, accompanied by a flashing smile. "Nippon ranch, sar. Ver' nice fruit, flower, all thing ex'lent! You come in, please."

He went ahead. Behind, in the obscurity, Rannals was conscious of other shapes; the prisoners were well watched. This did not prevent him, however, from murmuring to his companion:

"Slip a hairpin into my hand as we enter—quick!"

The girl's hand went to her hair.

An instant later, as they passed through the doorway, Rannals stumbled and half fell against Miss Anderson. The little Jap glanced around quickly, suspiciously. With a laugh at his own awkwardness Rannals apologized to the girl. They went on.

The hairpin was in his hand. He cursed himself for not having secured it earlier.

The three arrivals found themselves in a small, narrow hall which was quite bare, but well lighted. Here the chauffeur clapped his hands. Two figures appeared, a man and a woman—both Japs. The woman was deft, slight, large-eyed. The man was of the brutal peasant type, heavily nostriled, sullen of eye. To them the chauffeur spoke, then turned to Rannals.

"You be happy here maybe. If please, be quiet and obey nicely. Otherwise, ver' sad accident might happen, yes! Plenty people close by."

As though to emphasize this warning a door opened and two more Japs stood staring at the prisoners. The little woman beckoned and smiled to Miss Anderson, the man made an imperative gesture to Rannals.

"Good-by, and good luck!" said Janet Anderson. "I'll not forget."

"Good-by for the present," responded Rannals, and followed his jailer.

There was not far to go. Up a short flight of winding stairs and into a room whose door was massive and fitted with Yale locks. The door clanged shut behind Rannals, and he found himself alone.

He examined the room curiously. It was large and cheerful, well furnished and lighted. A bathroom adjoined. There were two windows, and he walked to the nearer. Through the glass he saw steel shutters on the outside. He had expected this, of course, being a prisoner.

A large table beside the bed held a few books and magazines, also a tray on which was an excellent repast. Rannals walked to the bathroom. There, upon a rack such as hotels used, he perceived his own suit case lying open. A single high window in the bathroom was small and fitted with bars.

Smiling slightly, Rannals sat down and examined his handcuffs. Now, a revenue agent, particularly one whose work lies with the narcotics squad, is very apt to have an extensive knowledge of steel bracelets: the opportunity at least lies open to him. Rannals had made use of his opportunities.

Taking the hairpin which Miss Anderson had given him, he bent it with his handkerchief, and took cloth and pin between his teeth. For a little he worked over his handcuffs. He had been shown how to do the trick by one of the most expert jail breakers on the coast.

Presently he stood up, stretched himself, put the handcuffs into his pocket, and went in to dinner.

"Tagashi is considerate of my comfort," he reflected aloud after his meal. "I'd better make the best of it while I can. A bath, a shave, a change of clothes—why not? Agreed!"

"By all means," said a voice—a caustic, powerful voice. "You have half an hour. Make the most of it."

Rannals stared about, but the room was empty as before. What terrible quality was in that voice—what piercing, cold energy that made him shiver? Then he must be under secret observation, of course.

He returned to the bathroom. He no longer felt elated over being rid of his handcuffs. Instead, he felt profoundly disturbed—even terrified. He could not get rid of the echo of that voice.

CHAPTER XII

P RECISELY HALF an hour after that disembodied voice had addressed him Rannals saw his door open. A strange Jap appeared.

Rannals, refreshed and cleansed, felt immensely more like himself. He looked at the Jap, who made a slight but imperative gesture and addressed him:

"You are to come. You remain free."

In those words, in that tone was a menace more potent than any threat. Rannals knew better than to jeopardize his new freedom by any vain dashing his head against the bars. He was held by an iron hand beneath a glove of silk—made in Japan.

He left the room, following the man. Another figure appeared behind him. Since no stairs were descended, Rannals knew that he remained on the second floor of the building. Presently they came to another man who stood beside a door; this man was clearly a Chinaman. Rannals set him down as no Cantonese, but a Manchu.

The Manchu opened the door and looked at Rannals with impassive eyes.

"Go in," he said. "Wait. The son of heaven will talk with you presently."

Rannals obeyed. The door was closed behind him.

He found himself in a small chamber which contained only a window, a chair, and a large, massive table of red teak. At one end was a curtained door. To this Rannals advanced and drew the curtain. He disclosed a heavy grille of iron, beyond which was another room luxuriously furnished.

At this instant the light in his own small room was extinguished.

Plunged in darkness, Rannals conjectured that for some unknown reason he had been set here to watch and listen. It was characteristic of him that he seized the occasion to do neither. A glance showed him that the large room beyond was nearly empty. Chairs stood about a table. In a large chair of red lacquer sat a man whose back was to Rannals, face invisible.

Turning swiftly, Rannals darted to the window of his chamber. To his quick relief he discerned moonlight outside, no bars. He opened the window silently and leaned out.

This window was set in a square recess of the building. To either hand, in the other two walls of this recess, were windows, one of which was lighted. Straight ahead, Rannals had a view of trees, a garden. Below, twenty feet below, was a concrete pavement on which the moonlight glimmered whitely.

Rannals looked at the lighted window, to his right. He looked into a room, handsomely furnished, in which sat Janet Anderson. She was reading quietly, as though she sat at home. Rannals stared, incredulous; then he once again heard that caustic, impersonal voice in the air:

"It is too far to jump. Come back. Listen!"

He whirled, startled, terrified by the frightful and inhuman tone of that voice. His little chamber, faintly illumined from the larger room beyond the iron grille, was empty. Who had spoke?

He turned away from the window, oppressed by this sense of helplessness. Now he saw the other men coming into the room beyond. As they came they nodded greeting to that immobile figure whose back was to Rannals.

Three men entered and took seats about the table. First of them was Tagashi, fat and ponderous, pig eyes gleaming. Behind him was a well-dressed, immaculate person whose air, voice, and dress were unmistakably English. This was Raymond

Pavitt-Beasley, of Vancouver, who represented the Chen or thunder Trigram. The third man was Charley Schwab of Chicago, or Tui; a thin, malignant person who wore many diamonds and whose vulgarity of person and speech was only belied by his heavy-lidded and piercing eyes—the eyes of one born to leadership and ability.

Rannals stood tense, his thoughts busied with himself rather than with the scene. Had it been meant that he should see Miss Anderson safe and in luxury? Beyond doubt. The way in which that cold voice had twice leaped out of the very air at him was more than startling; it was astounding, terrifying!

Suddenly Rannals heard that identical voice again. This time it proceeded from the man in the red lacquer chair, whose back was toward him.

"Good evening, gentlemen. We are all assembled?"

The three Trigrams glanced at each other.

"Gonzales is late, what?" said Pavitt-Beasely.

"Gonzales will not arrive, my dear Chen," said that inflexible, inhuman voice. "He is dead. As you know, Chien and Li are also dead. Of the six Trigrams in this country there remain the three here present—Kun, Chen and Tui."

Tagashi started. He looked at the speaker, and his heavy-rolled face was sweating.

"You are wrong," he said in a hollow, terrible voice. "Of the eight Trigrams in all there now remain three."

"Explain!" said that inhuman voice.

"I learned to-night—by Marconi-grams"—Tagashi spoke with some difficulty—"that K'en died to-day in Honolulu and K'an in Nagasaki. No explanations were given."

Pavitt-Beasley and Schwab glanced at each other.

"Evidently," drawled the Canadian, "It is our turn next. After you, my dear Tui."

"Not yet," snapped Schwab, his voice vicious. "I ain't a dead one till I'm a stiff, savvy? Now we're here, and we're fixin' to put up a scrap. Looks a whole lot to me, gents, like somebody had been a cursed fool. Three bumped off here in Frisco! If this here is to be a murder party I'm goin' to sit in with yeller chips, that's all."

The inflexible voice of the unknown cut across the others there like a whip, and quieted them.

"Sit down, gentlemen. You already know the circumstances. You know what we face—and who is against us. You are to be guests here for a few days. In this house you are perfectly safe—I guarantee it. I trust that is satisfactory?"

The three nodded, not without a suggestion of relief. Obviously Tagashi had been hard hit, badly shaken by the news from Honolulu and Nagasaki.

"First," pursued that deadly, toneless voice, "we must meet the enemy in this country, in San Francisco, and destroy him. Later we can regain all that has been lost abroad. It is evident that K'en and K'an were murdered by Chinese emissaries. Here, as you know, we have more than Chinese to face."

"I say," spoke up Pavitt-Beasley with his languid drawl, "why drag us into it, old chap? We were doing quite well at home, you know—"

"So were K'en and K'an," came the retort. Its significance was so deadly, so direct, that the Canadian nodded assent at once and sat back, stroking his mustache. He was a man with heavy, commanding eyes and reddish hair.

"More than the preservation of your lives," went on the unknown speaker, "is the immediate necessity of uniting our entire forces. Thus you were ordered to suspend operations and report here with all available funds. I have here the report of the defunct Hsun, our New Orleans chief. What interests us to-night is only the means of defense. According to this report and the certified check which accompanied it, Hsun brought to our fund the sum of seven hundred thousand dollars, cash. Your report, Kun?"

Tagashi fumbled some papers from his pocket.

"Of my own," he answered, sliding a check across the table,

"three hundred thousand. I have taken over the affairs of Chien, following his recent demise from regrettably consuming too much rice wine." At this a leer showed in his heavy face, and the other two smiled, betraying their knowledge of Mordaunt's death and its manner.

"Chien's affairs were in bad shape," resumed Tagashi, "but I salvaged a quarter of a million. This gives us, so far, a million and a quarter."

"Your report, Tui?" asked the unknown.

"Four hundred thousand," said Schwab, producing a check.

"And you, Chen?"

Pavitt-Beasley stroked his mustache. Rannals had already set him down for no Canadian, but an Englishman. Canadians do not favor the more-English-than-the-English manner, particularly in western Canada.

"I understand," he drawled, "that this is a time of emergency in which all moneys are to be pooled for the common necessity. Is this correct?"

"It is," was the response.

Pavitt-Beasley laid down a check. "Here is five hundred thousand."

The unknown collected the checks.

"This," he said, "gives us a total of over two millions. The sum previously cabled me from Honolulu and Nagasaki reaches a million; three million altogether. I am prepared to make this five million. With such an amount we may consider our finances sufficient. Now comes the question whether we shall fill the vacant Trigrams at once or conduct the fight ourselves and reorganize our business later."

"Do it ourselves," spoke up Schwab, chewing an unlighted cigar. "This ain't no time to monkey with dope. We got to forget business and bust this Solomon guy."

The other two nodded assent.

"Then it is agreed," said the inflexible voice of the unknown. "As regards the fight against Solomon. I would say that I have made full plans to-day—plans which will demand your full cooperation and assistance."

"How in hell," said Schwab, "are we goin' to fight a guy we don't even know by sight?"

"Here is a photograph of him," said the unknown. "Copies have been made for us and for our men. His history, to a certain extent, is known to me and—"

"But I say!" broke in Pavitt-Beasley. "These Chinese, you know—his whole crowd! They've jolted us quite a bit, what? Frisbie, you know—"

"Frisbie was careless and paid for it," said the inexorable voice. "Solomon got him, got his reports, his money. We cannot help it. To-morrow we open the fight. By to-morrow night we win the fight."

"How?" asked Tagashi.

"To-morrow afternoon falls the blow which I have prepared. At seven o'clock to-morrow evening Solomon will be here. He will not leave here alive."

At this moment Rannals softly stepped back to the still open window.

He now understood perfectly that it was the voice of this unknown individual in the red lacquer chair which he had twice heard proceeding from the air. This man was the actual but secret head of the entire *hui*—a person superior to the Trigrams. Probably a senior partner in the syndicate, as it were.

Thus there had been nothing supernatural about that voice. The man had been watching him, that was all—knew exactly what Rannals would do under given conditions. A man of most extraordinary intelligence—no more.

But, at the present moment, this man was busy with the three Trigrams.

From the window Rannals glanced back at the grille and the adjacent room. The murmur of voices came to him—the four persons there were deeply engaged in talk. He turned to the window. In the clear moonlight outside the grounds appeared deserted. The window of Janet Anderson's room had now been shaded.

"Too far to jump!" thought Rannals. "That's true, with concrete to land on. But—who said anything about jumping? Not I!"

At the window hung curtains of some stuff like monk's cloth, fairly heavy. In a jiffy Rannals had removed them and knotted together two corners. Holding this length of cloth by one end, he lowered it from the open window. Knotting the corner in his hand, he hooked this over the catch on the top of the raised sash.

The sash would come down when his weight came on the cloth, Rannals fully realized. Careful to make no sound, assuring himself by a glance that the attention of the men in the adjacent room was fully occupied by their own affairs, he wormed himself through the window opening, and at length stood on the sill outside. Then, inch by inch, he lowered the raised sash, pulling on the cloth as he did so until the sash had closed upon the cloth at the bottom.

An instant later Rannals was letting himself down, hand over hand.

It seemed too good to be true—too easy! As he went down, Rannals glanced at the window through which he had seen Janet Anderson. No chance to reach her now—he must get away and effect a rescue from outside.

All he needed was a telephone, a message to the authorities.

He came to the end of the improvised rope, glanced down, and let go. He fell only six feet, and thrilled to the sense of freedom as his feet touched the concrete. At last! True, he had nothing to serve as a weapon, but he might need none.

He looked around. In the clear, brilliant light of the full moon everything was clear cut and bright. He seemed to be at the rear of the house. Twenty feet away was a large garage, the doors closed; the space between was all concrete. Behind the garage, fruit trees.

"Got to go around and reach the highway," thought Rannals. "Wouldn't dare to get away with a car."

He could hear a chatter of voices from one side, where lighted windows betrayed what were evidently the kitchen and pantry; a rattle of dishes came to him. Obviously here was his chance. Rannals darted to the corner of the house. As he reached it the figure of a Jap appeared suddenly before him.

"You come this way," began the Jap, when the fist of Rannals caught him.

Thinking that the man had mistaken him for some one else, Rannals struck instinctively and hard. The Jap went sprawling to the pavement. Rannals dashed around the corner of the house—only to find another Jap, smiling, who covered him with an automatic pistol.

"You come this way, please!" said the Jap calmly.

Rannals halted, with a cold hand clutching at him. He perceived now, as before, that he was being played with—that his every move was anticipated, prepared for. The sense of paralyzing helplessness was frightful. He felt as though he were dealing with some supernatural agency.

Yet, even then, Rannals almost mechanically noted certain details of his surroundings. It was apparent that this house stood somewhere out among rolling hills, wide countryside. Yet to the house came both electric cables and other wires. There must be a telephone somewhere about—

A shadow detached itself from a side doorway, and shambled forward.

"Yah! Got him, did ye?" came a jeering voice, which made Rannals turn in wondering incredulity. "The boss said ye would. Hello there, ye low-down skunk! Know me, do ye?"

It was no other than Shuffles Beeson. He stood before Rannals, reviling the former revenue agent with a volley of oaths and imprecations. His awry head, his twisted upper lip, the vindictive malice of his eyes, all conveyed an impression of bestial malignity.

"C'me on in with him!" he snarled. "The boss gimme orders about this guy. Bring him along, Kato!"

Rannals felt the pistol held by the Jap thrust into his side. He accompanied the two men into the house, upon him a crushing sense of fighting against fate.

Nathan Rannals was more nearly broken than ever before.

CHAPTER XIII

A ND NOW, in that same handsomely furnished chamber upon which Rannals had turned his back to escape, the three Trigrams sat with Ch'ien-hsi and discussed certain detailed matters. Rannals would have found this discussion of great interest had he still been listening to it.

Both Charley Schwab and Raymond Pavitt-Beasley knew fairly well all that had taken place in San Francisco, but they were now informed of other details.

"This man Anderson," said Tagashi to Ch'ien-hsi. "I wish to remove him."

The cold, inhuman eyes of the Manchu regarded the Jap steadily, inscrutably.

"He is one of our best men, I understand," came the toneless response. "Is he not the brother of this woman you brought here to-night?"

"Yes. Therefore he is dangerous," affirmed Tagashi sullenly. "I distrust him, and I fear him."

"Very well," came the impassive reply from Ch'ien-hsi. "It is a small favor. He is yours."

"What about these two prisoners?" asked Schwab uneasily. "Believe me, boss, it ain't safe to keep 'em on the string. Get rid of 'em, I say."

Something like a smile flickered over the stern, stony features of Ch'ien-hsi.

"Never fear," he said. "They do not leave this place alive, yet they may have their uses. They die to-morrow night. From the man, Rannals, I shall get certain information about Solomon. By means of the woman I shall get Solomon here."

"Here?" The word broke from all three of his listeners.

"Exactly. Solomon is to come here to-morrow night. While he is to come here you three men are to destroy his Chinese friends and his organization."

They stared at him, astounded.

"But," said Schwab, licking his thin lips, "but—our reports—the money! I thought you needed money—"

The shadowy smile that flitted over the face of Ch'ien-hsi was terrible to see. In it was something dreadful, some frightful semblance of inhuman power and cruelty.

"True. To-morrow morning, early, each of you will go to San Francisco." Ch'ien-hsi took from his pocket three envelopes. He wore evening dress. As he sat there in the great temple chair of red lacquer the contrast between his clothes and his features was tremendous. One saw here a person of infinite power, of absolute resource; a person superior to race and to human limitations. Oriental and occidental seemed met in him.

To each man he handed an envelope.

"There are your directions. You are to see certain men, do certain things. If you do them, by noon to-morrow you will have spent three millions of dollars. If you do them, the newspapers will know only that a new tong war has broken out virulently."

In his repetition of the words "If you do them" there rang a warning, an unuttered threat which each of the three Trigrams understood.

"But one cannot bribe a newspaper, old chap," said Pavitt-Beasley.

"One can buy a newspaper," said Ch'ien-hsi. "By tomorrow night I shall have spent the fourth million. By Monday night the entire five million. By Monday night the *hui* will be supreme, our enemies will be gone, and we shall reorganize."

In the spectacle which his words presented there was a potent magic. This Manchu loomed up as more than a man; the three lesser men regarded him with awe, with terror. He sat there before them as one who held fate in his hand, one who juggled with life and death—and all the while remained aloof, supreme, omnipotent.

"By gosh, I believe you're the goods!" exclaimed Schwab under his breath.

Pavitt-Beasley smiled thinly. "Your directions shall be obeyed—quite so!"

Tagashi said nothing. His piggish eyes gleamed like black jade. He looked at Ch'ien-hsi as a yellow boy looks up to the enshrined image of Jizo.

The Manchu rose.

"That is all. Tagashi, wait for me. You, gentlemen, get a good night's sleep."

While these things were passing at the conference Nathan Rannals sat in a cheaply furnished downstairs room, a room such as might belong to any well-to-do Japanese rancher. Outside the closed door, the Jap guard had been left. Near Rannals sat Shuffles Beeson, pistol in hand; Shuffles had not ceased taunting and reviling the man he hated so venomously.

With the sense of failure strong upon him. Rannals had made no answer. But suddenly he made one despairing effort.

"Shuffles, listen to me!" he said, leaning forward. "You can make five thousand dollars in five minutes if you'll do something."

The twisted lip of Shuffles drew up in a snarl.

"Sounds likely!" he returned. "How?"

"Deliver a telephone message."

"Yah! Where's your five thousand?"

Rannals gathered hope as he regarded the creature before him.

"Listen! You run no risk. Nobody will ever know that you did it. Deliver this message and I'll guarantee that you get five thousand in cash within three days. Did you ever know me to break my word? Haven't I got a reputation for being good for a promise?"

Shuffles nodded. His eyes flitted about the room, his weak chin wavered.

"What's the message?" he inquired. "Who to?"

Rannals gave him Solomon's telephone number.

"Telephone that number. Tell where this house is and that I'm here. Say—this is mighty important—say that tomorrow Tagashi and his friends are going to strike a hard blow. To-mor-row means everything!"

"Hey?" Shuffles gazed at him inquiringly. "What about to-morrow?"

"I don't know. Just give that message—that the big blow falls to-morrow. Will you do it?"

Shuffles sat back in his chair and grinned.

"I look like it, don't I?" he jeered. Rannals' half-born hopes crashed down. "Yah! Catch me givin' me pals away—huh! You big stiff, I hope you croak by to-morrow night!"

A low laugh echoed in the air, and Rannals recognized the voice of the unknown. An instant later the door opened. Into the room strode Chien-hsi.

Shuffles fairly jumped to his feet, fear and a questioning terror in his eyes. But the Manchu, gazing at him and ignoring Rannals, held out a hand as though in reassurance.

"Very well, Shuffles," he said, his toneless, inflexible voice quite cool. "You may go and telephone Solomon as Mr. Rannals requests. But do not tell him where this place is, and do not mention to-morrow at all. Tell him that Mr. Rannals hopes to see him in a day or so, and is quite well. That is all."

Shuffles stared at the Manchu as though in paralyzed awe. So, indeed, he must have been. Suddenly he bobbed his head twice, turned and put for the door. Ch'ien-hsi glanced after him, smiled as the door slammed, and turned to Rannals.

"A poor half-wit—but useful," he said calmly. "Well, sir, I suppose you wonder who I am?"

The gaze of Rannals hardened upon him.

"I think you must be the devil," he answered.

Ch'ien-hsi inspected him appraisingly, curiously.

"Well, no matter. You heard enough upstairs to show you that I am master here. You are watched by others; do nothing foolish. Sit down. I want to talk with you.

Ch'ien-hsi took a chair. He sat stiffly upright, his gaze fastened upon Rannals, who seated himself again.

Rannals was astonished by this man, of whom he believed Solomon to know nothing. At first glance, the Manchu appeared only as a singularly handsome individual; then this impression passed. The remarkable self-mastery of the man, his lack of gestures or motions, the complete subordination of body to brain, became noticeable. The only hint of expression in his face lay in the deep and fluid eyes. Otherwise the face was stony, carved in old ivory.

Gradually the implacable power of the man was borne in upon Rannals. In the forehead was nothing of the dreamer; the bulge above the eyes showed the thinker, the hard materialist, the scientist. As Ch'ien-hsi seated himself Rannals noted one thing which startled him. There was no bulge to the back of the man's head—the skull rose straight from the neck. In such a person there is no human sympathy, no touch of kindliness. With an unutterable horror growing upon him Rannals perceived that this man was a creature set apart from his fellows—above them and apart from them.

"You comprehend," said Ch'ien-hsi suddenly, "that I am not a person to make threats. By to-morrow night, Mr. Rannals, your associates will be destroyed. I shall be supreme. This is a statement of fact."

The absolute finality of this statement made Rannals feel cold.

"You mean," he returned, "you think it to be a statement of fact. Even if it should come to pass—what then? You are nothing but a panderer to the depraved taste of men. You are a drug seller. I gather that you are the head of the entire drug syndicate—and what of it? You have nothing to gain but money."

"Money is power," said Ch'ien-hsi, but he said it as one who thinks of something else.

"Not in your sense," retorted Rannals. "A man of your evident ability can make ten times the money in legitimate ways. There are dozens of men in this country more powerful than you can ever hope to be from the sale of drugs."

A shadowy intangible smile flickered over that face, lending it a sardonic air.

"How little you understand!" repeated the Manchu, transfixing Rannals with his luminous, piercing gaze. "I bend all evil men to serve me—is that not power? I am above all human laws of right and wrong—is that not power? I am supreme to human passions and desires; petty fools like you, adorant magi before the little god of routine and things that must be—how little you understand!"

Now this was not boasting. It was said quietly, in a frightful earnest.

"Come into my laboratory, and I will show you what the emancipated will and intelligence can do. I will make for you a homunculus, a little mannikin of a man, all flesh and blood, who dances in a vacuum and prays me for a soul. I will show you how men are ruled by their desires—and how to play with men! Ambition? It is another name for grasping desire. I am above ambition. If it amuses me to see human folk grovel in the grip of opium—so much the worse for them. If it amuses me to play with the destinies of peoples—"

Rannals felt a sense of malefic strangulation, an oppression that choked him. It occurred to him that he was dealing with a maniac; yet this was clearly impossible. The light of sanity was incredibly strong in the face of the Manchu, horribly so.

No, not a maniac—a man! A man self-hypnotized, deluded by the auto-hypnosis of the Orient. A man greater than most perhaps, but only a man. With this realization, Nathan Rannals shook off the awful sense of fear that had threatened him. He was dealing with no superhuman creature after all. Rannals could see now how this Manchu hypnotized all who met him, as the snake mesmerizes the bird into actual paralysis.

A short laugh broke from him as he looked into those bale- fully gleaming eyes and felt his own manhood surge up anew in resistance.

"What's all this patter for?" he demanded coldly. "What do you want of me?"

The darkly burning eyes altered into ice.

"Information," snapped Ch'ien-hsi. "I want to know your exact relation to Solomon. I want to know all that you know about him."

Now it so happened that before starting his quest for Janet Anderson. Rannals had been empowered by the little cockney to give up any information of which he was possessed. He knew nothing that could hurt John Solomon, and he had been told, with a wheezy chuckle, that the more he embellished his actual knowledge with the work of his imagination, the better.

Thus Rannals answered the questions of Ch'ien-hsi.

CHAPTER XIV

EARLY SUNDAY morning Ch'ien-hsi accompanied Tagashi out to the car which was awaiting him. Pavitt-Beasley and Schwab had already departed.

In the glorious morning sunlight of northern California, the rich beauty of the flowering fruit trees surrounded the house with an ocean of fragrant pinkness. Half a mile distant lay the highway, a ribbon of concrete that was the artery of State traffic, yet invisible from the house. Twenty-odd miles to the west lay Oakland, while eastward stretched the rolling hills to the San Joaquin and Sacramento.

It was not of the beauty of the scene, however, nor of the remote quietude of this ranch house that the two men were speaking.

"Your work," said the Manchu in a low voice, his hand on the fat shoulder of Tagashi, "is to see that these other two men fail in nothing. Full instructions have been furnished you. The other two Trigrams are to do everything; you are to check them up and see that they do not fail."

"I understand," and the heavy features of the Jap flashed with cunning. "Being both strangers to San Francisco, they may do things that we could not. But I am sorry that you deprive me of Shuffles Beeson. He would have been of great assistance to me."

"I shall need him," said Ch'ien-hsi curtly. "Now Solomon arrives here at precisely seven o'clock to-night; by eight o'clock he will be dead. I think that you had better arrange to get here about seven yourself, or perhaps a little later. In case anything goes wrong beforehand, you are to telephone me instantly. Nothing will go wrong, however, if you obey instructions. By seven o'clock nothing can go wrong. Thus, you understand?"

"I understand," said Tagashi, and got into the waiting car. It rolled away.

Ch'ien-hsi went directly to the rooms occupied by Janet Anderson. He knocked at the door, which was opened to him by Mrs. Lee.

"I wish to speak with Miss Anderson," he said quietly, and waited.

A moment later Mrs. Lee conducted him to a room in which Janet Anderson had been breakfasting. She rose to greet her visitor. Ch'ien-hsi made a gesture to Mrs. Lee, who closed the door and left them alone.

"I believe that Mrs. Lee has told you who I am?" said the Manchu. He gazed steadily at Janet Anderson, who returned the look with her usual quiet poise.

"Yes," she answered simply.

The word held much significance, but her eyes of gold-flecked lapis were quite unafraid. Very rarely did Ch'ien-hsi encounter any person in his power who could look at his fearlessly, yet here, for the second time within twelve hours, this came to pass.

Decidedly it was a good thing that these two captives of his were to die soon!

"I wish you to deliver a telephone message for me," said Ch'ien-hsi. "You will call up Mr. Solomon and tell him that I, Ch'ien-hsi, am going to send my car for him at six o'clock. He is to come alone. I wish to see him in order that this entire affair of the opium *hui* may be settled at once, without further trouble."

Janet Anderson smiled in cool disdain.

"I'm afraid you've selected the wrong person to set your trap," she returned. "I will not deliver any such message. I imagine you would have a very hard time getting Mr. Solomon to trust himself in your power, but I certainly shall not be the means of helping to deceive him."

"There is no question of deceiving him," said Ch'ien-hsi calmly. "You may tell him whatever you like in addition to my message."

"Then why?" The girl's gaze scrutinized him with open suspicion. "Suppose you send me to him now. I will deliver your message orally."

"That is impossible." Ch'ien-hsi was quite inflexible, unimpassioned. "We desire you to remain here until your brother arrives—to-night, I trust. I give you my promise that to-night you shall be free."

Something in the mien of this man inspired the girl to believe his words. Ch'ien-hsi might be, possible was, above a lie. He was not above a double meaning, however.

"Just why do you want me to telephone Mr. Solomon?" she inquired.

"Because"—and here Ch'ien-hsi told the exact truth—"he does not know me. I doubt if he knows about me at all; my name would me nothing to him. On the other hand, when you speak to him he will realize with whom he is talking. You are at liberty to tell him anything you wish, remember. You will be left alone in the room to speak freely. All I ask is that you convey my message."

"Are you trying to learn how to reach Solomon?"

Ch'ien-hsi smiled in disdain. "I will give you his telephone number. More, I will tell you exactly where he lives. Can you not get suspicion out of your mind?"

"Certainly not," came the cool response. "Why should I? Why do you not get Mr. Rannals to telephone?"

Ch'ien-hsi did not tell her that Rannals knew altogether too much—knew things she did not know. Instead, he now stooped to a lie.

"Mr. Rannals has been taken back to town. He is to see Mr.

Solomon personally and try to arrange a meeting between us. Of course, if you refuse to telephone him—"

"I will do it," said the girl quickly.

"Then come with me, please."

She followed Ch'ien-hsi to a downstairs room—the same chamber in which the conference of the previous night had been held. The Manchu bowed slightly and motioned to the telephone on a side table.

"I will return in ten minutes," he said, and closed the door behind him.

Janet Anderson sat down at the telephone.

One must admit that Ch'ien-hsi had brought the impossible to pass, with a clever psychological twist. When he did stoop to a lie it was a crucial lie, and one that spelled success. Instantly Janet Anderson thought that Rannals was to interview Solomon and bring about the meeting, instantly she thought that that meeting would be brought about in any case—she realized the importance of warning Solomon against Ch'ien-hsi.

This was exactly what the astute Manchu wished her to do.

She reached Solomon on the wire, delivered her message, and followed it with a tense warning. Naturally she told Solomon all she knew about Ch'ien-hsi—which was enough to put the pudgy little cockney on tenterhooks. Her warning was imperative, but of course vague in content.

"Werry good, miss," said Solomon in conclusion. "I'll do me werry best for you—and if I was you I wouldn't worry none whatever. God bless you!"

Solomon rang off.

Janet Anderson hung up the receiver. She looked about her at the handsomely furnished room; the helpless misery of her eyes gradually quickened into interest as she realized that the furnishings around her were princely, wonderful objects. The very rugs and chairs were of velvet brocade and silver-inlaid ebony. The crimson lacquer temple seat at the head of the center table was extraordinary in its vivid beauty. Hanging almost over it was a large bronze temple bell, with a marvelously colored patina that ranged from full scarlet to an iridescent green—

Suddenly the eyes of the girl noted a singular thing.

She sat in the cove of a bay window, at one side of the chamber, and thus had an oblique view of the table and furnishings. Entirely by chance, her gaze noted a cord that ran up the wall. She followed one end of this cord or wire to the floor, and across the floor to the red lacquer chair. She followed the other end half across the ceiling, to the bronze chain from which depended the temple bell. The cord or wire descended the chain, being twined among the links, and ended at the bell itself. What was the purpose of this connection between the red lacquer chair and the bronze temple bell?

At this minute the door opened, and Ch'ien-hsi appeared.

"May I reconduct you?" he inquired.

The girl rose and followed him in silence. There were no questions. At the door of her room Mrs. Lee met her, and she returned to her prison.

Ch'ien-hsi went to his own place, and sent one of his two Manchus for the little surgeon's bag in which he had placed the saffron flowers they had picked for him.

In his own steel-barred room Nathan Rannals had remained closely confined since the previous night. The surly, heavy-browed Jap who appeared to be the caretaker of this house brought in his breakfast, but refused all attempts at conversation.

With a good night's sleep behind him, a good breakfast, and a pipe to hearten him, Rannals felt more himself than since his capture by Tagashi. And yet, all the while, all the night through, had been growing upon him the awful realization of what this day was to bring forth.

As the morning dragged along, Rannals slowly entered into a desperate mood. From what he had overheard the previous night at the conference, he knew that by night Ch'ien-hsi expected to destroy Solomon. He knew no details.

The sense of futility, of being unable to speak or move without being overheard by the listening Manchu, was horrible. But, as he stood at his window, Rannals suddenly perceived the figure of Ch'ien-hsi walking up and down between the rows of fruit trees; the tall figure paced back and forth, the cruelly handsome face uplifted as though his distorted brain were communing with the cloud dragons.

So the Manchu was not watching his prisoner!

Rannals, feeling hope impacting on his soul, examined this windows closely, examined every possible avenue of escape. He found nothing. Palpably this room had been constructed as a prison chamber. It was impregnable to evasion.

Cursing that steadily pacing figure among the blossoming trees, Rannals flung himself into a chair. No hope! Already it was wearing on toward noon. Already—

The door of his room opened.

Into the room came the sullen-browed Japanese jailer. In his hand, the man carried two nosegays of purplish blossoms, each wrapped about in thin waxed paper. Something in his manner, in the way he carried them, impressed Rannals with the notion that the man was afraid of the thing he carried.

But Rannals forgot this in the realization that here was his chance, unwatched from the hidden spy hole, to reach a telephone. Only a desperate person would have conceived such a plan. Rannals was desperate.

"The mase' say he send present," said the Jap, advancing to Rannals and holding out one of the flower clusters. "He say put in wate', ver' pretty."

Rannals rose, took the waxed paper roll—and caught the man by the throat.

Fortunately for himself, his right hand clenched about that yellow throat in a grip of iron, shutting off every sound, shutting off life itself. The Nipponese became a thrashing animal, struggling and grappling in a wild frenzy, but the grip of Rannals could not be broken.

The two men twisted about, and the Jap threw himself to the

floor, dragging Rannals with him. Still that grip held. The man's struggles grew more frantic as his breath and strength fled; he fought wildly, furiously, vainly. He had been taken so completely by surprise that he did not so much as try to draw any weapon.

Rannals gained the supremacy, shaking that contorted figure beneath him. With an effort he raised it in the air, dashed the Jap headfirst against the baseboard of the room—and again. The man went limp in his hands. Again Rannals sent his head crashing against the wood, to make sure.

Rising, panting from the struggle, Rannals looked down. The Jap was bleeding, unconscious—perhaps dead. No matter. Rannals could not hope to escape from the place, but he could hope for a few minutes at the telephone.

Stooping, he quickly searched the prone figure and secured an automatic pistol. With this in his hand, he turned to the door. He paused at sight of the two nosegays, their waxed paper torn, the blossoms crushed.

"Why did the devil send these flowers?" he thought, frowning. "Well, let it go!"

Rannals crossed rapidly to the door, opened it, and stepped outside.

Mrs. Lee was standing in the hall, facing him.

Rannals knew instinctively that she had been drawn by the sound of the struggle. She was startled by his sudden appearance; he was no less startled at thus coming face to face with her. Her eyes widened, her lips opened—

"Don't call!" said Rannals, almost with a snarl. The pistol in his hand leaped up, covered her.

"Would—would you harm a woman?" she stammered, shrinking before his eyes.

"Try it," said Rannals. He meant the words. He guessed that she acted as jailer for Janet Anderson; he would have shot her down in this moment without compunction.

And in his eyes the woman read this fact. She remained silent.

"Come into this room," said Rannals, holding open the door.

She obeyed, followed him inside. Already her presence of mind was returning, however. As Rannals silently motioned her into a chair, she caught up the crushed blossoms.

"What beautiful flowers!" she exclaimed. It was a tremendous effort that she made to regain her poise, to impress on Rannals that he was dealing with a woman, to put aside the crisis that was upon her.

"What kind are they? I never saw any just like these—"

"Sit down," said Rannals, his eyes cold upon her.

She obeyed.

Rannals stepped back a pace to the bureau. Not taking his eyes from the woman, who sat holding the two flower bunches, he reached out and caught up his pajamas. He tore the shirt into several strips, then came back to Mrs. Lee.

"Put your hands behind the chair back—no talk now!" he said harshly.

Frightened again, the woman obeyed. She sat slumped down in the easy-chair, the flowers fallen into her lap. Rannals tied her wrists tightly behind the back of the chair. Then, coming around to her feet, he tied her ankles.

"I won't gag you," he said, rising and looking down at her. "If you shout I'll come back and kill you. If you remain quiet, I'll come back and release you. That's all."

He turned and left the room. The eyes of the woman followed him; then, with a breath of relief, she saw him close the door. After all, she had been terribly frightened by that unexpected meeting, by the cold death in his eyes!

The fragrance of the flowers rose, and her nostrils widened to it. She bent her head forward, the better to catch that breath of sweetness.

Outside the room, Rannals passed down the hall, his whole energy now bent upon finding a telephone. He remembered suddenly a detail that he had noted only subconsciously that previous night—there was a telephone in that room where the conference had been held. Could he find the room again?

He paused to think. Yes, he remembered how he had been conducted to it. He turned, entered another hall, and paused before a door. Pistol in hand, he opened the door. It gave him entry to that same ante-chamber where he had been placed to overhear the conference. He stepped inside. The room was empty.

A moment afterward he stood at the iron grille which separated him from the conference chamber. That, too, was empty. He examined the grille, and found that it was a door, which opened to the touch of his fingers. He stepped into the larger room—and saw the little telephone table in the recess of the bay window.

Rannals fairly darted to it. Triumph—at last! He stooped over the table, unhooked the receiver—and heard the clear "Number, please?" of central.

He gave Solomon's number, his own name. An instant later he heard the wheezy voice:

" 'Ello! Is that you, Mr. Rannals?"

"Yes. You must watch out to-day. They are going to—"

A thin cord of silk fell about the head of Rannals. His hand and wrist, upraised to hold the receiver, were bound to his neck. He was jerked sharply backward. Two Japs fell upon him. A third seized his right arm. He could not even grasp the pistol which he had laid beside the telephone.

Rannals fought. One of the Japs staggered and fell across the big ebony table, vomiting blood. Another cried out horribly as the thumb of Rannals tore at his eye. A moment afterward Rannals looked up to see the snarling visage of Shuffles Beeson above him, saw an upraised pistol butt—and was stricken into insensibility.

Ch'ien-hsi stood in the doorway, coldly eying the scene.

"Have that table moved outside," he said to one of his two Manchus, who stood at his elbow. "I shall use this room to-night, but want no table. Have the place cleaned."

He came forward and looked at Shuffles Beeson, who returned his look and laughed shrilly, venomously.

"I got him!" said Shuffles, a snarling whine in his voice. "I always knew I'd get the dirty devil some day—and now I got him! I only wished I'd killed him."

"You may kill him," said Ch'ien-hsi coldly. "I have no further use for him. And the woman also."

"Her!" Shuffles started. Across his twitching face crept a look of unholy glee. "Say, boss—don't kill her! I want her. Give her to me!"

Ch'ien-hsi stood regarding the degenerate creature for a moment.

"Very well," he said at length. One of the Japs was snapping manacles upon the wrists and ankles of Rannals. Ch'ien-hsi ordered them to take Rannals to his room.

"The woman is yours," he said to Shuffles. "This man dies here to-night with Solomon. But the woman must be out of the way. Go to her now; she is your reward. At seven o'clock to-night she must be dead. Do you understand? Do what you like first, but at seven o'clock I expect to be told that she is dead. Go!"

From Shuffles broke a hoarse gasp. Then, an animal's cry upon his lips, he turned and ran toward the rooms occupied by Mrs. Lee and Janet Anderson.

Ch'ien-hsi strode to the room of Rannals. There, in the doorway, he paused at sight of the Jap lying on the floor, the woman sitting with bowed head in the chair where she was tied. Mrs. Lee did not move, did not even look up. The cold gaze of the Manchu found the flowers in her lap, and he understood her immobility.

"After all," he murmured, "the experiment is highly successful. It is perhaps as well to have removed her; she was of no further use. The flowers have not been wasted after all."

He directed his Manchus to open the windows, buy the flowers, and remove the bodies of the Jap and Mrs. Lee.

When Nathan Rannals came to himself he was seated in his chair by the window, ironed hand and foot.

He was still there when, shortly before seven o'clock that evening, he saw a car arrive below, and, in the blaze of lights, disgorge the pudgy figure of John Solomon, alone.

A groan broke from Rannals. His head sagged. He knew now that Ch'ien-hsi had won.

AT THE moment when John Solomon left the car, Ch'ien-hsi was seated at the telephone. He was not using the instrument, however; he was trying to use it, as he had tried more than once in the course of the afternoon, and with the same difficulty. The telephone would not function. Ch'ien-hsi could hear the slight click and buzz, knew that it was in perfect condition, but he could get no response from central.

He abandoned the attempt when apprised of Solomon's arrival, and seated himself in the red lacquer armchair.

This chair had been moved slightly. In front of it, and above the level of a man's head, hung the old bronze bell of wondrous patina. This bell, probably a genuine Han relic, was of the Han type on which temple bells have been modeled for two thousand years. It was studded with the usual large nipples arranged in patterns. It had no clapper, however, and no striker was in sight; it seemed to hang there for decorative purposes, not for use.

The chamber was flooded with light. Behind the seat of Ch'ien-hsi stood the two Manchu servitors, garbed in their black silk. To one side, against the wall, sat Nathan Rannals. He was ironed, hand and foot, and in addition was gagged. Behind his chair stood a guardian Jap. No one else was in the room.

Solomon entered, conducted by two more Japs, one of whom was his chauffeur. These three were the only brown men in the chamber. They remained, as did the two Manchus servitors.

On the threshold, John Solomon paused. His blank blue

eyes swept over the room; no hint of expression came into his pudgy countenance at sight of Rannals. His eyes came to rest upon the figure of Ch'ien-hsi, and he walked forward a trifle stiffly. He had left his hat outside; his hair looked silvery in the electric lights.

"You searched him?" asked the Manchu of the two Japs. He spoke English, as though disdaining to hide his meaning from Solomon.

"He has nothing but a notebook," was the response.

Solomon halted, and his gaze fastened upon Ch'ien-hsi. The Manchu returned the look. In this moment of appraising silence it became apparent that each man was weighing the other, and from the face of Ch'ien-hsi it was evident that the Manchu did not make the mistake of holding his adversary in contempt. From the face of Solomon, however, nothing at all could be deduced.

On the rug that stretched out before the seat of Ch'ien-hsi there was delineated a small dragon of gold against a blue background. Solomon had halted at this dragon.

Still the two men held each other in gaze, as though each were waiting for the other to speak. It was curious to watch them, to study the two men. In one was a tremendous dynamic energy held in leash, controlled, yet ready to blaze forth in a fury of destruction. In the other—what? It was hard to say. That expressionless face of Solomon held nothing, it seemed, except perhaps a vast and terrible patience.

"So you are Solomon!" said the Manchu suddenly. "You know who I am?"

"Yes, sir," answered Solomon. His wheezy voice sounded a trifle apologetic. "If I ain't mistook, sir, you're a werry close relative o' the last Manchu emperor, and your name used to be—"

"My name is Ch'ien-hsi," said the Manchu quickly. His face had changed slightly at Solomon's words. Undoubtedly those words had startled him.

"Werry good, sir," was the submissive response. The gaze of

Solomon lifted momentarily to the iron grille behind the chair of the Manchu. That door was curtained.

"You came here," said Ch'ien-hsi, "in order that all further trouble might be obviated between the *hui* which I represent and certain interests which you represent?"

"Yes, sir," answered Solomon's mild tone.

"That trouble is going to be obviated," went on the Manchu, "in the simplest possible manner—namely, by removing you and your associates."

The blue eyes of Solomon widened a bit.

"I was afraid o' that werry thing, sir," he responded, and sighed wheezily. "Dang it, I ain't 'ad no luck at all this trip, as the old gent said when 'e kissed the barmaid. It looked to me, sir, as 'ow you wanted to talk things over, so to speak, and so I come along to see you."

Ch'ien-hsi regarded him steadily for a moment, then spoke in heightened acerbity. The ineffaceable calm of Solomon seemed to mildly irritate the Manchu.

"I will show you how I intend to deal with you," he said, and motioned to the surly-browed Jap behind the chair of Rannals. "Find that man Shuffles Beeson. Bring him here."

The Jap departed. The eyes of Rannals dwelt upon Ch'ien-hsi in silent horror.

Solomon produced knife and plug, and whittled some tobacco into his palm. He brought forth his ancient clay pipe and proceeded to stuff it full. He seemed entirely unaware that these actions had produced an absolute stupefaction in the two Japs who had searched him—without finding knife or plug! In fact, he appeared quite absorbed in what he was doing, and he looked up with a start when Shuffles Beeson made his appearance.

The drug addict came shuffling forward past Solomon, his eyes upon the Manchu. Under the pitiless electric lights his close-cropped head, his livid countenance, his snarl of lip-scarred degeneracy were brought out remorselessly.

"Is the woman dead, as I ordered?" demanded Ch'ien-hsi. His look and words seemed to terrify the poor creature into paralyzed abjection.

"Yes, boss," answered Shuffles, licking his lips.

"Very well. Take this man Rannals and kill him. I'll have him carried to the same room. Do it any way you like, since you hate him enough to make him suffer, and bring me word when he's dead. You understand?"

A light of venomous exultation flashed across the face of Shuffles.

"Sure!" he cried hoarsely. "Sure! I'll fix him—"

He turned and shuffled hastily away, a frightful figure with the light of disordered reason blazoned in his dope-maddened countenance. Two of the Japs seized upon Rannals, who struggled vainly. With surprising strength, they lifted him and carried him away.

Solomon lighted a match and puffed his pipe alight.

"Now that we're by ourselves, sir," he said to the Manchu, "mebbe we can 'ave a bit o' quiet talk. If so be as money 'u'd tempt you to let me go free—"

Ch'ien-hsi laughed harshly. He leaned forward, searching Solomon's face with his burning eyes. That pudgy face remained imperturbable, inscrutable, blank.

Rannals, as he was borne from the room, was half paralyzed by the cunning fingers of those who carried him. Those fingers, trained to the jujutsu which was borrowed from China by Japan and converted into a devilish system of torture, searched out his nerve ganglia, his muscles, and brought a groan of pain from his gagged lips. He abandoned resistance, and allowed himself to be borne limply.

He was carried to the door of the rooms which had been occupied by Janet Anderson and Mrs. Lee. This door was open and the room was empty; the door beyond was closed.

As Rannals was carried in, the inner door opened, and Shuffles Beeson appeared.

"Dump him there!" he cried shrilly, pointing to a chair. "Yah! Tell me to come along for shovin' mud, will ye? Never again, mister officer!"

The two Japs, grinning evilly, obeyed the command and literally dropped Rannals in the chair. They departed closing the outer door after them, while Shuffles favored his victim with a flood of curses and objurgations.

Then, suddenly breaking short his tirade, the degenerate shuffled away and vanished.

Rannals eased his aching body into a more comfortable position, and waited grimly. With his hands manacled behind his back, he was practically helpless to avert whatever destiny Shuffles might have in store for him. His only prayer was that it might be short and speedy. The thought of that shuffling, cringing figure returning to inflict a painful and lingering torture was intolerable, beyond endurance.

The moments dragged horribly. There was no sound, although Rannals thought he could catch an indistinct voice from another room. He did not know what had become of Janet Anderson, and dared not conjecture. All was lost, Solomon had come blundering into the trap set for him, and there was nothing to do but to face complete disaster manfully.

The inner door opened. Rannals looked up—and saw the figure of Randolph Anderson crossing to him with quick, light step.

Meanwhile, in the chamber from which Rannals had been taken, the interview between John Solomon and Ch'ien-hsi had progressed to a more animated stage.

As though his beloved pipe had inspired him with fresh hope and courage, Solomon showed himself less impassive. The tall Manchu began to speak in cold, inflexible sentences, laying bare to Solomon the skeleton of what was then happening in San Francisco. Solomon listened, now and then injecting a word, and showed that pugnacity was rising in him.

And then, to make Solomon feel more poignantly the ignominy and contempt of his failure, Ch'ien-hsi proceeded to lay bare his plans, already in fruition, with a merciless brutality. He told how the three Trigrams had been sent to do certain work, with every detail provided for and Tagashi engaged in seeing that no detail went wrong.

"You left your home at precisely six o'clock," he went on, flinging the remorseless words at the rather pitiful figure of Solomon. "Thus you knew nothing of what was going on; the first intimation would have reached you shortly after six o'clock, when Lui Toy was killed.

"With his death, the chief man of the Six Families were destroyed—all, in fact, who were associated with you. At ten minutes to seven your home was raided, your men killed, and the building given to the flames."

"Beggin' your pardon, sir," broke in Solomon, "but ain't that 'ere program werry 'ard to carry off in a big city?"

"Why so? A tong war in Chinatown; an explosion and fire in an isolated apartment building—that is all. Local politicians bribed. The police force taken care of. The newspapers either controlled or bought. I am surprised that you would call it a difficult matter."

"Yes," said Solomon reflectively, "but you ain't sure about it! 'Ow do you know all this 'ere 'as 'appened?"

"Because I arranged for it to happen," and over Ch'ien-hsi's features flitted that singular, shadowy, sinister smile. "What could prevent my plans being fulfilled?"

"Well, I ain't right sure," said Solomon thoughtfully. "For one thing, Providence!"

"Providence?" repeated Ch'ien-hsi with a slight rising inflection in his toneless voice. "Providence? But what providence is there to interfere with my wishes? None."

"Prowidence is a werry mysterious thing, as the Good Book says," reflected Solomon. "It's mortal 'ard to figure out the ways o' Prowidence, as the old gent said when 'e buried 'is third. Who 'ud think, sir, as 'ow there was eight o' them 'ere trigrams alive and a-prosperin' only a few short days ago—and this mornin' there was only three left!"

"This morning?" repeated Ch'ien-hsi, his eyes suddenly acid keen. "And why not to-night?"

Solomon sighed wheezily.

"I'm werry much afraid, sir, as 'ow all 'o them 'ere three ain't alive to-night."

An imperceptible frown darkened the eyes of the Manchu. He shot a lightening-swift glance at the telephone in the window recess. Solomon chuckled.

"Yes, sir—it quit workin' this afternoon, just like that."

"What do you mean?" demanded the Manchu coldly.

"Well, sir, if you want it straight—the serwice quit at noon on your line. And that's why Tagashi ain't been an' called you up."

Ch'ien-hsi regarded his opponent, unmoved by this signifi-cant information.

"So!" he said softly. "Then you knew where this place was. But you knew too late. The forces I set in motion could not be stopped."

"Except by Providence," said Solomon.

This bland repetition seemed to irritate Ch'ien-hsi. Before he replied, however, Solomon felt in his breast pocket and produced a thin red notebook. He stood thumbing over the pages of this for a moment, carefully intent upon his task; every eye was fastened upon his pudgy figure.

At length Solomon found the place he sought, and extended the notebook.

"Ah, 'ere it is!" he said. "If you'll be so good as to cast your eye on this 'ere, sir, you'll find it all writ down, shipshape an' Bristol fashion."

"What is it?" asked the Manchu, leaning forward to take the notebook.

"It's me accounts wi' you, sir, all up to date."

Ch'ien-hsi took the notebook and glanced at the writing it contained.

As he read, the man's face changed in a singular manner.

Solomon struck another match and relighted his pipe, but Ch'ien-hsi paid him no attention. The features of the Manchu altered, lost their aloof dignity, became suffused with a slow tide of color. A storm of passionate fury gathered in his burning eyes. His lips were clenched in a thin scarlet line.

What was written there which could so powerfully affect this invulnerable and superhuman individual?

Suddenly Ch'ien-hsi dashed down the book to the floor. His eyes fairly blazed as he looked at Solomon. Fury thickened his throat.

"Dog that you are!" he said hoarsely, slowly slipping one hand along the lacquered arm of his chair. "Dog that you are! You shall die, you liar—"

"Beggin' your pardon, sir, I ain't no such thing," affirmed the little cockney mildly. "If you'll 'ave a bit o' patience that 'ere Tagashi will be 'ere in a minute to see you. 'E'd ought to be 'ere right now—"

At this instant there was a noise at the door. One of the three Japs opened the door and listened. Then he turned and stared at Ch'ien-hsi.

"Tagashi is coming!" he cried out.

"So 'e is, sir. If I was you," added Solomon, "I'd wait and 'ear what 'e 'as to say, just like that. Werry bad news you'll find it, too."

As though by magic, Ch'ien-hsi became his cold, far-poised self again.

"Very well," he said. "You shall die in your turn. If he has failed, then he shall die. And you shall see the manner of your death."

Barely had the Manchu ceased speaking when the door was flung open.

Into the room burst Tagashi, running, panting. The great lump of a man had become a horrible sight. His eyes protruded.

The rolls of flesh about his face formed a great livid dewlap; the man ran heavily, stumbling, in his entire manner wearing the look of one who has just been witness to some fearful and incredible horror.

"Failed!" he gasped out as he came forward. "Failed!"

"Who failed?" demanded the cold voice of Ch'ien-hsi.

Tagashi came to a halt, shoving Solomon away carelessly and staring at Ch'ien-hsi from those terrible, protruding eyes. He was standing before the bronze temple bell, exactly upon the little gold dragon in the rug.

"Both—dead!" he croaked. "Schwab arrested, shot—the other killed—I tried to reach you—they prevented me—"

His voice died out in a sob. Ch'ien-hsi sat motionless for an instant, as though this report of disaster had left him entirely unmoved. Then:

"I warned you of the reward of failure," he said coldly. "This is your reward."

His hand moved slightly on the red-lacquered arm of the chair.

CHAPTER XVI

THE MOTION of Ch'ien-hsi's hand was imperceptible.

Tagashi, who was looking only at the Manchu, did not know what happened. But Solomon was looking at the bronze temple bell, and he saw a curious thing.

One of the bosses, or nipples, with which the old Han bell was studded, seemed to omit a tiny jet of vapor. There was a slight hiss, as though caused by compressed air. Tagashi suddenly threw both hands to his throat and toppled forward. As he fell the shock of his limp weight made the house fairly shake.

This entire affair passed in the fraction of an instant.

"Carry him out," said Ch'ien-hsi, addressing himself to the three Japs.

Only then did they realize that the Manchu had somehow, by some devilish ingenuity, slain Tagashi. One of them uttered a cry and ran forward, whipping out a pistol. Before he could use it the choking report of a weapon sounded from behind Ch'ien-hsi.

One of the two Manchus had fired. The other covered the two remaining Japs.

These two were cowed. Their comrade fell across the huge body of Tagashi, dead. Now Ch'ien-hsi repeated his cold, unimpassioned order. There was a tense silence as the two bodies were removed, the Manchu servitors aiding in the business.

All this while Solomon stood unmoved. Though the heavens might fall, this pudgy little man would stand unperturbed, wide-eyed, emotionless. Only, as the body of Tagashi was carried out, his blue eyes lifted to the curtained grille that was behind the seat of Ch'ien-hsi. This time, as Solomon looked at it, the curtain flickered faintly, as though in a draft of wind.

There was no draft in this chamber, however.

The two Manchus came back into the room, shutting out the Japs. At a gesture from their master they returned to their places behind him, their eyes fastened upon John Solomon.

Ch'ien-hsi regarded Solomon also. For all the iron inflexibility of the tall Manchu's countenance the light of hell now smoldered in his deep eyes.

"It appears," he said slowly, "that you have beaten me, well, so be it. At least one thing is certain: You will not escape me. Clever as you are, you cannot escape the death which is upon you. Before you die tell me who betrayed me to you."

Solomon produced a handkerchief and mopped his face. It was not warm, yet he was perspiring rather freely.

Undoubtedly he believed in this moment that the Manchu spoke the truth. He could not escape the mysterious, instantaneous stroke which had fallen upon Tagashi. It had some connection with that temple bell, yet Solomon could not fathom it. Only a very close scrutiny, or a very lucky chance, would have revealed to him the connection between that bell and the lacquer armchair in which sat Ch'ien-hsi.

Therefore, in spite of everything, Solomon must have given himself up for lost.

"It was Providence as betrayed you," he said in a new voice. Into his wide blue eyes crept a new light—a light that was accusing, menacing, terrible. "I learned about this 'ere place yesterday, and I made me plans. When your Trigrams returned to the city this mornin', me men caught 'em at the ferry. Them 'ere instructions you wrote out was all werry fine—only they didn't work, just like that. 'Cause why, I nabbed them 'ere three men.

"I give orders to let Tagashi come 'ere to-night. You, Ch'ien-hsi! You who 'ave been a prince! Dang it, you ain't nothin' but a dirty Mongol dog! You've been an' set yourself up, sittin' in the seat o' the scornful as the Good Book says, and makin' a mock o' Prowidence—and now see where you be! It's all werry fine to be a prince o' darkness, but it's danged slippery walkin', I says.

"But," and his voice dropped, "if so be as you wants to know who give you away, why, I'll tell you."

"Who?" demanded the Manchu coldly.

"That there gent," and Solomon lifted his eyes to the curtained grille.

Ch'ien-hsi started. He half turned his head. The two Manchus servitors glanced around. They did so, only to look into the mouths of weapons. In that doorway stood Nathan Rannals, and by his side was Randolph Anderson. Behind these two, dimly seen, was the face of Janet Anderson.

Ch'ien-hsi half rose from his seat.

What happened then came suddenly, violently. The two Manchus, without orders, reached for their pistols. Both Rannals and Anderson fired. Then, with a leap, Anderson was in the room and covering Ch'ien-hsi with his weapon.

"Sit still!" he cried out. "Before I kill you—listen!"

"See 'ere," began Solomon in an agitated voice. "You wait—"

"Shut up!" Anderson flung him a terrible look, his eyes wild. "I'm running this show. You, Ch'ien-hsi! Do you know me?"

The Manchu stared at him, paralyzed by the sudden apparition, by the death of his two servitors, by his transition form the place of judge to that of victim.

"Yes," he said in a low tone. "I have seen you—you are—"

"I am Randolph Anderson." As he said this Anderson smiled. It was not a nice smile; in it was the fanatical lust for vengeance of one who has long suffered in silence.

"And," he added, "I am also—"

A swift motion of his hand. From his head fell the glossy black wig. From his upper lip swept the straggly black mustache. His body slumped into a cringe, his head fell somewhat askew.

From the man Randolph Anderson had suddenly been evolved the lip-scarred degenerate—Shuffles Beeson!

A fearful cry was wrenched from the lips of Ch'ien-hsi. His head fell forward upon his breast, his eyes closed. In a flash Anderson turned his head toward Solomon.

"Quick!" he articulated. "Quick! The door—"

At this instant Janet Anderson came forward as though to enter this chamber from the one adjoining. Instantly Solomon was galvanized into life. He darted forward, seizing the girl's hand, and fairly threw her back into the next room. As he stood there he caught Rannals and pressed him backward. The pudgy little man had been transformed into a whirlwind of energy.

And with reason.

For, behind them, a terrible thing was taking place. The eyes of Ch'ien-hsi had opened, his fingers had slithered forward along the arm of the red lacquer chair. From that hanging bronze bell one nipple after another seemed to dart forth tiny, half-visible jets of vapor. They fell about the head of Randolph Anderson.

And, as they fell, the pistol in Anderson's hand barked out its shattering report.

In the adjoining room Solomon hastily drew the curtain across the grille, as though to shut out the sight of the two figures who had fallen to the floor. He turned to the astonished, horrified Rannals. Janet Anderson had fallen unconscious.

"Take 'er out!" he said. "Take 'er out, quick! Them 'ere poison fumes—'urry up! Dang it, 'urry up! Me men will be in directly—"

From somewhere outside came a shot, a yell, another shot. Then a sound of battering at doors, of pounding feet.

Rannals picked up the form of Janet Anderson and staggered from the room.

He carried her downstairs, seeking only to get away from this house of evil, out into the cold night. He was not sure what had happened—his brain was awhirl with the swift rush of events, the piling of tragedy upon tragedy. Somehow he gained a door, caught the girl up more firmly, and stumbled down the outside steps. An electric light blazed above, the lights of automobiles were concentrated upon the house entrance. As Rannals emerged he came upon Lui Toy calmly smoking a cigarette.

"Good!" exclaimed the Chinaman. He stood there unconcerned, his bland presence acting like a shock to Rannals. "Good! May I help you? Here, let me bring cushions—"

Rannals found himself laughing foolishly, weak with reaction.

He lowered his unconscious burden to a makeshift seat formed from automobile cushions. His brain cleared gradually. Lui Toy offered him a cigarette, struck a match for him.

"Quiet, my friend. All is finished. Solomon will be here in a moment."

It seemed unreal, this peace. Presently Solomon came. He exchanged a few low words with Lui Toy, stooped to glance at the face of Janet Anderson, then rose and took the arm of Rannals in his.

"I want to 'ave a look at the stars!" he said simply.

The two men walked a little apart. Rannals asked a question; Solomon shook his head. The little cockney was trembling slightly.

"What 'appened? Dang it, why, it was fair 'orrible! We didn't know what to look for. And when it did 'appen I couldn't make out 'ow it was done. That 'ere bell was fitted up to shoot out poison gas from the nipples. Inwisible it was, too. Dang it, we got out o' there just in time! 'E fair filled that 'ere room wi' fumes, 'e did! I 'adn't no 'opes at all until Anderson come along—"

"Did you know that he was Shuffles?" queried Rannals.

"I 'ad me suspicions, yes. But 'e didn't know I knew. And you?"

"I never suspected, of course," said Rannals. "Who would? He was, in reality, the dope fiend Shuffles Beeson. He didn't play at it; that was his real identity. What a frightful irony it was, Solomon!

"And he played at being his former self, the old Anderson. Think of the man, able to transform himself for a little while into the person he had been! Doped up, keenwitted, with wig and mustache and a bit of color on his eyebrows, he became straight-bodied and alert. Then back again to the slouching, twisted degenerate."

Solomon drew a wheezy breath.

"Do you know what 'e was, Mr. Rannals? 'E was Doctor Jekyll and Mr. 'Yde backwards, that's what! Instead o' makin' 'isself into a degenerate, 'e was makin' 'isself into a man again—only there wasn't no 'ope for 'im—"

The figure of Lui Toy approached them.

"Miss Anderson is herself again," said the Chinaman.

"Take 'er for a walk," said Solomon to Rannals. "I've got to see to things 'ere. We'll be busy a good 'alf 'our. Take 'er for a walk, I says."

It was good advice.

For half an hour Rannals and Janet Anderson walked under the stars. They spoke of Randolph Anderson; the girl faced the matter quietly, bravely. She told of how her brother had cast off his identity of Shuffles that afternoon, how for a space he had become his old self again, how they had spent a few precious hours together while Ch'ien-hsi imagined that she was delivered over to the degenerate.

"He told me that there was no hope," she said quietly. "He realized it fully, Nathan. He knew that the Manchu had some infernal means of destroying himself and every one with him, and while we suspected it had some connection with the bell we did not know the secret, of course. Randolph wanted to—to end everything by saving the rest of us—if it could be done."

"It was he who kept Solomon apprised of things, then?"

"Yes," she answered, not without a touch of pride in her voice. "Oh, he fooled that terrible Manchu completely! And when you tried to bribe Shuffles to warn Solomon last night, and Ch'ien-hsi told him to telephone Solomon, he did so. But he gave full warning. He called him up again this morning, told him more. Solomon was able to—"

"Solomon is a clever man, but he took long chances," said

Rannals soberly. "Come, let us put all this away from our thoughts, if possible. Do you know what Solomon said when we came out of the house? He said: 'I want to look at the stars!' I like that. Let us look at the stars, too, and forget—"

By the entrance of the house Solomon and Lui Toy stood together.

The work was finished; the cleaning up was done. There was nothing to delay the return to San Francisco. But Solomon, who was puffing contentedly at his clay pipe, made no haste. Lui Toy followed his placid blue eyes to where, down the drive, two indistinct figures were visible in the clouded moonlight.

"Let 'em be," said Solomon. "We ain't in no 'urry, Lui."

"No, that is true," assented the Chinaman. "The work is done. The *hui* is destroyed. Some day it will have to be done all over again, of course; there will always be evil men seeking the huge profits of the traffic. But that day is far distant. And do you realize that it has all been done in less than a week's time?"

Solomon sighed wheezily.

"Do I realize it?" he said. "O' course I do, 'cause why, I've been a werry busy man this past week. And I'm a-growin' old, just like that. Dang it, I ain't 'ad me sleep for two nights! And now, Lui, it looks werry much like I'd 'ave another job on me 'ands."

"What?" demanded the Chinaman in surprise.

Solomon chuckled and waved his pipe. "You see that 'ere Mr. Rannals? Well, Randolph Anderson, 'im that was Shuffles Beeson, cleared 'is character. But what's 'e goin' to do now? Don't 'e need work?"

Lui Toy laughed softly.

"Don't worry about the future of Mr. Rannals," he responded. "If he will trust to my advice, his fate will be secure. Unless, of course, now that his character has been cleared, he wants to go back into the revenue service."

"No," said Solomon positively. "No, 'e don't! 'E ain't a-goin' back into the serwice. It ain't no job for a married man."

"But you mistake!" protested Lui Toy. "I have known Mr.

Rannals for a long time. I know quite well that he is not married—"

"I didn't say 'e was," and Solomon chuckled again. "But that ain't no sign 'e ain't a-goin' to be. And that 'ere is the werry job I got on me 'ands—to find a weddin' present for 'im and Miss Anderson!"

"Oh!" said Lui Toy.

Solomon's chuckle was wheezy, but none the less hearty.

ABOUT THE AUTHOR

H. BEDFORD-JONES is a Canadian by birth, but not by profession, having removed to the United States at the age of one year. For over twenty years he has been more or less profitably engaged in writing and traveling. As he has seldom resided in one place longer than a year or so and is a person of retiring habits, he is somewhat a man of mystery; more than once he has suffered from unscrupulous gentlemen who impersonated him—one of whom murdered a wife and was subsequently shot by the police, luckily after losing his alias.

The real Bedford-Jones is an elderly man, whose gray hair and precise attire give him rather the appearance of a retired foreign diplomat. His hobby is stamp collecting, and his collection of Japan is said to be one of the finest in existence. At present writing he is en route to Morocco, and when this appears in print he will probably be somewhere on the Mojave Desert in company with Erle Stanley Gardner.

Questioned as to the main facts in his life, he declared there was only one main fact, but it was not for publication; that his life had been uneventful except for numerous financial losses, and that his only adventures lay in evading adventurers. In his younger years he was something of an athlete, but the encroachments of age preclude any active pursuits except that of motoring. He is usually to be found poring over his stamps, working at his typewriter, or laboring in his California rose garden, which is one of the sights of Cathedral Cañon, near Palm Springs.